ENGAGE

SAVAGE DISCIPLES MC #3

DREW ELYSE

Let Jager make you his pet!

Drew Elyse ♡

For Michael
Because nine years later,
we haven't gotten sick of each other.
And, really, it's about time
you got a dedication.

PROLOGUE

Ember

THE SOUND WASN'T what woke me. I had no idea why I'd stirred in the middle of the night. Usually, I was a sound sleeper.

No, the sound came after I'd already started to wake. I lost the seconds I had trying to place it. It came from the hallway, a mix of solid knocking and rattling.

A picture frame, the answer came to me.

It was only that knowledge that had me moving. There was no reason for any of the frames I had hanging in the hall to make that sound. Not unless...

The door to my room flew open. There were men there, three of them. I didn't waste time staring. Instead, I scrambled to the side of the bed. I just had to get to the nightstand. There was a gun in the drawer—the gun Dad had taught me to shoot and insisted I have.

I got the drawer open, but never reached my only saving grace. One of the men was on me, grabbing me around the chest and hauling me backward. I fought. I kicked and hit at him, my training lost and raw instinct to fight or die kicking in. Another man came close, and I screamed with all I had.

I tried to fight him back, both legs kicking out, but his partner turned me. I felt the sharp prick at my arm. It didn't take long. Even as I continued to scream, to try to break away, darkness took over the edges of my vision, closing in until there was nothing left.

1

WHEN I WOKE, I was facing a wall covered in its own layer of dirt, broken up only by a rust-colored track of water from a leak above.

Where was I?

I tried to remember, tried to fight the fog to grasp onto anything that would tell me how I ended up in such a place.

I was home, in my room. I'd gone to bed...

The picture frame.

Like a dam breaking, it came back. The men, fighting them off, losing consciousness.

My head swam, my vision hazy. I had to figure out where I was, how to get out of here. I moved, feeling an ache like I had never known through every muscle. Then, a stinging pain in my arm. I looked there, seeing the IV. I followed the cord from my arm to a bag hanging on the wall above my head.

It was only then I noticed I wasn't alone.

I shot to sitting, jerking back to the wall. But what I saw wasn't a threat. What I saw was three women, all of them frail, malnourished, and dirty. To my left were iron bars. We were in a cell, me and those women. Soon, I would look like they did.

"Where are we?" I found the voice to ask. My throat was dry. So much so, it hurt to speak. That was when I noted how my skin felt like I hadn't showered in days.

Had it been days?

"We don't know," one—she looked to be the oldest—answered. Her voice sounded as rough as mine. When was the last time they'd been given water?

"How...how did we—"

She shook her head sadly. Beneath the grime, I realized she was, in fact, the oldest—maybe five years older than me, no more. Her dark hair was long, matted, her skin pale, her eyes flat.

"Sometimes, they take us, sometimes..." she trailed off, looking to her side. I followed her gaze to the woman next to her. She was blonde like me, and looked to be about my age from what I could see of her face as she peered over her knees. "Sometimes, we are sold to them."

Oh God.

My eyes moved past the blonde, terrified someone had given her over to this fate. What I saw hit me harder than anything I had experienced since I'd woken up.

The last woman was no woman at all. She was just a girl. She had light brown hair that needed washing weeks ago. Her cheeks were sunken in. She had been down here a while.

"How old are you?" I couldn't help but ask.

She didn't talk, just hid her face behind her hands, the woman who had spoken to me already answered for her.

"Fifteen."

Fifteen. She was still a child. What were they doing with a child?

What were they doing with any of us?

IT WAS hours before the man came down the hall, appearing in front of our cell. I'd long since dealt with the IV. I didn't have the finesse to pull the needle free without it tugging and scratching beneath the surface, but the discomfort was worth it when I watched a small flood of whatever they were injecting me with escape. Tricia, the woman who had been talking to me since I woke, told me it was a sedative mix. If I left the IV alone, I'd go back under. I'd already been there for three days. How long I'd arrived after they'd taken me was anyone's guess. The last thing I wanted was to lose any more time in this place.

Tricia also told me the names of the others. Katia, the blonde, and Sarah, the young girl.

"I've been here about two months, I think," she explained. "Sometimes it can get hard to track how long it's been. They come once a day with food and water. That's the only real way to tell time down here." There was something in her expression when she mentioned the provisions they were given, something disgustingly similar to longing.

"But why are we here?" I asked, not even sure if I expected her to have an answer.

She didn't respond, but I could see in her face that she did know.

I met her eyes and repeated, "Why are we here?"

Her gaze turned sympathetic, as if she weren't down here as well, as if she hadn't been here far longer than I had. She felt bad for me because whatever she was going to share was going to make this whole nightmare worse.

"They intend to sell us."

Sell us. I wouldn't even let my mind wander to what that might mean. I forced myself to seal off thoughts of who would want to buy us. I had to keep myself together. Letting my mind go there was not the way to do it.

After that, there wasn't much to say.

Then, the man came to the cell. He was brutish, large, and outright intimidating. He didn't say a thing as he approached the metal bars holding us captive. He simply inspected the nearly empty IV bag, seeing I'd freed myself from the line attached to it.

I had no idea if what I was about to do was stupid—whether it would get me punished, hurt, or worse. I just knew where I was was about as bad as it could get. I had to try something.

"There's a motorcycle club, in Hoffman, Oregon. They'll buy me. They'll pay whatever you ask," I practically shouted at him.

He stared at me, not responding.

"The Savage Disciples. They'll buy me."

He walked away without a word.

CHAPTER 1

Jager

"WHAT THE FUCK am I looking at?"

On some level, the answer was pretty fucking obvious. I was looking at a woman. Tall, blonde, nice body. What I really wanted to know was what she was doing here, seeing as she wasn't straddling the lap of one of my brothers or grabbing him a beer. She was passed out on the damn couch—and not the lightweight who passed out at a party either. Her arms and legs were bound with duct tape, a strip of which was also adhered to her mouth.

Behind her were two motherfuckers in suits who had no business at all being in the Savage Disciples' clubhouse, let alone when most of the brothers were out on a run and wouldn't be back until morning.

And, lest I forget, that meant not for another seven hours or so seeing as it was three in the goddamned morning.

Ace, who was still recovering from a couple gunshot wounds and hadn't gone with the rest of the brothers, spoke up. "These two fuckers said she told them we would buy her."

Buy her?

"The fuck you say?"

One of the suits decided to take that one. "She recently came into the ownership of our employer," he explained. The words came out stilted, like he was remembering a script. Probably because whoever his "employer" was—and I had a pretty solid

6

guess—wanted his lackeys to sound moderately intelligent, if not sophisticated. Seemed he wasn't quite getting the product he was after.

The goon went on with his thesaurus routine. "She was quite adamant the Savage Disciples would be willing to pay for her release. Our boss is not a frugal man, but he does like to turn a profit. He is also disinterested in trouble with motorcycle gangs. Selling her to you dispenses the need to find another buyer and pay for the man-hours involved in such an endeavor."

Jesus Christ, but I was getting twitchy. I focused on cracking my knuckles to keep from burying them in one of the fuckers' faces.

Motorcycle gang. Fuck, I hated that phrase. We weren't a damn gang, running around in the streets shooting each other and dealing dope on corners. But that was beside the point.

Whoever the chick was, she'd thrown our name out when she'd been taken. I had no doubt that was what happened. The Disciples weren't in the trade—even back in the days when the club's shit wasn't clean, we didn't deal in pussy—but trafficking wasn't completely unfamiliar to us. You live outside the law, you see shit. Peril of the life.

This woman—chances were she was an innocent victim in this case. Taken off the street, sold by her parents, who knew. What it meant was she was in the hands of some seriously not good people who had plans for her—plans she was certainly not going to like.

I looked her over again, trying to force any sort of recognition, but there was still nothing. She was cute, no doubt any guy here would be glad to have a go at her, but that didn't explain why we'd buy her. If she had a connection to the club, it wasn't one I knew about.

Even as I conceded she was a stranger to me, I kept my face

passive. There was no reason for the hired muscle in front of me to know one way or another whether she was familiar.

I shot Ace a look, but his answering stare and the minute shake of his head told me he wasn't having any more luck with identifying her than I was.

We were stuck in a shit situation, but the club was under my charge while our brothers were away. It was on me to make a decision.

"How much?"

"Fifty thousand."

Fuck. This could blow up in my face, but it didn't seem I had much choice. If I said no, they'd find another buyer—and from the look of the girl, they wouldn't have a hard time with that. Most likely, she'd end up in some pimp's stable, selling her ass for his profit. And that was probably one of the better possible outcomes. I couldn't risk that. She named us, which could mean she was important to one of the brothers.

"Twenty-five," I shot back.

The other goon chose to chime in then. "You's already gettin' a damn deal."

Seems he was instructed not to talk by the big man because he had even less of a way with words than his buddy.

"Your boss wants to avoid the hassle of selling her. I want to avoid the hassle of going after the asshole for taking a woman who belongs to the Disciples. Twenty-five."

The one who'd pulled rank since they walked in studied me. I met his stare straight on, not hiding the fact that I knew I had the upper hand. If he failed to make the sale or brought the wrath of the Disciples to his boss's door, he was fucked. He had no moves.

"Twenty-five," he submitted.

With a nod, I turned to Ace. "They don't fucking move until I get back," I instructed. A jerk of his chin met my demand.

Without a word, I left the room. Stone, the pres, had left me the key to his office. It was a good fucking thing too, seeing as the safe was in there. I felt like shit about taking twenty-five large from the club's funds without the okay from my brothers, but it had to be done.

If it came down to it, if buying her was a total fuck up on my part, I'd forfeit my cut of the money from this run. The payout would be big enough that the club wouldn't be hurting anytime soon. Safe escort of the kind of firepower our benefactor was moving didn't come cheap, particularly when escorting that kind of shit meant it could be Disciples who landed their asses in a cell.

I carried the fat stack of bills back out to the main room and handed them off, mentally cursing every-fucking-thing about this situation. The goon with half a brain took the cash and counted it out—twice—before nodding.

"Everything appears to be in order." Jackass.

"You've got your money. Now, you got one minute to get the fuck out of our house before your boss can make his way down here himself to pick up directions to your fucking bodies," I explained.

The two of them decided to waste a whole twenty seconds of that minute staring me down. A dare. After ten, I grabbed my piece from the back of my jeans and held it down against my thigh. They spent the next ten sizing me up. If they knew jack shit about anything, they'd know I'd have them both down before either could get to the guns clipped on their belts.

Whether they read that or not, they moved just about the time the countdown hit thirty. Neither said a word—which was a good call with the way my trigger finger was twitching—as they left. I moved my attention back to the girl who had just cost the club twenty-five grand.

"Go strip one of the rooms. One with a bathroom. Nothing left that could be a weapon. You know the drill," I instructed Ace.

"And call Slick in. Need to flip the lock around on the door. You know how he gets when we touch his work."

"On it," he answered.

I called after him as he walked away. When he turned, I added, "Take the room across from mine. Want to be able to hear if she wakes and gets up to anything." With a nod, he got to it.

I crouched down in front of the girl so I could get a better look at her face. Damn, she was a beauty. Real fucking cute. If goons one and two were working for who I thought, then she had no business being in their hands. Those boys weren't known for being gentle—or waiting for a "yes".

She might be a trap. Could be she was meant to report back on anything she could get her eyes or ears on. Until we knew for sure, she'd be guarded. Still, I couldn't help but hope she was clean. Fucked as it was to think it in that moment, I wanted a taste of this one.

Although, that would depend entirely on whether or not she could handle me tasting. Lots of women couldn't. I hoped she wasn't one of them.

When Ace had the room ready, I moved Sleeping Beauty to the bed, brought in a chair, and sat across the room for a while, mulling over the decision to untie her. No way in fuck she could overpower me, drugged or not. She wasn't tiny for a woman, but that didn't matter. I didn't know a man twice her size who could get the drop on me. Still, I wasn't exactly yearning for the job of having to restrain her if she went rogue when she woke.

Fuck. That wasn't entirely true. I was all for restraining her. That shit might have even been part of the hesitation I was having over cutting her loose. There was nothing quite like a bound woman.

It was that thought that had me grabbing the switchblade and releasing her. I was a lot of things—most of them bad—but I wasn't so fucking lecherous I'd make a move on an unconscious woman. It didn't matter whether she meant something to one of my brothers or not, that was a line I'd never cross. It was a line I'd gladly castrate a motherfucker for crossing.

Cutting through the rope took no time at all. Whoever had done the job didn't know a thing about binding someone. Had she been awake, she'd have been able to slip free easily enough. One rotation of her wrists was all it would have taken. Amateurs.

Once she was loose, I settled my ass back in my chair and waited. She didn't even stir—not a movement. She was out cold the entire forty-five minutes it took for Slick to arrive, and she slept right through us talking. She didn't even wake when he got to work on the lock. Whatever they'd given her, it was doing its job.

"Nothing?" I asked Slick again as he grabbed his repacked bag of supplies a while later. The door was outfitted with a new lock we'd control from the hall. Not so much as a knob on the inside for her.

"Don't recognize her, man," Slick replied.

"Fuck," I muttered. That made three of us. Not a good sign.

"You made the right call, brother," he assured me.

I seriously fucking hoped so.

I followed him out of the room, taking the chair with me. I had no idea if a girl her size could break the thing, but I wasn't taking chances. Slick handed over the key and we locked her in before he took off.

As I went back to my own room for another couple hours of no sleep, I shot a text off to Doc. He needed to come in and check the girl over. No telling what issues the drugs they'd given her might have caused. Old man probably wouldn't get it until morning, but that would have to do.

CHAPTER 2

Jager

I MANAGED to nod off at some point. I'd seen the sky lighten and the sun rise through the window, but I was out when the commotion started. Pounding, and a female screaming.

Shit.

I shook off the sleep and went into the hall just as Ace approached.

"Guess she's up," I muttered.

"She's gonna hurt herself the way she's running on that door," he said.

The piercing screams weren't relenting at all. On the contrary, they seemed to grow sharper as the seconds wore on. With the thumps and scratches sounding through the door, she was going to fight until it gave way or her hands did. No part of the clubhouse construction was cheap, that door included. The fucker was solid oak. She'd destroy her hands long before she made an impact.

"I've got her," I told him before turning back to my room. I threw on a shirt and my cut, and grabbed the key Slick had given me from the bedside table.

I slid the key in the lock, but didn't turn it. Instead, I pounded my own fist full force against the door.

"Back up," I ordered.

Her cries broke at the sound and her assault on the barrier halted. I turned the key, but lifted my arms to block my face. In my experience, women went for the face first. She didn't have a weapon, but nails and eyes were a bad fucking combination.

I was right to brace. The second I swung the door open, she attacked. Unfortunately for me, I was wrong to block upward. She didn't pounce like a cat with claws bared; she went right for an uppercut to the gut. It was smart—smart enough to outmaneuver me. In my moment of hesitation after the blow, she threw an elbow right at my sternum.

It was coordinated, practiced. She knew what she was doing. Despite her small size, she managed to get momentum behind the blows. With that surprise on her side, she would have been able to take down most men.

I wasn't most men.

As her left arm pulled back toward her body and her right arm began to swing forward, I recovered. Then, she was fucked.

Her right fist never made contact. I got my arm beneath hers mid-swing and forced it off course. The pull of her own movement sent her listing. She were a dude, I would have used the moment to return the favor with a fist to the abdomen. A girl that size, I could do some irreparable damage with a move like that. Instead, I grabbed for her left arm, getting a hold she wasn't going to be able to break on the slim thing. In one yank, I had her back to me, and grabbed hold of her other arm. I held her tight, but far enough away from my body to make a head-butt out of the question.

"Let me go!" she screamed, trying to shake me off.

"I'm not gonna hurt you," I told her. "Not the one who took you. Just trying to figure out who the fuck you are."

That seemed to grab her attention. She pulled away, and I let her. Her ice blue eyes were wild and surrounded with what I hoped were dark circles, not bruises. She looked me over with more than slight speculation in her gaze until she took in my cut.

Her eyes stayed on the Savage Disciples patch for a long moment.

"You're a Disciple?" she asked.

I gave her a jerk of my chin in answer and braced for the freak out to continue. As much as I loved my cut, it might've been best to leave it in my room. She might have named the club to those fuckers, but that didn't change the fact that most women weren't going to be real comforted in her situation by realizing they were in the hands of an MC.

She wasn't most women.

Her knees gave out and I had to move quick to keep her from slamming to the floor. On a broken exhale, she whispered, "Oh thank God."

That was when the tears started.

Shit.

I didn't know what to do. She was going into a full breakdown, but unless I was very mistaken, it was from relief. Sobs racked her body as she held onto my cut with a death grip. If that shit wasn't genuine, she was the most talented actress I'd ever seen. It seemed maybe she really did have ties to the club.

As much as I wanted to find out what those were, there was no getting that kind of intel out of her in the state she was in. I couldn't exactly blame her. However she had gotten here, it had not been a good journey. Honestly, the fact that she held it together until she seemed to think she was safe was impressive. She was strong. Had to give her that.

When the sobs lost some of the power—something I figured had more to do with exhaustion than her calming down all that much—I wrapped my hand around the back of her head, trying to get her attention focused on me. The moment I did, she let out a sharp cry and flinched away. Looking down, I noticed the blood on my hand.

I twisted her torso so I could get a look. There, in the

somewhat matted tangle of her hair, was red. There were flakes of dried blood littering the spot. It must've happened before she was brought to us, but the strain of the fight opened it back up.

"Ace!" I bellowed toward the open door.

His hurried, but uneven footfalls proceeded him. "Yeah?"

"Call Doc. Keep ringing the fucker 'til you wake his ass up. Get him here ASAP. Girl's got a head wound."

He ran off to do just that and I carried the girl to the bed. I pulled a chair back in the room and sat beside her. Someone had to make sure she didn't hurt herself until Doc could take a look at her. He'd be able to tackle it, or tell us whether we needed to get her to a hospital. Doc got his road name because he'd been a surgeon for years before he walked away from medicine to join the club.

She kept crying quietly, a mix of pain and relief, I figured. Life had given me enough lessons to teach me to trust my instincts, and they were telling me she was no threat. She seemed like she needed protecting.

The club could do that, protect her.

The club, not me.

Jamie had always seemed like she needed protecting.

I hadn't done that. Maybe it hadn't been my job, but I hadn't protected any of them.

Mom.

Dad.

My sweet little Jamie.

I wasn't taking on that kind of job again.

Doc came in an hour later. He didn't even make it through the doorway before he stopped dead.

"Ember?" he asked, shocked.

She stirred on the bed, having dozed off half an hour before. She rubbed at her red eyes before focusing on Doc. "Uncle D?"

Uncle?

"What the fuck is going on here?" Doc roared, surprising me. The brother was a crotchety fucker, but he was usually pretty quiet.

"You know her?" I had to clarify, if only because I had no damn clue how we'd gotten here.

"Know her?" he asked, like I was fucking dense. "She's Roadrunner's fucking daughter!"

Well, shit.

DOC SURMISED the wound was minor. Shit bled a lot, but I knew as well as anyone head injuries did that. He decided it didn't even need stitches, just to be cleaned and looked after.

Good news.

And speaking of news...

"You ain't said much, Jager," Doc pointed out as he drew some of her blood. He was going to take it to a friend at the hospital, make sure we weren't looking at any lingering issues from whatever they drugged her with.

For whatever reason, Ember wouldn't let me go far. While Doc had examined her head, she'd held onto my arm to keep me close. Doc's eyes lingered on that hold more than once, his face tightening beneath the white beard. He could say something if he wanted. It wasn't like I was inserting myself there. Fact was, I was happy to get some space, but I wasn't going to do anything to push her back into hysterics.

She'd been through hell. I could deal.

"Don't say much a lot," I answered.

Ember's lips kicked up at one corner, but I didn't give her anything.

"You reach out to the boys last night?" he asked.

I shook my head. "They're due back any time now. Wasn't going to get them here much faster. Figured there was no point."

Doc nodded. "You didn't want to spook anyone."

Exactly.

Silence lapsed, broken only by the sounds of Doc messing with his equipment. It reigned until he stood, announcing, "Going to run the sample to the hospital, try to beat them back here."

He wanted to be here when Roadrunner found out what happened. Seeing as he was one of the only people who had been around Ember before, that was a good call.

After he left, Ember seemed to become aware of the way she was holding on to me. Her eyes settled on her hand on my arm, roaming up and over me, before dropping. She pulled her hand away and brought both arms in tight to her body.

"Sorry," she muttered.

"No problem."

"What's your name?" she questioned.

It hadn't occurred to me that that shit hadn't come up sooner. With everything else, it hadn't been important.

"Jager," I answered.

She nodded in response, but said nothing else.

So there it was again, the silence. I preferred it that way. I wasn't one for talking just to fill the void. She seemed to feel differently. When Doc had been checking her over, he'd talked more than I was used to hearing. She was more at ease then, whereas now, she was curling in on herself.

"You okay?" I asked. A fucked question, I knew. Physically,

she already laid it all out for Doc while I was right there. Mentally, there was no way she was copacetic at that moment.

"Why haven't you asked?" she shot back instead. We both knew what she meant. Neither Doc nor I had posed a single question about what happened to her. Even while Doc was checking her over, he didn't ask how she got hurt, just stuck to how she was feeling.

"Your dad's going to want to hear it himself, not have one of us relay that to him. Not about to make you relive it more than needed," I explained.

"Oh." That was all she gave in response, but I wasn't looking for more.

After a few minutes, she shifted gingerly, until she was lying on her side, curled up like a child. Her head was flat on the mattress a few inches from my legs. Stripping the room meant Ace had taken the pillows out. I considered going to get her one since she clearly wasn't a threat, but I stayed put. Despite Doc telling her she was safe at the Disciples' clubhouse, her eyes kept shifting to the door nervously. I didn't think leaving her alone was the right call.

Her head moved around, trying to get her neck comfortable. Only a short pause passed before she did it again. By the third time, I was done watching her squirm. Snaking my hand beneath her arm, I pulled her toward me, lifted her head gently, and laid it on my thigh. I wasn't going anywhere, might as well give her that.

She settled then, and within ten minutes, fell asleep.

I stayed awake, as always, listening for the roar of tailpipes while wondering if the Disciples were headed for war.

CHAPTER 3
Ember

THE SOUND WOKE ME—A low rumble from a distance. It was a sound I knew, one I learned to love when I was just a little girl. No one in the neighborhood I grew up in with Mom had a motorcycle. That roar meant one thing: my dad was there.

I used to spend all day listening for it when I knew he was coming. Just then, I knew this sound meant the same thing and tears pricked at the back of my eyes.

Doc's arrival hadn't made that kind of sound. If it were him coming back, I wouldn't have heard it. This was several bikes, their engines making enough noise to carry through the walls.

I sat up and Jager stood once I was out of the way. I couldn't read him, not that my mind was clear enough to read anyone. I wasn't sure whether he had been waiting for me to release him all morning or preparing for Dad to come in. He didn't give anything away. Even when I attacked him earlier, his face had been stoic.

And what a face it was.

I was so past the point of being able to deal, I wasn't really feeling anything. It was like a wall had gone up in my head so I could exist without feeling everything it was containing.

Still, I had enough headspace to notice Jager. I might've had to be dead not to. He was so *there*. His presence was something that couldn't be ignored, even if it seemed he was happy to fade into the shadows and observe.

He looked like he could belong in the shadows.

It wasn't the black clothes, exclusively black and grey tattoos, or even the black leather cut on his shoulders that I knew as well as anyone meant he wasn't rainbows and sunshine.

It was his eyes. They weren't dark in color—they were actually an amazing grey I wanted to get a closer look at—but they were dark, nonetheless. There was pure shadow behind those irises that somehow permeated out of him. If he managed to make a room darker by entering it, I wouldn't be surprised.

He had a face and body that could make a woman want to give living in the dark a try—at least for one night. Tall, not dramatically, but definitely tall even for a man. Muscular through both arms in a way you could tell it continued throughout his body. It wasn't just about show or getting women either. He radiated power. His body was a weapon more intimidating than the gun he probably carried.

I'd been intent on taking all of this in, even knowing I was doing it to distract myself. Jager made a good distraction, even if he wasn't an active participant in that goal.

I looked to the door again—something I couldn't seem to stop doing. I knew why. I'd seen them in the doorway to my room when...

Nope. No. Not going there.

Instead, I focused on the sound coming through the doorway. The engines had shut down and voices were carrying, becoming louder as they came inside.

"Shouldn't you..." I trailed off, indicating the hall with a tilt of my head.

"Ace is handling it," he answered.

He wasn't leaving. The breath that left me at his answer told me I wouldn't have been able to let him go.

The voices quieted. I barely picked up one speaking to the others, but wasn't able to catch any of what was said. It went on for a while, which surprised me. I figured Dad would be rushing right through the building. Unless Ace didn't start with me being there. Maybe he was telling them about last night. I didn't remember any of it, but something had to have happened to get me from the cell I'd been in when I'd woken up the first time to being in a room at the Disciples' clubhouse.

Then, there was a yell. "What the fuck?"

That voice. I knew it. My heart soared at the same time my throat closed to the point where I could barely breathe.

Loud, fast footsteps sounded, getting closer and closer until he was standing there. He froze in the doorway, staring at me with wild eyes.

"Daddy," I whispered as tears spilled over.

He had me in his arms a second later, holding me close and squeezing me tight. That wall my mind had built came crumbling down and I fell apart, feeling the security only my dad's arms had ever given me.

"Ber-bear," he said in a gruff voice against my head and I completely lost it. He was here. I was with him. He would keep me safe.

I cried for what felt like hours, Dad moving only to situate us on the bed so I was in his lap, my face pressed to his chest and soaking his shirt.

Somewhere in my mind, I knew it was killing him. He'd never been able to handle my tears. I could still remember how he reacted when I'd broken down crying as a little girl because I fell off the first bike he got me. One of the training wheels had come to a complete stop when it hit a pebble on the ground. He'd thrown the whole thing out, bought a new one, and wouldn't let me ride it until he'd checked over every piece with his mechanic's eye, tested it, and swept the driveway and sidewalk.

Seriously, he got out a broom and swept it.

All because I'd shed a couple tears over a little road rash.

Seeing me falling apart like that, he was going to lose it.

It was that thought, the knowledge that he was suffering too, that eventually gave me the strength to rein it in. He heard it, felt it, and gave me time to get myself under some semblance of control. Only then did he ask the question I knew he'd been dying to get an answer to since he walked in.

"What happened, baby girl?"

Through hiccupping breaths, I settled myself on the bed beside him and forced out the words. "It was really late. I was asleep. I didn't even hear them until one knocked into one of the picture frames in the hall. It was too late by then. By the time I realized what was happening, they were already at my bedroom door. I went for the gun, but one of them got a hold of me before I could get it and release the safety. They stuck me, I felt the needle, and whatever they gave me knocked me out."

The anger radiating from Dad made me stop there, but he insisted, "Keep going."

With a sigh, I continued, telling him the whole thing. The sobs came back, even though I had no more tears left. I had to stop frequently, unable to get the words out. Dad didn't pressure me, and neither did the other men I could tell were in the room even though I hadn't looked around. In fact, Dad didn't say anything else until I explained how I told my captor about the club.

"That was good, baby girl," he assured me. "That's what got you home."

Home. Good God, I hadn't known whether I'd ever be able to return anywhere that could be a home.

I nodded at his assurance. "The guy, he locked us back in and came back with someone else. He was in a suit. I told him the same thing. They both left, then came back a while later with a syringe. They put it into my IV and I went out again. That's the last thing I remember before I woke up here."

Reading that I had nothing more in me, Dad moved and again pulled me into his arms.

"You're here now. We'll keep you safe," he promised.

I sighed. I had no idea what was coming or why life had led me here, but I knew, with absolute certainty, that he was telling the truth.

CHAPTER 4

Jager

WHEN EMBER WAS DONE TELLING her tale, we got the fuck out of there. Roadrunner needed time with his daughter and neither of them wanted us standing around like a nosey fucking audience.

"You recognize the two who brought her here?" Stone, the Disciples' president, asked me.

I shook my head. "Got a guess who they work for, though."

"That man Russian?" Stone inquired.

"Seein' as both his boys were..." I let that answer itself.

A heavy silence sat over the brothers gathered outside the room, that being Stone, myself, Tank, and Gauge. The rest of the club was staying back, waiting for their update.

Gauge spoke first. "We thinkin' retribution?"

Stone looked to me. "The price you negotiated, that include a caveat that we stay clear of their operation?"

Like I'd make a fucking deal like that. "No. Only that them not giving on their asking price would guarantee we wouldn't."

Pres nodded as he pinched the bridge of his nose. The whole situation was a mess. The Disciples didn't have the manpower to take on an organization like Kuznetsov's alone. Even with backup, we'd be looking at a fuck of a war.

When Stone gave Gauge his answer, he did it strained. "We are rushing into a battle we can't win. First off, I want to know why the fuck they took her. Odds they knew her connection to us

24

are slim, not with how they seemed interested when she shared that intel. They aren't above snatching random women, but that's usually off the street or out of clubs. Breaking into her house is odd. I want to know when they went there, why they picked her."

"Not thinkin' they're gonna offer that shit up," Tank pointed out.

He wasn't wrong.

"We need to see what we can find on our own." He leveled his eyes on me. "Get whatever you can on her and anyone close to her. Search what you can with her info now, then we'll ask questions to help widen the net once she's in better shape."

"Start running it today," I told him.

"Right," he replied. "Best go tell the rest of the boys what's going on."

HOURS LATER, I had the initial run on Ember on Stone's desk. The girl was smart. There wasn't a lot out there beyond the basics and she didn't post every fucking thing she did online. My gut was leading me to a Daniel Louis I came across. She never listed it as such, but I got the feeling he was a boyfriend recently made ex. He was my next focus, but Stone wanted to wait until Roadrunner had a word with her about the guy.

Officially off duty, I went back to my room to change. When I came out, I was facing off with an unsure looking Ember.

"Hi," she said before biting her bottom lip. Nervous habit,

but I wondered if there were more fun ways to make her sink her teeth in that plump flesh.

I didn't reply, but nodded my head at her.

"Ummm..." Biting her lip again, she looked down the hall and then back to me. It was then her eyes moved down my body. I'd put on sweats and a white tank. Her teeth sunk deeper into her plump bottom lip as she took in my torso. I shifted to keep myself where I was and her eyes snapped back up to my face.

"Sorry." The apology was immediate and embarrassed, like it bothered me that she had her eyes on me. "Going to work out?"

I gave her another nod while I watched her struggle to keep her eyes up.

"What do you do?" she asked.

"Box."

"That's cool. Dad's had me in kickboxing since I was a kid," she offered.

Girl was a talker, it seemed. Whether it was a nervous trait or a general one remained to be seen.

When I didn't answer, she went on. "I was actually...ugh... looking for him. My dad, that is. He was going to talk to someone, but he hasn't come back. I'm kind of...um..."

She didn't finish that thought, but the rumble from her stomach did it for her.

Roadrunner would be in with Stone, going over the info I delivered.

"Take you to him."

"Really?" she asked with a smile, then went on without needing an answer. "Great. Thanks."

I turned and started walking to Stone's office. She followed.

"I wanted to thank you," she said after a few steps. She caught on that I wasn't going to speak just to fill inane conversation gaps, so she went right on. "For earlier. For staying with me. I'm...not usually a crier. I just—"

"Messed up shit," I put in.

"What?"

I looked down at her, but pulled my eyes back quick. "Messed up shit you went through. Kind of shit that would break anyone."

She cleared her throat before giving a husky, "Yeah."

"Held it together better than most. Still are. Says a lot."

She didn't speak that time, but I felt her eyes on me.

"Gotta say it—whether I'd take the advice myself or not. Find a way to let that shit out. Talk about it, whatever. You need someone, I'd recommend Ash—Sketch's woman. She's been through some shit, got to the other side. She'd be good to talk to."

Might get her off my back too. I didn't regret opening the door to Ash after that shit went down when we both shot the man who killed her dad, shot Ace, and meant to kill her. She'd been drowning. I had a lifeline to throw, so I did. Still, I could do without the fact that she now seemed bound and determined to fix me or get me to open up.

"Yeah. I'll..." she hesitated, likely thinking out an answer that would keep her from lying.

I let her off the hook. "Not asking you to make promises. Just keep it in mind. You find you want to talk, she'd be a good choice. That's all."

I heard the breath she released at that. Shit, she was tying herself up in knots for no reason. She could have just lied to me. It wouldn't have mattered.

"Right. I'll remember that," she said.

We were outside Stone's office by that point, so I said nothing else. Instead, I pounded on the door for her. When Roadrunner opened it, I left without a word.

She didn't need my help anymore and I needed to hit the gym.

CHAPTER 5
Ember

FOUR DAYS I had been at the Disciples' clubhouse and I slept for a lot of it. Doc said it might take a couple days to get whatever they'd given me out of my system entirely. He said this in a pissed off, grumbly way. Because I'd known the man since I was born, I knew there was more to Doc's anger than just the very obvious fact that I'd been kidnapped, drugged repeatedly, and sold—as if that all weren't horrific enough. It was in the way he cut off his tirades mid-stride and switched gears. If I had to guess, I'd say it had to do with what they'd given me or how much of it.

I knew I wouldn't get an answer on that, so I didn't ask. They always felt they had to protect me. I was a little preoccupied with feeling like crap from whatever was running amok in my bloodstream anyway.

It took all of two days for me to eat solid food again. My first meal after my awkward encounter with Jager hadn't gone so well, so I'd been on a diet of broth and Jell-O since. I wasn't exactly sure which biker got sent to the grocery store for Jell-O and flip flops—since I'd been wandering around barefoot—but I managed to distract and amuse myself for a while wondering.

The one person I knew it wasn't was Dad. Aside from when he'd gone off to talk to Stone—undoubtedly about me, and certainly not anything I was going to be made privy to—Dad scarcely left my side. He even brought a blow up mattress into the room I'd been given. I'd told him I would be fine, that he could sleep in whatever room was his on a real bed, and it was a good thing he didn't listen. The first night, I woke up screaming and terrified because I couldn't remember where I was. Unlike the exhaustion and nausea, the nightmares showed no signs of slowing down any time soon. Part of me wondered if they ever would. I tried not to think about that.

In fact, trying not to think about things was becoming an essential part of my life. Every couple minutes, I would have to turn my mind away from the long list of things I was determined not to think about. Seeing as there was very little for me to do in a biker clubhouse I had not taken the initiative yet to explore at all, this was a tiring effort.

So, on the fourth day, it came time to do some wandering.

Everyone seemed to be giving Dad and I privacy, and I appreciated it, but I also hadn't really met anyone, which made the exploring plan a bit more nerve-racking. I knew Doc, of course. I'd met Stone a couple times over the years, and he'd been in to talk with me and Dad a few times as well. I'd met a guy closer to my age Dad introduced as Slick when he came by to flip the lock around on my door, something I learned he'd done just a few days before so I could be locked in. He'd given me three keys to the lock, promising those were the only copies. He could get in if absolutely necessary—he was a locksmith, after all—but no one else would have access unless I gave it to them. This, I didn't admit but felt down to my bones, was very comforting.

And last but most definitely not least in my mind, I had met Jager.

Talk about things that made me nervous about exploring the clubhouse.

Actually, talk about things that made me nervous. Period.

Shaking off thoughts of Jager, something I'd done quite a bit the last few days, I ventured down the hall. Dad had left my room about an hour before, saying he needed to check on things in the club's garage he managed. He'd been absent from it for days. Him going in to work meant I was going to be by myself unless I grew a pair and left my room. So, that's what I was doing.

I'd showered and dressed with toiletries and clothes Dad told me Cami had gone out to get, which was very sweet. Cami, I knew, was Tank's daughter. Since Dad liked to keep me up to date with the club even though I'd never been around it, I also knew she married one of the brothers, Gauge. When I'd remarked I would pay her back, since all the clothes still had tags on them, Dad had gone all commanding on me.

"No. I gave her the money for it. You're my baby girl, I take care of you," he'd laid down the law. That was my dad. I swore, if I let him, he'd still be taking care of everything for me.

I'd have to thank Cami, though. Not only did she go out of her way, she got me some decent clothing choices to get through the next few days. At the moment, I had on a black tank top and a pair of olive-colored fabric shorts with a reasonably stretchy waistband, which was probably a purposeful choice to ensure they'd fit without me being there to try them on.

As I neared the end of the hall, I hesitated. There were voices, and quite a few of them. It didn't sound loud and raucous like a party or anything, but I wasn't sure I wanted meeting everyone to start with a huge group. Still, it was becoming impossible to keep my mind occupied while I sat in a small room with only Dad coming in to keep me company.

At the mouth of the hall, I stopped. There were a handful of people sitting around on the couches and chairs together. Three couples, each pair sitting very snug, and I could see three of the brothers kicked back. One of them was gesturing with a beer in hand and I wasn't sure exactly what time it was seeing as there was no clock in my room and my phone was probably still on the bedside table in my apartment, but I was certain it was before noon.

"Look, I'm just saying, you fuckers getting balls and chains is the real problem. Ain't my mouth or anything that comes out of it that's changed. Certainly not the fine ladies who service those of us smart enough not to get tied down. It's you," he said, berating the men with women on their arms.

One woman sitting with her legs pulled across Slick's lap, shot back, "Ladies? That's what we're going to call them now?"

"Hey, now," the guy with the beer chastised, "no need to be nasty. Nothing wrong with a woman who wants to find a man to get her off, no strings attached. If I remember correctly, that was how you met our boy."

Clearly choosing to ignore his last words, she said, "No, there's nothing wrong with that. But the women you guys get to hang around here, clean shit up, and jump the second one of you says the word, are not *ladies*. They're club whores."

"Whatever. Tomato, tomahto."

I sensed the movement beside me and my head flew to the left. There was another person in the room I hadn't noticed, Ace. He was here with Jager when I'd...arrived.

Ace was attractive in a cuter way than Jager. I'd guess he was about my age—twenty-four or close to it. He had a leaner build than Jager or Stone, who both were very obviously opposing, but he in no way appeared anything less than formidable. He had a few days' worth of stubble on a very nicely defined jaw. His brown hair was cropped short from what I could see sticking out at the edges of the slouchy black beanie he had on. I'd only caught a glimpse of him twice in the time I'd been there up to that moment, but he'd had that hat on each time. I wondered if he always wore it.

He had been leaning against the wall a few feet from where I was at the entrance to the hallway, but he pushed off and stepped toward me. I glanced out the corner of my eye and saw the rest of the room had not noticed his movement or my arrival.

"Thinking of turning back?" he asked, his voice low.

"No," I answered, lacking conviction.

"They all want to meet you. The women in particular. Got a babysitter for all the kids to be here when Roadrunner told them you might be up to it today," he explained. "Daz is running his mouth like an asshole now, but he'll cool it if you go over. They're all wanting to check in on you."

"They don't even know me," I said, though he already knew.

"You're Roadrunner's daughter. That's all that matters. Your old man means a fuck of a lot to everyone here, but particularly to Ash and Cami."

I knew that was true too. I knew it from the way Dad talked about them, the way he always had, and if I was being really honest, it was something I'd once resented a bit. Dad thought it was best Mom raise me, even when she decided that meant moving away from Oregon and, thereby, the club. He was in no way an absent father despite the distance. Still, I often wished I'd had him every day. Ash and Cami had gotten him in person way more.

I didn't hold that grudge anymore. In fact, I was glad Dad had them around. He was paternal by nature—or he always had been since I'd been around. Cami and Ash growing up around the club meant he got to put that to use.

Realizing I hadn't actually answered Ace, I looked at him. He seemed to get that I'd digested what he'd said because he went on, asking, "You want me to walk you over there? Start off the introductions for you?"

If he hadn't offered, I never would have asked. Since he had, I was absolutely going to take him up on it.

"Please."

He surprised me by throwing an arm over my shoulders as he led me to the group. Slick and at least one of the other guys turned their eyes our way as soon as we started moving, revealing they knew I'd been there the whole time. They'd just hidden it so I could have a moment without everyone—the women, in particular—cottoning on. It was sweet, and I appreciated it.

Once they'd broken the seal, all eyes started to come my way. The women got to their feet. Slick's woman was very pregnant and needing a hand up from him. The other guys who had women with them stood after they did. There it was again, me thinking these guys were sweet. The way they were literally at their women's backs spoke to just how much they cared.

One of the women stepped toward me first. She was a few inches shorter than me, but that wasn't uncommon since I was five-nine. I was used to being a bit taller than most women I met. She had long, deep brown hair that was wavy in an obviously natural way. She was beautiful and rocking some serious curves. There was no question in my mind why she would turn the head of the seriously hot, but intimidating, guy behind her.

"Hi. I'm Cami," she introduced herself with a warm smile. Then, she nodded over her shoulder. "And this is Gauge."

Her obvious excitement to meet me made my smile come easily as I responded, "Hey. I'm Ember."

She moved right in and gave me a hug. Alrighty then.

As she pulled back, she said, "Sorry. That was probably weird. It just feels like you're family. Roadrunner is like my uncle. It's like we're cousins or something." I was going to tell her it was fine when her eyes roamed over me and she instantly went on. "Oh, it all fits you great! Awesome."

"Yeah," I answered, looking down at the clothes myself. "Thanks for getting all of that stuff for me."

"No problem," she said with a flick of her hand. "I was happy to do it. Though, it would have helped if Roadrunner gave me a little more than 'she's about your size, but taller' to go on."

I shook my head. "That sounds like Dad."

As I said it, I moved my eyes around the group, landing on a cute blonde with curly hair pulled up into a ponytail. Her face had fallen, her eyes growing so sad, it stole my breath. I knew in an instant this was Ash. Her father, Indian, had been Dad's best friend until he was killed years ago. Dad had never really gotten over the loss. Clearly, she hadn't either.

Almost as quick as the weight of her loss had settled over her, the seriously gorgeous guy covered in tattoos behind her stepped in tight to her back, wrapping a fully inked forearm around her upper chest and kissing her hair. *That would be Sketch,* I thought. As soon as he had her in his embrace, the sadness disappeared.

After a second, she gave me a shy smile. "I'm Ash," she offered.

"Sketch," her man put in with a nod to me.

"Hi."

Introductions continued through the group. Slick stepped up, introducing me to Deni, his petite wife—so petite it seemed amazing she could support the size of her pregnant belly—who seemed to be bursting with attitude. Then there were the brothers, Ham, who was a freaking giant, and Daz, the guy with the beer, who was a ridiculously blatant flirt.

Before I knew it, I was settled in with the group, sitting on one of the couches, shooting the breeze with them. No one asked about what had happened and I think I loved them all a little bit for it. I didn't feel like the freak show, but just like Cami had described me—a part of the family.

CHAPTER 6

Ember

"WAIT. SERIOUSLY?" Deni gawked at me.

"Well, yeah. Dad got me into kickboxing when I was just a kid. I teach it to teenagers and have a self-defense class for women," I answered.

"So, you're like a total badass," she shot back.

I smiled and shrugged.

"You totally are. Damn," she seemed to say to herself. "Could you take on one these assholes head-to-head?"

I looked around at the guys. Ham seemed like a definite no. Big guys could go down hard, but only if they were unskilled enough to let you get their weight out of their control. I got the sense Ham was not that type of guy. His content half-smirk said he knew I was aware of that. I moved my eyes to Slick, Gauge, Sketch, and Ace. They were all definitely formidable opponents. In a fight or die scenario, I might have been able to hold my own enough to get away—assuming I could outrun any of them—but I sincerely doubted I could take them down.

Then, my eyes moved to Daz.

His cocky ass smile had me issuing the dare with a lifted eyebrow. It wasn't so much that he seemed like less of a fight than the others, just that I knew he didn't see me as a challenge. When I was still in pigtails, Dad had taught me my ace card was men would always underestimate me. I'd learned that lesson well and had been using it to my advantage my whole life.

I looked from him back to Deni with a smirk. "Well, I could take Daz."

He put his beer down and gave me a once over that had nothing at all to do with sizing up my fighting prowess. No, he was checking me out. Again.

"You think you can take me, baby?" he asked, his ulterior meaning not at all veiled.

I met his kelly green eyes that were all sex. Really, Daz was attractive. My guess was his constant flirting wasn't even necessary. Plenty of women would jump at the chance to be with him without it. Of course, that would be jumping for *one* chance, just a single time hitting his bed, after which he'd promptly forget their names—if he learned them in the first place. Still, it'd probably be a night—afternoon, twenty minutes in a supply closet, whatever—they would never forget. I knew this just from talking to him. Even if I hadn't overheard their conversation when I came in the room, Daz just reeked of player.

If manwhore types weren't a complete turn-off for me, I might be tempted to give him a try.

"I know I can," I shot back at him.

He got to his feet, all calm and cocky. I kicked my flip flops off and shifted my weight to get a sense of the traction I got on the floor.

"Um...just to say, I wouldn't trust the floor in here to be go-barefoot clean," Ash offered.

I shrugged. There was no way I was taking Daz down in flip flops. It was what it was.

Daz took a few steps toward me, all swagger, no sense. While he was picturing my tank and shorts on the floor, I was sizing him up. There weren't any noticeable weaknesses, no favor to one leg while he walked, no gaps in his musculature. I would be screwed in a real fight with him. Luckily for me, he wasn't giving me that.

We faced off, neither gunning to make the first move. His

body was completely at ease, a nonverbal statement that he was going to let me get a free shot. Fat chance of that.

"You want me, big guy, come and get me," I taunted.

And, like a damn fool, he took the bait.

He was on me in a moment, swinging out, but not with a fist. He wasn't going to even attempt to hit me. Instead, he was trying to grab hold and subdue me. I twisted my body out of his reach, turning toward him so I could land my elbow—solidly, though not full force—into his gut. As he doubled over, I moved around him and swept his feet, sending him headlong onto the floor.

The girls cheered and the guys clapped and laughed at their fallen brother.

And then, I heard, "What the fuck?"

I turned and kind of choked when I saw Jager standing there, legs planted and arms folded across his huge chest. Besides his presence, what had me swallowing my own tongue was the fact that he'd gotten a haircut. More accurately, he'd shaved both sides of his head down to nothing, leaving a long, sleek mohawk in the middle. If there were such a thing as haircut kryptonite, mine was a mohawk. It always had been. Some women liked the scruffy look, some liked clean-cut, I liked the edge. Something about a mohawk—in general and on Jager specifically—was so hot, there was a serious possibility I was about to orgasm in front of an audience without him even touching me.

Just as I was trying to figure out something to say—anything so I'd stop standing there staring at him like an idiot—arms closed around my chest and hauled me off my feet.

Suddenly, the clubhouse was gone and all I saw was the slate blue I'd painted my bedroom walls six months ago, the gauzy white curtains on the window, my white and silver damask bedspread a mess and falling to the floor, all shrouded in darkness. And in the meager moonlight coming in from the window, three men I didn't know, guns aimed my way as the fourth tried to grab a hold of me.

I fought. I kicked, hit, screamed as loud as I could. I wouldn't let them take me. I couldn't. I...

"Ember!" someone yelled.

But that voice—it was one I knew. It sounded so far away.

"Ember!" it called again.

I blinked and my bedroom was gone. I could see it all again, the clubhouse lounge I never left, familiar faces around me.

Holy shit.

Holy, holy, holy shit.

"Flashback," Jager muttered, and I realized he was kneeling next to where I'd crumpled to the floor.

Trying to swallow back the tears welling, I moved my eyes from him and up the legs standing a few feet away until reaching Daz's face. The cockiness was all gone and he looked stricken.

"Fuck, Ember," he said in a strained voice, "I'm so fuckin' sorry."

At his words, Jager shot to his feet. "What the fuck were you thinking, asshole?" he demanded.

"We were just messing around," Daz returned.

I watched as Slick stood and got between them. "Jager, man, back down. We were all here. They were screwing around. It was all good."

Jager's head shot his way and he bit off, "Then you're all fucking responsible. That shit shouldn't have fucking happened."

Shit. Okay. Things were getting way out of hand. "Jager," I called.

He ignored me. "You didn't think this shit might be too soon?" he demanded to the room at large. I watch the men get pissed, particularly Gauge and Sketch, who were inching in front of their women on the couches.

"Jager," I called more earnestly. His head came my way as I

got to my feet. "It wasn't anyone's fault. I was fine. And then, I wasn't. It could have happened anywhere."

"It didn't happen anywhere," he snapped. "It happened because Daz was acting like an idiot and scared the shit out of you."

"It wasn't his fault," I insisted. Then, because I couldn't let him think otherwise, I stepped around Jager and walked to Daz. "It wasn't your fault," I told him.

His eyes said he didn't buy it, and I hated that.

"Jesus Christ," Jager bit off quietly, then his heavy footsteps pounded from the room.

I didn't turn to watch him leave. Honestly, I wasn't sure I could. I was barely keeping myself together without that visual.

"I'm sorry," I offered to the room. It hardly scratched the surface, but it was all I had.

Daz wrapped an arm around my shoulder. "Nothin' for you to be sorry about."

I took the comfort he offered even if I wasn't sure I deserved it after the scene I'd caused. Daz, I decided, was a good guy.

"I just..." I coughed, trying to clear my throat of the emotion clogging it. "I think I need some time alone." As much as it was true, it was a shitty excuse, but everyone let me get away with it.

They offered a few goodbyes and the girls promised they'd come back around tomorrow. I didn't respond to that. I wasn't sure whether I was going to make an appearance or not, but I appreciated that they were going to come even though they knew that might be the case.

Then, with my head scrambled and no clue how to fix it, I walked away.

CHAPTER 7

Jager

"CARD IS SET FOR FRIDAY. Got five guys lined up," I told the room.

It was time for church—club meeting, closed doors, patched members only. The room was one used solely for that purpose. If the Disciples weren't in church, it was locked. Once we were in the room, the fucker was also locked. There was no way for anyone outside the club to get in and try to bug the place or any shit like that.

Every brother in the club was seated around a table with Stone at the head to run the show. Behind him, the Disciples' insignia stood proud on the wall. Around us all, the walls were like a museum for the club. Pictures at rallies, mugshots—any kind of shit with sentimental value was hung in here.

Personally, I thought it was all just shit. Aside from that image on the wall that was patched on all our backs, the rest of it meant nothing to me. Sentimental crap like that, it went away easy. Pictures got lost, damaged, burned to fucking ash. Then, they didn't mean a damn thing. The patch, that fucking meant something. My cut was destroyed tomorrow, that patch would still be my life.

I'd had sentimental crap once. It wasn't what I missed.

"Simultaneous fights?" Tank asked.

"Not this time," I answered.

Stone turned to Tank. "Officer Andrews get his payout?"

40

Tank nodded. "Cops will be otherwise occupied Friday night. At least, the on duty ones who don't come out for the show."

There would be plenty of those. The club might be clean enough to get in fine with the P.D., but that didn't mean we were fucking spotless. Fight nights were a fat payday, particularly when you knew the house fighter would be the one with the takedown. Somehow, fuckers still showed up every time to bet against me. Served them right when we took their money. Plenty of the local officers were regulars, throwing their tax-payer provided paychecks into the betting pool at their local MC. Fine by us, so long as they left their badges at home.

"Alright, that shit's taken care of then," Stone surmised. "We've got one more order of business before you fuckers get out of my face."

"Love you too, Pres," Ham shot back.

Stone gave him the finger as he went on, "Didn't get a chance to cover it with all the other shit last time. Jager used club funds to pay off those assholes who had Ember—"

Roadrunner sat forward and said, "I'll cover it."

Stone kept speaking. "I'd like a vote. All in favor of the club covering that charge, payouts from this run gettin' cut to eat that, say 'aye'."

Unanimously, with the exception of Roadrunner, the brothers voiced their assent.

"Right. Done. Get the fuck out of here." Stone smacked the gavel on the tabletop, ending the meeting.

No one said another thing about it, just got to their feet and left the room. I noticed Roadrunner didn't move right away, no doubt others did too, but everyone let it lie.

In the main room, a couple of the club girls were hanging around behind the bar, passing out drinks. I gave the brunette a nod and she poured me a glass of Jägermeister. She handed it off to me, bending over until her fake tits nearly came out of her top. I took the glass, passed on the other offer, and grabbed a seat by Ace, who was listening to Daz talk about some parts they needed to order for the garage and not being able to find a good supplier.

That was how I killed the next few hours—with my brothers and an always topped off glass.

I WAS HEADING BACK to my room, calling it a night, at least for the social shit. Ember stepped out of her door as I approached mine. She hesitated when she saw me, her eyes automatically going down. She didn't scurry away, though. It wasn't fear or shyness that had her averting her eyes.

"Look at me," I said.

She did. Immediately. Eyes up and right on me, not even a pause.

Fuck. Just like I thought.

I needed to get the fuck out of there, or she did, and fast—before I decided against caution, against respecting my brother, and did something that couldn't be undone.

Ember's eyes stayed on me, expectant. I lost control for a second, letting myself look down at the thin t-shirt and tiny sleep shorts she had on, her long, long legs revealed like a goddamn offering.

"Shouldn't walk around here like that," I found myself saying.

She finally moved her eyes to look down at herself. Finding nothing amiss, her gaze turned questioning.

"The guys here respect your father. Roadrunner is our brother, so no one'll treat you like free pussy. Still, don't need to be tempting the boys into forgetting that shit."

And by "the boys", I meant myself first and foremost.

Her mouth widened, but she said nothing. I hadn't asked her to speak.

Fuck. Fuck. Fuck.

I moved passed her, knowing it had to be me. I had to put a stop to this shit before it got seriously fucking out of hand. She would let it. She would let me do whatever I wanted. Whether she realized it yet or not, she was submitting to me. I got to my door, unlocked it, and shut it without saying anything more to her. There was nothing else that could come out of my mouth that would be good for either of us.

Sitting down on the side of the bed, I pressed the palms of my hands to my eyes, like the lack of sight would get rid of the image in my head. Those fucking shorts. She needed to burn those. If she didn't get what kind of ideas those things were giving any man who saw her in them, she was a fool. Ember didn't strike me as a fool.

No, Ember knew exactly what kind of effect she had on men. She might have too much shit in her head to focus on it, but she knew all the same.

I didn't need that. I didn't need her and her complications.

Shifting where I sat, I tried to get my solid cock into a position that didn't feel like I'd locked it in a vice.

I might not need her, but I needed something to take care of that.

There were plenty of women around. Women who would fall on my dick just because of the cut on my back. Women who hung around hoping for the opportunity to fuck a Disciple. But I had no interest in them.

I needed a woman who knew what I wanted, who knew what was expected of her. I didn't need to train club pussy I wouldn't be using again. I didn't need some chick thinking she might hook herself an old man if I went back for seconds.

No, I needed a woman who came without all the bullshit attached.

And, I was thinking, a blonde sounded good.

I made a call, instructing her to meet me at the apartment I rarely used. She had an hour to be there waiting, and I knew she would be.

When the time came, I was there. I let her in without a word, and she kept her mouth shut like she was meant to. Without instruction, she stripped and stood before me, eyes downcast.

"Kneel on the bench," I ordered.

"Yes, sir."

That was the last time she spoke. The ball gag ensured that. I didn't need to hear a thing from her. I didn't need the sound reminding me who was bent over the bench, taking the cracks from the flogger, taking my cock.

Though I let the fantasy play out in my mind, I couldn't forget who was actually there, and who wasn't.

CHAPTER 8

Ember

"THIS IS PRETTY."

I was out with Cami, Ash, and Ash's daughter, Emmaline. Deni, regrettably, said her "overbearing, controlling husband" was keeping her home because she'd been experiencing some mild Braxton-Hicks contractions. She was none too thrilled about missing shopping.

Emmaline, or Emmy, was four years old and obviously a little princess. The all-pink outfit proclaimed that clearly enough, particularly the t-shirt announcing she was, in fact, "Daddy's Little Princess" in glitter. According to Ash, Sketch was the one who dressed her, which explained the shirt.

"She's got five shirts that all say something about 'Daddy' on them. If she's wearing one, it's probably because *Daddy* was the one who dressed her," she'd gone on to say.

I couldn't help but picture Sketch, and all his tattoos. I'd seen him a couple times since I'd been around. He, like the rest of the Disciples, it seemed, owned two colors: black and white. White only being the occasional shirt, still always worn under their black leather cut. That he had dressed a little girl in all pink still struck me as crazy.

When I shared that, Ash laughed. "Well, I say he dressed her. What I mean is he let her do whatever she wanted—like he always does—and just not-so-subtly suggested the shirt."

That made much more sense.

I absolutely bought that Emmy had decided on the flouncy pink skirt she had on. Particularly since it was her who had just spoken, pointing out another piece of clothing she thought I should get. Pink, again.

My eyes went to the clothes strewn over my arm. I wasn't averse to pink myself, but there was quite a bit more than I would normally grab. I was finding that I, like Sketch, had trouble saying no to Emmy. I wasn't necessarily going to buy them all, but I'd try them on for her.

Ash saved me from this one. "I think Ember has enough pink, baby."

Emmy looked at her mom like the woman was speaking Portuguese. "But pink is the bestest."

"Best," Ash corrected.

"Right," Emmy nodded, glad her mother was agreeing. Ash just shook her head in amusement. I grabbed the pink sweater.

The girls and I were out shopping because, frankly, I needed some clothes. Cami's little drop off had been amazingly helpful, but she'd only grabbed a few things. Now, I was wearing those while I actually stocked up, something Dad had given me cash for and insisted I do. He and I hadn't made a plan about getting any of my things from my apartment. I think he was waiting for me to bring it up, not wanting to push too soon, and I was waiting to figure out what the heck I was going to do.

If I were honest, there was no part of me that wanted to step foot in that apartment again. The flashback I'd had with Daz and the nightmares that hadn't stopped since the first night I'd been at the club made that clear enough. I barely slept because I knew I'd wake up terrified. I wasn't sure what would happen if I saw my old bedroom, but I was certain it wouldn't be pleasant.

It wasn't like I had much to go back to. Mom had moved us to Olympia, Washington when I was too little to remember. It was where I'd grown up. I'd gone to college up in Seattle and ended up staying there afterward. I'd gotten a degree in Business Administration because I'd thought it would be useful and had no idea what to study, but ended up working part-time at a local gym and part-time as a bartender. It wasn't a long-term arrangement, but it paid my rent and kept me fed. Aside from that, I was just drifting.

Did I want to go back to drifting?

"Ember, you okay?" Cami called.

Alright, maybe in the middle of a trip to the mall wasn't the time to sort all that stuff out in my head.

"Fine. I think we've seen everything. I'll find someone to open up a fitting room," I answered.

"Yay! Dress up!" Emmy cheered.

Seriously, she was flipping adorable.

Half an hour later, we were in another store, repeating the process, when Cami asked, apropos of nothing, "So, what do you think of the boys?"

"The boys?"

"The Disciples," she explained.

What did I even say to that?

"They're great. Rough around the edges, obviously, but I worked at a fighter gym and a bar that wasn't a stranger to rough guys. Not to mention, you know, Dad. They don't faze me." That sounded pretty good.

"What was up with Jager the other day?"

I froze, my hand locking into a fist around the romper I was checking out on the rack.

"What?" I wheezed.

"The other day, with Daz. Jager seemed pretty intense, even for him. He doesn't usually step into things like that," she hedged.

"I have no idea," I told her, and I meant it.

"Is something..." she trailed off, but it was impossible to miss her meaning.

"No." There wasn't. I mean, he was hotter than sin and could probably have me begging just by saying the word, but there was still nothing there. I was pretty sure he found me to be a nuisance for the club.

"Really?" Cami pressed.

"Really."

Shrugging, she went back to perusing the racks while I forced my hand to relax around the now-wrinkled romper and move like I was a normal, functioning person.

Cami had no idea how much asking about Jager affected me. I'd been thinking about him nonstop. Well, I'd tried to stop, but the alternative to thinking about him was thinking about a host of things I wanted in my head far less. So, Jager it was.

The other night, when I ran into him in the hall, I could swear he was going to make a move. Or, maybe not. Maybe moves weren't his style at all. I got the distinct feeling Jager was more about demands. This feeling didn't help my attraction. I happened to be quite fond of demands.

Not that I knew this from experience. I'd never been with a man who took control. Still, I knew what I fantasized about. On those long bouts of not finding a man who seemed worth letting into my bed, when my creativity dried up and I turned to porn for inspiration, I knew there were always certain things that got my attention.

Bondage, for example.

"What about Ace?" Cami queried.

Shit. File bondage and any prospect of doing that with Jager under another thing I shouldn't be thinking about while shopping with the girls.

"What about him?"

"He's cute," she said.

"Are you trying to play Disciple matchmaker?"

"What?" Cami evaded. Ash laughed.

Cami deflected the attention by holding up a cobalt blue bodycon dress. "This would look amazing on you."

The dress was hot. Like, really hot. It wasn't necessarily my go-to style, but none of the clothes I was buying were. The clothes I really loved weren't the kind you could always get easily at a mall. They required shopping online at specialty shops or hitting up higher end resale places. Still, I could rock that dress. There was just one issue.

"Where would I wear it?"

"Fight night," she said immediately.

"Fight night?"

"Friday," Ash answered. "The club hosts fights from time to time. People bet. It's a whole thing."

"And you're supposed to dress like you're going out clubbing?" I clarified.

"Not necessarily," Ash replied.

"Things are a little different for us," Cami countered. "Gauge and Sketch don't really want us drawing extra attention."

"Sketch doesn't even want me going, he just doesn't really want to leave me at home either," Ash amended.

"So, you guys will be wearing...?"

"Jeans," Ash answered.

"Probably shorts, but that depends on how long before we have to leave Gauge sees me. And our property cuts. Absolutely."

"So, since I don't belong to any of the guys, I dress up?"

Ash had her eyes on Cami. Cami had her eyes on me, and answered, "You don't have to, but you can. There are going to be a lot of guys there, the club and people from town. Maybe you'll meet someone."

Seriously. What was with her trying to set me up?

"Is my being single offensive to you in some way?" I teased.

"Of course not. But that doesn't mean you have to be either," she shot back.

She handed me the dress and walked a few feet away to look at another display.

I turned my attention to Ash. "What am I missing?"

She bit the inside of her lip in indecision before saying, "I think we're all just hoping you find a reason to settle here. We like you. We love Roadrunner and know he likes having you close. And, honestly, we're worried about you. What happened..." she let that hang for a moment because neither of us wanted to talk about it. "The guys can keep you safe here."

My eyes moved to the cobalt fabric on my arm. "And the dress?"

"Cami and I both came back here for different reasons," she explained, "but we stayed for the same one: our men. The right guy gives you roots. If you find him here," she shrugged to indicate the unsaid *maybe you'll stay.*

I didn't tell her I was thinking I might stay either way. I just studied the dress like it might have some answers.

"You should know," Ash spoke again, "Jager is fighting on Friday. He always does. He's undefeated. That's how the guys make most of their money, on people who make the mistake of betting against him."

I didn't know what to do with that, but the way she went back to perusing and talking to Emmy told me she didn't expect anything. I didn't really know what to do with any of it. Staying, dating, fight night, Seattle, Hoffman, the club—it was all just a jumbled mess in my head. Like the practiced hand I was becoming at it, I shoved everything into the increasingly crowded back of my mind.

I WAS HANGING clothes and arranging them into the closet of what had become my room at the clubhouse. Shockingly, the clubhouse had a top of the line washer and dryer squirreled away. I had to guess it was the myriad of slutty girls using it and keeping the little laundry room stocked. I couldn't even picture the guys doing so themselves.

The dozen bags' worth of shopping I'd done—which did include, though I asked myself why a thousand times, the dress— were all clean and ready to be worn. So, despite the fact that I was avoiding dealing with pretty much everything, at least I had clothes. I was counting it as a victory.

A knock came at my cracked door, followed by Dad stepping through. He was around a lot, usually spending most of his time with me, or me hanging out in his office at the shop while he worked. Some people might get tired of it, but I wasn't one of them. I'd always loved my Dad. Mom and I had a rocky relationship—to put it lightly—and now I found it was best to distance myself as much as possible. I'd never had that problem with Dad.

"How's my girl?" he asked.

"Okay," I answered.

He eyed the two shirts I still needed to hang. "You get what you needed?"

"All set. I have your change in the purse on the dresser," I told him. Clothes weren't all I'd had to buy. I had nothing. The purse was one of the first purchases, along with a wallet, so I wouldn't be pulling loose bills from my pocket all day.

"Keep it. In case you need anything else. Whatever."

I didn't argue because I knew better. "Okay, Daddy-o."

While I finished hanging and sorting, I told him about my day with the girls and he told me about a '72 Camaro that had been brought in to the shop for a total facelift. When my task was done, I sat on the bed next to him, leaning into his side like I always did.

"Need to get you a TV in here," he said.

"You don't have to. I'm fine going into the lounge."

"You say that until the guys give you shit and take over when you're watching something. Or until you walk out there to Daz watching porn."

"Right there for anyone to see?"

"Fucker keeps it in his pants, but that doesn't mean he doesn't turn that shit on."

Jeez.

"Okay, maybe a TV then. I'd like to avoid that."

"Good call, Ber-bear."

After a moment, I decided it was time to address something I'd been thinking about a lot over the last few days. "Can I ask you something?"

"Anything," he answered right away.

"Why did you keep me away from the club? Everyone's been so welcoming. And Cami and Ash said they were raised by all the guys. Why wasn't I?"

"Figured this'd come up," he sighed. "Look, I never wanted to say shit about it before 'cause I didn't want it to be a problem," he started, but didn't finish. I figured out where he was going.

"It was Mom. She's the reason. It's why we moved to Olympia, isn't it?"

He sighed, knowing exactly how easily Mom made me blow up. "Ember..."

I jumped to my feet, pacing around the room. "Why? Why would she do that? Why take me away and make it so I only had two people to make up my whole family when I could have had all this?"

"Look, baby girl, back when you were born, the club wasn't the same as it is now. We were into shit..." He ran a hand through his hair, yanking at the ends in frustration. "Fuck. I didn't want to get into this. Back then, we were involved in a lot of shit, all of it illegal, some of it fucking dangerous. It was not a great time for the club as a whole. We've gotten free of that. We're not exactly a bunch of upstanding citizens, but we're a fuck of a lot better now than we were. When that shit was going down, when brothers were getting hurt, getting locked up, getting *killed*, I understood where your mother was coming from. She didn't want that for you. Then, I had to be here while my baby girl was three hours away. I had to watch Cami and Ash grow up here with the club, the two of them never being touched by any of the bad shit we dealt with. I tried—for years, I tried—to convince your mother you could be a part of this in a good way.

"She wouldn't have it. When I started to push, she threatened to go to court, fight to get my custody taken away, to limit how much I could see you. Didn't matter what kind of money I threw at that, there was no way for me to win that fight. I've got a record, and not just one stint inside. You know that. I'm a known member of an MC with a long history of involvement in shit no judge would want a kid around. I could have gotten the best lawyers out there, but she still would have destroyed me in court."

I wasn't pacing anymore. I was frozen to the spot at hearing what Mom had done to him. It was hard to breathe knowing it.

"She threatened to keep you away from me?" I whispered in horror.

"She thought she was protecting you," he offered, but even he didn't really accept that as an excuse.

"By keeping you from me?" I started to yell. "How the fuck would that have been good for me? How the fuck was missing out on having a bunch of men who would have treated me like family and done whatever they had to to keep me safe protecting me?"

"Ember..." Dad got to his feet, coming toward me.

"No. She's so unbelievable. I wanted to be here! I like it here. I want to stay," I ranted.

Dad grabbed my arms. "You want to stay?"

His disbelieving voice drew my focus back to the room and I looked up at eyes that matched mine. "I want to stay," I repeated.

Then, I wasn't looking at anything because he yanked me into his arms. "You want to stay," he said gruffly above my head, "then you fuckin' stay. I want nothing fuckin' more than for you to stay."

Well, there it was. It was decided.

I was staying.

CHAPTER 9
Ember

I FELT LIKE AN IDIOT.

Or, really, I looked like an idiot.

It was Friday. Fight night. Dad tried to talk me out of coming, but I didn't know why. He just said it "wasn't the place" for me. When I asked what that meant, he'd just shaken his head and walked away.

Whatever.

It had only come up once more when he made me swear I'd stick close to one of the brothers at all times. I figured I would do it just to humor him. He'd given me the keys to a loaner car they had for the shop, told me how to get there, and taken off about two hours before I needed to follow.

I drove Cami over too, since Gauge was also going early. He met us as soon as we arrived, giving me my first Disciple to attach myself to.

Now, we were inside. The inside in question was the basement of a gym. From the brief glance as we walked through, I knew immediately it was a fighter's gym. I'd worked in one that wasn't much different. From the looks of things, their focus was on boxing or MMA, maybe both. The basement was finished, but barely, and as we went down the stairs, a taped off circle meant to be the boundary for the fights came into view.

It seemed to me the basement of a gym that trained people to fight was not the best place to hold an underground fighting ring.

"Isn't having this here a little..." it took me a second to find the right word, "obvious?" I asked Gauge.

He looked at me, smirked a little, then answered, "Only need to avoid that if the cops are looking to shut you down. Seein' as we've got several of Hoffman's finest in the crowd tonight, doesn't much matter if it's obvious."

Oh, well then. That settled that.

The place was packed and we were still early. Mostly, the crowd was made up of men. A lot of them looked like the Disciples—big, burly, lots of tattoos, and facial hair. There were plenty in cuts, not all of which bore the Disciples' insignia. Some of the men looked more like clean-cut, suburban types, but they were less in number. I wondered if they—or some of them, at least—were cops.

Then, there were the women.

A few women, like Cami, were dressed simply in jeans—or, in Cami's case, shorts, something Gauge had given her a displeased look for when we arrived. Some wore property cuts like hers, but all were right at the side of a man whose body language clearly said she was not to be fucked with.

The rest were scantily clad in the most extreme sense of the phrase. Most of what they were wearing could scarcely by deemed as clothing. Little crop tops, the tiniest of daisy dukes, and miniskirts so short, ass cheeks were actually visible. Seriously, I had underwear with more coverage, and I wasn't talking granny panties. There were also girls wandering around with nothing but bikini tops covering their chests—and to call it "covering" was a stretch.

I looked hot, I wasn't going to deny that. The dress was a perfect fit, meaning it was skintight. It was short, though by comparison, it probably looked matronly since it actually came down at least five inches below my ass. It had thin straps and a Vneck I'd thought was pretty low before I'd gotten there. My hair was straight down; it was the only thing I had the supplies to do. I'd gotten makeup on our epic shopping spree and had finally broken the stuff open. To me, dress and heels meant makeup, every time.

So, I was feeling good about how I looked, until I walked in. Now, I felt ridiculous.

I pinched Cami's arm.

"Ow. What the hell?" she cried.

Pinching wasn't a good call. Cami's response had Gauge swinging around, ready to fuck someone up for messing with his wife. Oops.

"Sorry. My bad," I told him right away, hands up.

He backed off, muttering, "Sorry, Ember."

"What the hell was that?" Cami demanded.

"Why would you tell me to wear this? I look like a freak. I should have just worn normal clothes like you."

"I'm dressed like this so I *don't* turn heads. You're single. You should be getting attention," she explained.

"You're insane. A, I don't want attention. B, I'm hardly going to get it with all the nearly naked chicks wandering around," I pointed out.

"Leaving something a mystery does more with these guys," she stated firmly. "They get the slut look all the time. It gets boring."

I somehow doubted men ever found half-naked, stacked, skinny women boring to look at.

Cami's eyes moved around the room, then fixed right over my shoulder.

"Oh man," she muttered. "You might say you don't want attention, but you're definitely getting it."

I turned just as Jager stepped close and wrapped a hand around my bicep. He was shirtless. Like nothing at all on top, not even his cut. Just his huge, muscled, tattooed chest. I feared I might start drooling.

"I've got her," Jager rumbled to Gauge, who gave him a chin lift in response.

Then, we were on the move. Jager pulled me through the crowd, which parted without hesitation for him. I was practically jogging to keep up, giving all my attention to not tripping in my heels.

At the back of the huge space everyone was standing around in, he pulled open a door, charged through, slammed it behind us, and backed me against it in complete darkness. Before I could say anything, he hit a switch to turn on the single bulb above us. It seemed like a janitor's closet, but I didn't have a chance to get a look since Jager was right in front of me. He pressed in until my back was flush to the unyielding door and my front was tight to his even more solid body.

"What the fuck are you thinking?" he demanded.

"I...what?" I stuttered.

"Why the fuck would you wear something like that here? Fuck. Why the fuck are you even here?" he kept at me.

I shook my head a bit. "I don't..."

"Are you trying to make me fucking crazy?"

"No."

He stared down at me, his eyes on fire, jaw clenched, nostrils flaring. He looked terrifying and hotter than anything I'd ever seen in my life. I wanted to run away, I wanted to kiss him, and I wanted him to shove up my dress and take care of the ache between my legs.

His hand came up, grasping my neck, his thumb pushing at the underside of my jaw. I capitulated, letting him raise my head.

"You dress like that to get one of those motherfuckers out there to take you home?" he growled.

"No."

He leaned in even closer, his hold at my neck getting firmer. He was nearly there. If I stretched up at all, I'd be able to kiss him. But I couldn't, not with his physical and mental hold on me. I couldn't go anywhere until he said.

"You dress like that to get me to fuck you?"

I didn't hesitate. I gave him the answer even I hadn't known was true until that moment.

"Yes."

He kissed me, his mouth taking mine with a savage force. His hands locked under my jaw, keeping me still for his onslaught. My submission only seemed to incite him more. He kissed me hard and deep, and I only gave back as much as he let me.

For the first time since I woke up to unknown men who had broken into my apartment, I felt my mind relax. There was peace in my head even as my body lit up for him. His power, his complete control, gave that to me. I sank deeper into the freeing intoxication.

He ripped his mouth from mine and the intense gaze he hit me with halted my protest before I voiced it.

"You go back out there, you stick to one of the brothers. Not Gauge or Sketch who are too occupied with their own women. You stay on one of the guys who won't be fucking distracted. When I'm finished, they take you to the office and lock you in. I'll get you when I can. Then, you're on my bike."

I didn't say a thing, just nodded my agreement.

"Tonight, you're mine, pet."

Oh my God.

I was too dumbstruck to even move my head to agree.

"Ember?" he demanded.

"Yes," I squeaked.

"Yes, sir," he corrected.

Oh. My. God.

"Yes, sir," I echoed.

His mouth crashed into mine again, kissing me for an unrelenting moment until my lungs ached with the need for air. Only then did he pull back and grab onto my arm, hauling me out into the fray. He led me once more through the parting crowd until he came to Ace.

Over the rumbling noise of the room, I heard him order Ace not to leave my side and to put me in the office when it was done, just as he'd demanded of me. Then, without a goodbye to Ace or a word to me, he disappeared into the mass of people.

Ace looked down at me, his eyebrows raised, his face contemplative.

"What did you get yourself into?" he asked.

I didn't answer him.

I had no idea.

CHAPTER 10

Jager

I NEEDED TO FOCUS. I needed to get my fucking head together, but all I could think about was Ember. How she looked in that goddamn skintight dress. How she submitted like a fucking dream. How I could feel the heat of her pussy against my leg.

For the first time in my life, I didn't want to fight. I wanted to get the fuck out of there and take her.

I got through the crowd, going into the hall where we'd put together rooms for the fighters. Knocking on the doors for the first two up, I hollered, "Ten minutes!" I didn't stick around for their responses. I went to the last room and stepped in.

Doc was already inside, ready to get me out to the ring, but there were two fights before mine.

"Water, now," he demanded.

I wanted something a fuck of a lot stronger than water, but that wasn't an option. The air conditioning didn't function fully in the basement and the room was warm already. After the first two fights were finished, it would be hot—too hot for a fighter who wasn't hydrated.

Without argument, I did as Doc told me, chugging down half a bottle. By the time I went out, I'd have a full two down.

"Any concerns?" he asked.

"Right shoulder's been tense."

He came over, standing behind me while he worked my right

arm with no finesse whatsoever. I had no fucking clue if he'd once had a decent bedside manner, but he didn't have one anymore.

"You going out to watch the other fights?" he asked.

"Yeah. One of 'em wants to challenge me. Told him he had to earn it. Need to see what I'll be dealing with if he wins."

"Then you ain't got time for heat. Try to keep moving it a bit while you're out there. Don't let it tighten up," he said with a slap on my back.

When I stood, my shoulder already felt looser. Doc knew his shit.

I got out into the main room just as the first two fighters were announced and made my way forward to the circle, not a soul saying a goddamn thing as they let me through. I was positioned right at the edge when the ring-card girl made her way out and the good shit started.

The guy I was there to see, Dustin, was practically a kid. Twenty-one, obviously trained, but I'd put him through his paces with one of the trainers at the gym before I'd give him a place on the ticket. He told me he'd been in boxing and martial arts classes since he was a kid. Had to be said, I had no fucking clue if that meant he'd hack it down here. Fighting in sanctioned competition was nothing like the no-holds-barred shit we did. I would know. I'd done my share of both. Only time I'd come anywhere close to having real competition was in the underground shit.

Dustin's training was obvious, and it was also obviously hindering him at the start. He was holding back from the kind of hits that would have a ref on his ass. But he caught onto the fault quick. Once he stopped holding back, he took control fast. He was scrappy, but with skill and training behind it that made him formidable. He didn't realize it—and neither did his opponent— but he was losing his guard on his left every time he struck from the right, and he was favoring his right a lot. That kind of opening, in the right hands, would have him down.

It took the kid six and a half minutes to K.O. the guy he'd been fighting. His opponent was known on the scene, so the win was met with a chorus of groans from those who lost their bets. It also meant the club was cleaning up.

With a glance across the room to verify Ace was still on Ember and all was good—something I forced myself to do quickly so I wouldn't be tempted to go over there and taste her again—I left the room while the crowd kept up their applause for Dustin.

I stayed in the back hall until the kid came through. He looked at me, waiting for me to speak rather than heading off for the water I could tell he needed.

"You got another fight. Lining up someone harder. You take him down, you get a shot at me. Hydrate next time and stop dropping your left guard."

Then, I went into my room so Doc could get me taped up and ready for my own time in the circle.

TWO SHOTS. That's all the motherfucker facing off with me got in. I gave him the first. It was bad fucking manners not to let them have one. Not to mention, if I never let them land a hit at all, it was harder to get people to bet against me. The best money came from the morons who did.

The second hit came when I saw the flash of blue in my vision. I couldn't fucking control it. My eyes went to her. Her gaze was fixed on me, her fisted hands up high below her chin, like she was so into the fight, she was planning out the next move I should make.

The fist had hit me then, right at the shoulder, and I'd earned it. It was not the fucking time to be distracted by her.

I dodged the next two swings he took, then landed a kick to his ribs. He stumbled back, then charged in an uncoordinated, rage move. That's when I was done. I'd fight a decent opponent, but I wasn't going to deal with some sloppy fuck letting feelings into the circle.

It took ten seconds, three moves. One elbow to the ribs I'd already hit, one kick to the knee he'd been babying the whole time to take him to ground, and a kick to the head for the knockout. Then, it was over.

Daz stepped over the passed out fucker and yelled into the megaphone, "And the motherfucker takes it again!"

I let him lift one of my arms in the air, giving everyone a chance to cheer or boo, like I gave a shit whether they'd won or lost cash on me. My eyes moved back to where Ember had been. She was still there, but Ace was preparing to take her away. Before he got her to move, though, I saw the big eyes, the slight part to her lips, the flush in her cheeks. She was aroused. Watching me destroy that bitch had worked her up.

Fuck. It was time to get the fuck out of there.

I didn't say a word to Daz, just pulled my arm free and walked away. He knew the drill. I wasn't in it for the fucking attention. I was in it for the fight. With that over, I had much better things to do.

Doc was ready when I got to the back, water bottle and towel in hand. He didn't talk through the fight with me or give me pointers. I knew my strengths, and I knew when I made a mistake the second I made it. I could analyze my own fight at twice the speed someone else could. Doc was there to see to my body and because he wouldn't fucking run his mouth endlessly while he did.

"Anything off?" he asked. I shook my head. "Then I'm out." And he was, a second later.

I wiped myself off with the towel, drank the bottle of water, and ripped the tape from my hands. Throwing my shirt, shoes, and cut back on, I got out of there too.

The place was, like always, a madhouse with the fights over. Those who had done their betting wisely were seeking out whichever brother they'd placed them with. Payouts were being handed out, but not without the club taking their cut. The crowd was a big one and there seemed to be a lot of people walking away with nothing. Some would have bet against me, some would have lost on the second fight, but the majority had bet against Dustin. The kid would get a cut of that money—a cut that would be substantially larger because the point spread hadn't been in his favor.

I saw Ace a few feet away, counting bills to hand to one of the shop's mechanics. He met my eyes and tilted his head up the stairs. He'd deposited Ember up there like I'd asked. Good deal.

It took ten minutes to get up to the main floor. The stairs to the basement weren't exactly wide and the night's losers were all heading out. It could have been a chance for me to shake off the adrenaline from the fight. Instead, I felt myself get more amped with each step. She had me ready to fucking blow and I wanted to punish her for it.

I broke away from the crowd, striding full speed across the dark gym and up the half flight of stairs to the office door. I never spent much time in there. I had no fucking desire to be stuck behind a desk. If I was at the gym, I wanted to be on the floor, watching how the training was going. Mostly, I used the room because of the elevated view and one-way mirror. I could watch without everyone knowing I was checking in.

The door was locked, like I'd asked, and I didn't have the key. The second I pounded on it, Ember pulled it open and I charged, slamming it and flipping the lock again behind me.

"You didn't ask who it was," I pointed out.

"I saw you coming," she answered.

I took that mouth. I didn't want to hear words, I wanted to taste her and feel her give me what I wanted. She did, spectacularly. That submission, it wasn't a fluke before, it wasn't even a decision she made. It was instantaneous, intuitive, natural. It was fucking perfection.

With my hand at the back of her neck, fisting in her soft hair, I pulled her back.

"I wanted to wait. I wanted to take my time to show you how I feel about how fucking crazy you're making me. That'll come later. Now, I need to fuck you," I told her.

"Yes, sir," was her breathy answer.

I backed her into the leather sofa sitting on one wall, half of it beneath the window.

"On your knees, face the glass," I instructed. She did right away.

Forcing myself to step away from her ready, willing body, I walked over to the desk and rifled through a drawer. I knew there were condoms in the fucking thing. More than one of the brothers had brought someone up here during a fight night. Finding one, I snatched it up and went back to stand behind Ember.

She didn't turn around to look at me. She kept herself facing the window where we could see the crowd still filing out from the basement. I ran a hand up the side of her thigh, feeling her jump a bit at the touch before she settled into it.

"Good girl," I praised. "Keep your eyes forward. Keep looking at all of them. Do you think they can see you?"

I hoped like fuck she hadn't noticed the one-way mirror when she'd walked through the gym. I wanted her thinking the only thing that might keep the men down there from seeing me fuck her was the darkness.

"I don't know," she whispered with a tremor in her voice that was all desire.

My rising hand pushed her dress up around her waist. She had on a thin pair of panties that cut high across her ass cheeks, highlighting the curves of each smooth cheek even more. I didn't want to play then, I wanted to take the edge off and get her back to my place where I could use her properly. But that ass was too fucking tempting.

I brought my hand down hard on one cheek, then the other. She cried out a bit, but arched her back in a silent request for more. I gave it to her, landing ten more smacks, five on each cheek, until they started to glow.

That was all I could take. Her red cheeks, her moans, and the way she had her ass arched up high for me had me ready to fucking burst. Getting my cock out and sheathed took seconds, but they were seconds I hated taking. I couldn't wait any more. Even taking her panties off was too much time wasted, so I just pulled them to the side. Her bare pussy came into view, swollen and dripping wet from the spanking I'd given her. Fuck, I was going to have fun with her.

"You ready for me?"

"Yes," she whimpered.

I slammed into her, full force, barking out a curse at the feel of her tight, hot cunt squeezing my dick. She cried out, but pushed her ass back against me, holding me deep. I grabbed onto her hip, my other hand going into her hair to grip it hard at the base of her head. Then, I gave it to her.

I fucked her hard, fast, unrelenting. I pounded into her sweet little body, holding her in place so she had no choice but to take my cock how I gave it to her. She gripped my cock tighter with every thrust, until I was nearly blinded by the feel of it.

"You need to come, pet," I warned her.

"Oh God," she moaned.

I pushed her head down, bringing her ass up even higher, and let loose. She screamed as I fucked her for all I was worth, feeling her wetness soak down her thighs until, just in fucking time, she flew apart. As she spasmed around my cock, I buried myself in as deep as I could get and came on a roar I couldn't contain.

CHAPTER 11
Ember

HOLY. Shit.

I couldn't...

I didn't...

There were no words. There was barely a coherent thought in my head.

I came so hard, for a moment, I thought I was going to black out. My heart was still pounding, my lungs burning, my body so overwrought, I couldn't move.

"Jesus. Fuck," Jager muttered.

Yeah, what he said.

He pulled out of me slowly, then collapsed beside me. I didn't move except to let my head fall onto the couch and my back to relax. We spent a long time like that, coming down from what we just shared. It was about the time I relaxed, my body finally catching up, that he stood. I heard him moving, the crinkle of the condom wrapper he'd thrown aside as he disposed of it, his zipper going back up. Then, he placed his hand softly on my back.

"Up, pet. I'm not done with you yet."

Oh, God. I didn't know if I could take more, but I got up anyway. He handed me some tissues to clean myself up and stood silently while I did. When I was decent again, my dress and panties fixed, my hair finger-combed back into place, he went to the door and led the way out.

Silence seemed to be Jager's modus operandi, which made

me super uncomfortable. Generally, talking was mine. I didn't like quiet, particularly not the awkward, weighty kind that followed being fucked within an inch of your life by a man you barely knew. The urge to talk just to fill the space was intense. I tried to quell it, but it was no good.

"Where are we going?" I asked.

"My place."

Huh. His place. Since I'd been around, I'd seen him at the clubhouse every day and was almost certain he'd spent every one of those nights in his bed there. Not that I was keeping tabs on him or anything.

I totally was. But whatever.

The point was, I hadn't expected him to have a place of his own. I thought he just lived at the clubhouse. Now, I not only had that information, but I was going to see his home for myself.

I followed behind him, trying not to stare at his huge back while I thought about all this, until we made it to the bottom of the half flight of stairs leading to the main gym floor. I was surprised to see people still milling about, casually making their way from the basement stairs to the front door. I expected everyone to be gone in the time we'd been...well, occupied.

"People are still here?" I voiced the thought.

"Takes a while to get payouts dealt with," Jager explained as he kept walking.

That meant most of the Disciples would still be down there, handling that. None of them would see us leaving. Or, they wouldn't see us leaving from the office upstairs. Who knows who saw Jager pulling me from the basement. Ace knew. Gauge had to know something.

Crap.

This I hadn't thought through. They were my dad's brothers, all of them, Jager included. It's not like I lived under any delusion that Dad thought I was still a virgin or anything, but that didn't mean he'd be comfortable with me starting whatever this was with one of the Disciples. Not to mention, he usually came to my room at night before turning in. What would he do when I wasn't there? He'd have no clue where I was and after what had already happened...

Shit. I was a terrible daughter.

"Dad," I said aloud, hoping Jager would understand.

"Knows you're with me," Jager answered.

"What?" It came out like a shriek, but I couldn't help it. Dad had seen me leaving with Jager—was I supposed to be calm about that?

Jager finally stopped just before we made it to the doors. "He's not an idiot. He knew there was something up when you insisted on coming tonight. Already handed me shit about that too. You're a grown woman, so he isn't going to tell you what to do, and he knows it'll only cause problems if he tries to pull that with me. Didn't tell him shit. Didn't plan on shit happening 'til I saw you in that fucking dress. But Ace taking you out, and me leaving, he'll know where you are. That's all there is to it."

I was floored. Not only by the knowledge that Dad knew something was up with me and Jager before anything had even happened. Not only by the fact that he'd seen me leaving, knew where I was going, and didn't stop it. Not only by the fact that Jager had told me Dad knew these things and I had to deal. No, what really shocked me was the sheer quantity of words Jager had just used. I was certain beyond a doubt I'd never heard him say so much at once before.

My shock and the honest to God fact that he was right—that was all there was to it—had me saying, "Okay."

Jager didn't hang around to process or talk that information out. He got back to walking out of the gym and led me to his black-on-chrome Fat Boy. It had been a while since I was on the back of a bike. A thrill went through me knowing I was about to be again, while holding on to Jager. He climbed on first, then waited for me to settle in behind him before he took off.

The ride was great. Jager's big, hard body, the open air, that throaty growl of the engine. Part of me was almost disappointed when he pulled up to an old-looking building that seemed once industrial. Any ideas of wanting to stay on the bike disappeared as soon as the thought of what we were doing there took over.

Jager led me into a plain looking lobby with a bank of five mailboxes on one wall and stairs and an elevator on the other side. Nothing ornate, but nothing battered or unkempt either. The elevator had key slats next to each floor but the first. Jager inserted his key next to the fourth floor, turned it, and hit the button.

"You have the whole floor?" I asked.

"Not a big building. Every unit's a whole floor."

Huh. Interesting.

"How do you let guests in?"

"Gotta come down and get them."

His short answers didn't faze me, though part of me wondered if they should.

"That seems like a lot of effort," I commented.

"Not really."

The way he said it made it clear it wasn't much effort because he didn't get a lot of guests. This was not surprising.

The elevator opened into a living room with high ceilings. One wall was made of exposed brick and windows. The ceiling was interspersed with exposed ductwork. There was a kitchen divided from the living room only by an island. To the right was a small hallway with what looked to be three doors off it. None of it looked particularly lived in. There was furniture, but it was sparse, and there were no decorations or personal things anywhere.

"This way," he said, heading down the hall to the second door on the right. Opening it, he went straight in and I followed, until I turned within the room and got a look. What I saw had my feet cemented to the ground.

The room was like something I'd only seen on a computer screen. It wasn't a room for sleeping or living in—it was a room where Jager could tie a woman up and fuck her.

No decorations, no color on the walls. There was a full bed on a plain, wooden frame with a slated headboard. The bedding was simple white and just sheets. No blanket to make it a place to sleep. That wasn't what it was for. This was punctuated by the hand and wrist restraints at each corner of the bed.

There were two support beams in corners of the room with chains attached to them. One wall was kept clear, chains dangling from the ceiling in front of it as well as anchors screwed into it. A few feet away was a padded, leather spanking bench.

It was a room much like ones I'd imagined myself in, a room from my dirtiest fantasies I would never have spoken aloud. Yet, there I was. It was real, and I was alone in it with Jager.

The ache I felt between my thighs was like nothing I'd ever experienced. I was wet, soaking, and the feeling only drove me higher. I wanted this, whatever he was going to do. I wanted it so much, I was ready to beg and he hadn't even said anything.

"Nervous, pet?" he asked. I'd been so caught up looking around, I hadn't realized he came back to my side.

I moved my eyes up to his, seeing the dark heat in them that made me want to moan. I bit my lip to hold it in before saying, "No."

He stared at me for a moment before his eyes flared. "Strip."

The shoes went first, the relief in my feet as they adjusted to being flat on the floor making me bite down hard on the inside of my cheek to keep quiet. Everything, even the feeling of my clothes moving on my skin as I removed them, seemed to be driving me higher.

Jager's eyes followed every move, but he said not one thing. When I was bare before him, he stepped closer. One hand came up to cup my breast, a finger running over my taut nipple. It wasn't play, it was like he was inspecting, learning my body now that it was revealed in full. His hand moved to the other breast and I was ready to scream if he didn't give me more soon. Then, that same blasted hand went down my stomach and dipped between my legs. A single finger ran through my slit and I cried out as it brushed over my clit.

"So fucking wet." His voice was approving and I felt a surge of pride at the sound.

I whimpered as his hand left me, but kept my lips sealed. His eyes stayed on mine and I knew I was doing nothing to hide the battle I was fighting. I wanted to beg, to demand more, to haul off and touch myself, but I remained still and quiet. This was a test, his eyes made that clear.

It felt like I'd been standing there for hours when he said, "Good girl."

There it was again. His praise lit me up. I felt it in every part of my body.

His next words came more swiftly. An order—one I was all too ready to obey.

"On the bed."

I moved without hesitation, walking across the room and reclining on my back. Jager followed, moving slower, pulling off his shirt as he came. His eyes roved over my body while mine fixed on the bulge in his pants.

"Have you done this before?"

Crap. I wanted to lie. I wanted to tell him I was a pro. I didn't want him to hold back or find me lacking. Still, as much as I'd thought about it, I'd never even been restrained during sex.

"No."

"But you've wanted to," he shot back immediately.

"Yes."

He nodded as he grabbed one of the ankle restraints, pulling my right leg out and fastening it. The process was repeated with my left leg. He said nothing, but I was deafened by the sound of my own heavy breathing.

When he came up near my head and grabbed my left arm, he spoke again.

"I won't go intense. But I'm not holding back, giving you a taste. You don't like it, you say 'I quit'. You say stop or no, I'll keep at it. You tell me you quit, we're done. I let you loose, stop what I'm doing. Understand?"

I understood. I even understood the unsaid part of that instruction. If I told him I quit, that meant permanently. "Yes."

"I'll be aware of your reactions. I think you genuinely aren't getting off on something, I'll move on. I'm not sure, I'll ask and expect honesty," he went on.

"Okay."

He strapped in my right arm, and I was completely at his mercy. There was an inch or so I could pull in each direction, but no more than that. Restrained, naked, and staring up at Jager as he took me in, I felt completely at ease and more desperate than I had ever been all at once.

"Okay," he echoed, then his hand went between my legs.

His fingers hit their target right away, landing against my clit, and I cried out. He rotated them, pressing lightly against that bundle of nerves until I was mindless, pulling against the bonds holding me down, trying to get more pressure.

"Still," he chided.

I did as he said, and he instantly pressed harder, giving me more. A reward for being good. I decided right then I could be good for him any time he wanted.

Doing so proved difficult a few minutes later when he stepped away right as I was about to come. I wanted to cry out at the injustice of it, but I bit down on my lip so hard, I thought I might draw blood.

My body had never felt more alive, more vital. There was a humming beneath my skin, an energy I hadn't realized until that moment had been completely silent. I'd shut it down, everything in the wake of what happened. Jager gave that life back to me.

He returned, his hand at his side holding something I couldn't get a good look at. Seeing him, the way he emanated power in that moment, I realized I was bringing something to life inside him too. There was light in those eyes, a brightness I thought I'd never see. This was the real Jager. He was dominance and power. I caught a glimpse of it when he'd been in the ring, but it was nothing like what I was seeing now.

He lived in the day-to-day world he had with the Disciples, but here and in the ring, he was truly alive.

I would have let him keep me tied up there forever just to bask in the sight.

I was broken from these thoughts when his arm went high, then came down with a sharp crack. Dozens of small stings exploded on the skin of my thighs and that time, I did cry out. There was slight pain, but it was unlike any I'd ever experienced before. It brought me from my mind and straight into my body. It awoke every nerve and the pulsing of my building orgasm grew stronger.

"My pet likes her flogger," he commented.

He didn't want a response, not more than what my body was already telling him. He made that clear when he landed the flogger again, this time across my stomach. Then again and again, until it felt like that humming beneath the surface was going to break out of me—until I could barely contain the raw feeling inside me.

His hand went back between my legs and if my mind were engaged at all, I might have been ashamed of the wetness seeping onto my thighs. Instead, I was all about feeling his fingers as he pushed into me and thrust unrelentingly.

I felt the first spasm of my orgasm move through me just as he pulled his fingers from my body. That time, I couldn't contain the keening whine. I needed to come. Why wouldn't he let me come?

"Not yet, pet. You've got a long way to go before you get that."

The flogger came down again, right at the juncture of my legs, hitting my swollen, desperate pussy. The feeling was so intense, I was blinded by it.

I heard screaming.

I was too lost to realize for a long time it was mine.

CHAPTER 12

Jager

IT HAD BEEN over an hour since I'd strapped her in. There was a glorifying pattern of pink and red lines decorating her skin. Her pussy and thighs shone, soaked from her arousal. Beneath the patchwork of marks the flogger left behind, her skin was flushed. She was panting, the exertion of being kept right on the edge of coming for so long getting to her.

She was perfection.

I'd alternated between the flogger and my hand for the first half hour, then I'd replaced my fingers with a dildo she lost her mind over. Every time I'd thrust it in and pull it out, she'd scream in triumph or desperation. Next time, I'd gag her. This time, I wanted to hear those screams.

I pulled the dildo away again, eliciting another cry of frustration from her. I watched her try to get herself under control, physically pulling at her restraints in the effort. Her body was undulating wildly, wanting the release the slightest friction could give her in her state.

Then, in a sweet, broken voice, she started pleading. "Please. Please, sir. Please. Please."

There it was. I'd been waiting. I'd been pushing, wanting her so worked up, even her desire to do as I said was gone. Still, she didn't try to demand of me. She begged, without having to force herself, without feeling any shame. She begged me openly.

I got a condom, not wanting the fucking thing between me

and all that wet I'd worked to get. Ember wasn't in any state to talk about that shit, though. We'd sort it later, then I'd take her ungloved.

I nearly groaned just at releasing my cock from my pants. She had me so fucking hard. Her submission, the way she never once fought what I gave her, never even said 'no' in response to me keeping her from her orgasm—nothing could have made me harder.

I climbed onto the bed and Ember flinched, jerking when my body touched hers. Her whole body was sensitive from the treatment I'd given her. I didn't go lightly because of that. As I settled myself over her, my cock ready to take her, I made sure I touched as much of her as I could. I wanted her raw nerves to feel me as I took her.

My cock glided right in, sliding through that soaked cunt even as she clamped down on me. Ready to reward her, and not willing to wait another minute, I fucked her hard. She flew headlong into an orgasm as soon as I started, screaming until her voice broke. I kept on thrusting, taking what I needed and getting her there again. Before the first orgasm left her, a second took over. The third hit even sooner, her pussy barely letting up on my cock between the two. It was on that third, when she was clamped down on me so tight I had to fuck her with all I was worth just to move, that I let it come over me. That drenched, tight as fuck cunt wrapped around me, hotter than anything I'd ever felt, sheathed me completely as I came.

And fuck, I came hard. Even with her already giving me that, Ember made my dick feel like it had been pent up for years. It was worse than the stint I did inside. How she managed to make me hornier than a year and a half without pussy did, I had no fucking clue.

As soon as my head cleared enough to move, I got off her. She'd be sore. She didn't need my weight on her. I got right to loosening her restraints, taking time to rub down each arm as I guided them back to her sides. She'd been on her back, so the blood flow was not impeded the way it would have been if I had her upright with her arms tied above her, but that didn't mean they didn't ache from being locked in that position.

I let her lay there after releasing her while I went to the bathroom and filled the tub. Aftercare wasn't usually a part of my encounters. The women I played with weren't amateurs and I never pushed the limits we discussed. I wasn't fucking callous enough to think a woman could be taken to that place without being cared for, so I avoided going there.

There was no avoiding it with Ember. She might have wanted it, might have gotten off huge, but she was still new to it all. It was another reason I should have steered clear, or just stuck to vanilla fucking. I just couldn't resist the draw of her, or the desire she clearly had for what I gave her. If that meant taking care of her in the aftermath, I would. The way she'd taken what I'd given her was fucking worth it. And it was worth the effort to secure the chance of doing it again, doing more.

Ember had fallen asleep by the time I got back to her. I went to pick her up when the memory of her flashback after Daz grabbed her halted me. Instead, I put a hand to her shoulder, giving her a little shake.

"Ember."

She stirred, her eyes blinking open. There was a tiredness there that had nothing to do with what we'd done. It was deeper than that, the kind of exhaustion I'd been living for years.

"Hmmm?"

"Got a bath for you," I told her. "Relax your muscles."

"Mmmm. Bath is good. Sleep is better," she murmured in response.

I didn't smile. I didn't laugh at how she was fuckin' cute, too tired after I fucked her to even get in the bath and relax. But I felt the stir of those reactions, something I hadn't experienced in a long time.

Something I hadn't had since Jamie gave it to me.

I chased that thought out.

"You can sleep after," I told her.

"Nope. Gotta go back to the gym, get my car, drive home."

"You can stay here. Take you to get your car in the morning." The words were out of my mouth before I took a fucking second to think them through.

As soon as they were out there, I realized how fucking stupid I was being. Stay here? Women didn't stay here. I fucked them, they left. The bath was already more than what was usually offered. Now I was letting Ember stay the night?

"Really?" she asked, maybe almost as surprised as I was for suggesting it.

No, I thought.

"Yes," I said.

Fuck.

She didn't get excited, though I wondered if that was a forced reaction. She just said, "Okay."

Okay. I helped her up, knowing better than she did how unsteady she'd be. I gave her a hand getting to and settling into the bath, then left her to it. Both of us weren't fitting in that tub, and anyway, I didn't need to do anything else to get her on the wrong page about what was happening here.

While she did that, I swapped out the sheets on my bed, since it had been a while. With that done, I went to the living room. I didn't have cable. Didn't think it was worth paying for when I was here so little. I hadn't been in the place long. I moved here from the farmhouse the club owned just a couple months ago, but still spent most nights at the clubhouse.

I grabbed a book, one I'd read before, which was a good choice because I wasn't retaining any of it. Instead, I was listening. There were muffled sounds of Ember moving in the water. Eventually, more motion followed by the gurgle of the drain. I went back to my room so I'd be there when she got out.

After a few minutes, she emerged from the bathroom. Drops of water clung to her exposed skin above and below the towel, catching the light as she moved. Her hair was wet and messy from her drying it off. Moving to the dresser, I pulled out a shirt for her to borrow and held it out to her without a word.

"Thank you," she offered, turning away from me to pull it on. I might have demanded she not turn away, but seeing her bare from the back, her ass that I hadn't had the chance to mark properly, did just as much for me as her facing me would have.

Ember went right to the bed, climbing in on the left side. It was farther from the door, and I was glad. If she'd chosen the other side, I would have made her move. She watched me, her eyes tired but expectant.

"Get some rest," I told her as I left the room. I didn't wait to see the expectation die. I knew it would and that was enough.

For hours, I kept myself planted on the couch, that same book I wasn't reading in my hand. Fuck, even as I set it down and finally gave in to joining her in my bed, I couldn't say what book it was. I lay down on my side of the bed, careful not to disturb her or settle too close.

I didn't sleep. Not just because I couldn't, but because she didn't need the shit scared out of her when the nightmares woke me. So, I was awake when hers woke her. She didn't scream, didn't thrash about. She just shot up to sitting on a gasp. It took her a while to calm her breathing and lay back down.

All the while, I pretended to be fast asleep.

CHAPTER 13
Ember

THE KNOCK CAME at my door not long after I got back to the clubhouse. Jager had kept his word, taking me back to the gym for my car first thing and I came right back because, honestly, it wasn't like I was going anywhere on a Saturday morning in a hot dress and heels. I didn't need to be the walk of shame girl at the coffee place. I only had time to change into a pair of comfortable shorts and a tank before the knock.

"Come in," I called, figuring it was Dad.

I was right, and his face spoke volumes.

"Hey, Daddy-o," I said, trying to diffuse the tension.

"Figure you know I know," he replied.

He was right, of course, so I didn't respond.

"Not gonna give you a lecture or any shit like that. You're a grown ass woman and I trust you. This is somethin' you wanna do, not gonna be me to stop you."

None of this was said harshly. Dad wasn't pissed. He was just laying it out like it was, something we'd agreed to do with each other a long time ago. I loved that we had that, even if it made for awkward moments like this.

"Just need to say my piece," he went on. "Jager's my brother. Not gonna bad mouth him. I trust him, 'bout as much as I trust you. And I'd trust him with your life, just like I would any of the brothers. What I can't say I trust him with—what I want you to be cautious of trusting him with—is your heart."

He was right. I knew that, so I set him at ease.

"I know this isn't that. It's not heart and flowers and forevers. I'm good," I told him.

He looked me over, that penetrating Dad look where he tried to see right into my head and read me. When it left without turning to concern, I knew he'd let it go.

"Alright, then we got other shit to sort," he changed the subject.

"Like?"

"Your shit. You got some new clothes, but that doesn't mean you should just leave everything in your old place."

Right. Of course. But...

"I don't know if I can go back there and pack," I told him.

"I know, Ber-bear," he said quietly. "Got a couple of the guys together. Daz, Ham, Tank. Gonna go up there, move all your shit out."

I thought about the brothers having to pack up all my stuff. Then, I thought about Daz taking charge of packing my underwear drawer. The horror of that thought must have showed on my face.

"Not going through everything," Dad assured me. "It's in the dresser, your nightstands, whatever, it goes on the truck in them."

Well, that was a little better. I hadn't even thought about the unmentionables in my nightstand.

"Okay."

"Gonna head up there today, might crash there tonight, then be back tomorrow with your stuff. Still got your room at my place. We'll move your things in, store the stuff we can't," he explained. "You stay however long you want. Fuck, you stay forever if you wanna. But, if you get a place, you'll still have everything to do it up."

Part of me, the child who had always wanted it, was ready to jump for joy at the idea of living with Dad. Even if it was only temporary. I loved him, but there was no way I was moving in forever.

"Okay."

"Headin' out," he said. "Gotta get the truck and grab Tank. He's gonna drive it back down so I can get your ride."

He'd thought of everything. Damn. I was so lucky.

I went to him and wrapped him up in a hug. "Thanks for taking care of all this."

"Anything for my girl," he said with a kiss on my head.

He meant that, completely. Anything for me. He'd proven it time and again.

God, I loved my Dad.

When he was gone, I sat on the bed. I meant what I'd told Dad. I knew what this thing between Jager and I was and what it wasn't. I had no delusions it was something big that was going to last.

Still, it was hard not to feel the enormity of what we'd shared. To him, it may not have felt like it—I couldn't be sure. He was probably used to the intensity, but I wasn't.

Yet, he hadn't acted like it was just run-of-the-mill for him. Those eyes, the active ones I saw for the first time while he had me tied, didn't lie. Even as I lost control, I saw something in them that reassured me he at least understood the gravity of what I'd given him. It was reverence. Not avowals of love, let's-spend-the-rest-of-our-lives-together reverent devotion, but reverence all the same.

It was that that convinced me. Even if things between Jager and I were never going beyond what they already were, I was absolutely not ending it any time soon.

THE NEXT AFTERNOON, I was sitting in the forecourt of the clubhouse, waiting. Dad had called saying they'd be back any time. The guys were headed right to his place with the truck to start unloading, but he was swinging by to get me.

Behind me, the front door opened. Ace and Jager strode through it. Jager gave me a look, a heated, heavy look I felt run through me, but he didn't approach. Ace came right over.

"What're you doing out here?" he asked.

"Waiting. Dad's going to be here in a minute with my baby," I explained.

I saw his confusion, but was focused on Jager, who kept moving toward his bike. He hadn't acknowledged that he was in the conversation, didn't look my way again, but his body noticeably tightened.

"Your baby?" Ace repeated.

"Mmmhmmm."

"Fuck. Are we talking about one of those little yappy dogs or some ridiculous shit like that? Didn't pin you for the type."

"Me? A yappy dog person?" I shot back. "Yeah, no."

"Thank god."

Then, I heard her. That sweet purr coming closer just as she came into view.

"Fuck," Ace muttered. "That your baby?"

"Yep," I replied.

"A nineteen thirty-two Roadster?" he asked, like he couldn't see it right there.

"Yep," I said again, putting an extra bit of pop in the P.

"Fuck," he repeated.

I left him there, heading out into the drive more so Dad pulled up right in front of me, but I sensed Ace moving behind me. I also sensed Jager's eyes tracking me.

Dad stepped out of the driver's seat. "Beauty drives like a dream," he said by way of greeting.

"Well, she was restored by the best," I answered.

I grew up around cars. Dad loved his bike, always had. He loved the freedom of it. There was something amazing about the open air. Still, that didn't make him any less of a car man. He loved anything with an engine. He had the name Roadrunner for a reason, after all. It was because of his perfect condition 1972 Plymouth Roadrunner. "The bird", as he called it. It was his baby. If I didn't know he loved me, I might have gotten a complex over the way he loved that car. Instead, I got a love of cars instilled in me by my motorhead father.

When I was twenty-one, he surprised me with the fully restored hot rod for my birthday. That was the day it became my baby and I'd been treating it as such ever since.

"Did you treat her good on the drive?" I pestered him.

"You givin' your old man shit after he just hauled his ass up to Seattle and moved all your stuff?" he grouched.

"Absolutely. Now, did you treat my baby the way she deserves?" I sassed.

Dad gave me an indulgent grin. "Opened her up on the highway, let that engine do what it's designed for instead of that cooped-up city driving you've stuck her with."

"Whatever," I groused. "Give me my damn keys."

He tossed them my way. "Gonna grab my bike, meet you at the house."

"Alright, Daddy-o," I replied, getting behind the wheel.

I started my girl up, loving that purr just as much as always.

Then, because I couldn't help it, my eyes moved across the forecourt to Jager. His eyes were already on me and there was a look to them that told me I'd be feeling whatever he was thinking about me and my car soon. It took all I had to ignore the shiver that went through me as I focused on maneuvering my car out onto the road.

When I pulled up to Dad's place, the guys already had the moving truck pulled into the drive and were unloading boxes. Dad had an almost shockingly suburban abode. A two-story colonial on an acre and a half plot. It wasn't the sort of block where the houses were all so similar you could easily pull up to the wrong one, but they were all similar. Small family homes in a decent neighborhood; a decent place to raise kids as long as there weren't too many for the size of the houses.

Dad had gotten it for me, for the occasion when I came to stay with him. Unfortunately, in what I now knew was my mother's attempt to keep me from the club, that had happened less than I would have liked. He always came up to Olympia to see me, and now, for the first time, we were going to get some decent father-daughter time in the house where he'd always planned to share that with me.

I wasn't choking up a little bit. Nope, not me.

Dad pulled up on his Harley right after me. We walked up to the truck together to take a look at all my stuff inside. He put his arm around me as I pondered how crazy it was that my whole life was right there in that truck. It hadn't even taken the guys long to load it all up and bring it down to Hoffman.

"Gotta head inside, Ber-bear," Dad said. "I've still got the bedroom set you replaced the kiddie stuff with a few years back in your room. We brought all your stuff down, but I figured you might want a change. Whether that's your furniture with new sheets and shit, the stuff that's in there, or you wanna go out and get everything all new. We can do whatever you want, just gotta know."

A change. I knew exactly what he meant. It might not be my bedroom in my apartment, but if I filled the room here with all the same things, it might feel like it. It might trigger me. I thought about waking up from the nightmares and seeing the curtains, the bedding, the dresser. I remembered waking during the real thing and seeing those things.

He was right, I needed a change.

We went inside together and I felt some of the anxiety that had started rising with those thoughts ease. I might not have gotten to live with Dad, but that didn't mean I wasn't with him. There were pictures all over—of me, of us—like a timeline of my life. In the living room, on the mantle over the fireplace, you could see baby me the day I was born, elementary school me missing teeth, my high school senior picture, graduation days from high school and college. Then, right in the center, a picture Doc had taken. It was on my twenty-first birthday, right when Dad surprised me with my hot rod. I'd thrown myself at him and Doc snapped the photo just after I hit. Dad's arms wrapped around me, my smile huge and eyes closed as I hugged him, my baby gleaming in the background. I had the same picture framed. It was sitting in one of the boxes on the truck outside.

Dad noticed my eyes on the picture and smiled. "Love that picture," he rumbled.

Yeah, I did too. It was us, plain and simple.

It was then, seeing that, I decided the furniture upstairs—furniture I'd picked even if it had been a few years now—would be perfect. I didn't need to recreate my apartment in Seattle. It had just been a place to live.

Right then, I was home.

CHAPTER 14
Jager

I WALKED into the clubhouse yard and drew to an immediate stop when Emmy darted across my path, giggling as always. Right on her tail was the only one here with enough energy to keep up with her, Daz.

"I'll get you, little princess!" he cried.

"No, Uncle Daz!" she shrieked back. I hadn't noticed until then that she'd managed to say "Uncle" correctly. Ash had been trying for as long as any of us had known Emmy to get her to stop saying "Untle".

Now that she fixed it, I had to admit, the old way was kind of cute.

"Hi," I heard from beside me and saw the older Davies woman sidle up.

"Hey," I replied to Ash.

"So," she went right on, "where's Ember?"

"How should I know?"

She looked innocent, but it wasn't some showy, wide-eyed, porn-acting look. It was just her keeping her expression clear. She shrugged. "You two seem...close."

There were a lot of ways to define close. Ember and I might have been a fuck of a lot of one of them, but we weren't any of the rest.

"No."

"Huh." I didn't know whether Ash was playing a game or just

90

using this as a way to continue her mission to get close to me. She'd been at it for a while, always seeking me out when the opportunity arose, like right then when the club was hosting a party. Those opportunities weren't exactly few and far between, and she always took them.

"She seems really sweet," Ash went on. "It makes it even more horrible, what she went through."

She wasn't wrong. That shit was always fucked, knowing it happened to Ember made me fucking homicidal.

In a softer, deeper voice, Ash said, "I don't think she's dealing with it."

She saw the breakdown that afternoon in the clubhouse plain as I did. She saw Ember around with the brothers acting like everything was normal. She hadn't seen Ember wake from a nightmare, something I knew was a common occurrence from the way she reacted. It was clear she didn't need to to suspect the truth. I was pretty fucking certain Ember wasn't dealing with any of it.

I expected the next thing out of Ash's mouth to be a suggestion that I try to help Ember, like I'd helped her, but that was not going to fucking happen. I'd laid that shit out for Ash—as much as I ever had, anyway—because I wasn't sure anyone else was going to be able to help her. Not to mention, Ash had already been very spoken for. I could have unloaded all that shit, given her every fucking part of my messed up past and dropped to my knees to beg her to be mine, and it wouldn't have mattered. Ember's situation was different, and there were a fuckload of people around ready to do what they could. To add to that, our situation was different. I kept on fucking her and burdened her with all that shit, she'd get ideas she had no business getting.

I wasn't in the market for an old lady. Not now, not ever.

Ash didn't preach to me about helping her. No, the next thing from her mouth was, "Oh, wow."

My eyes followed her line of sight, landing on Roadrunner, who had just come around the side of the clubhouse. He wasn't alone.

Fuck.

Good fucking God, Ember was trying to fucking kill me. First with her excitement over that goddamn car of hers. I'd never cared for the bimbos they put in bike and car magazines, sprawled out half-naked and oiled up on whatever vehicle they were spotlighting. If I wanted that kind of thing, I'd get porn. It had always been about looking past them to whatever actually had my interest. Watching Ember, not even done up a bit compared to those women, leaning all around that hotrod of hers to give it a look, I found I really fucking understood. Ember and that beauty were the shit teenage wet dreams were made of. I thought the hard on she gave me right then would never fucking deflate.

I wasn't even going to start in on that tight ass dress she wore to the fight.

With both those and the images burned in my brain of her tied up and creaming for me, I thought I'd gotten a good sense of how crazy the woman could make me.

I hadn't even scratched the surface.

It seemed, being stuck with just the Hoffman mall to get herself stocked, she'd had to settle. Now, with Roadrunner and the guys getting Ember's shit from Seattle, she was able to give it all. And that all was a fuck of a lot more.

She strutted into the yard on a pair of red heels I was damn sure she'd be wearing with nothing else. I'd work her until her skin was as bright as the fucking things before I fucked her in them. That was how fucking hot she looked. I was ready to lose it over the fucking shoes alone.

The rest of her...there were no words. She looked like the hottest fucking pin-up ever. If they'd been able to photograph her and stick her on the postcards they sent to the boys during the world wars, morale would have been at an all-time high. Fuck, you put her on postcards now, you'd have guys enlisting just to get a copy.

She had on a pair of short shorts that went up to her waist. I couldn't see her ass, but the way they fit her like a glove everywhere else told me that view would be spectacular. On top, she had a red and white striped halter shirt. It looked like a sailor get up, and if I had to get on a fucking boat to get it off her, I would. Her blonde hair was all pinned up away from her neck, her bangs rolled, and she had a red bandana tied around her head. Even from across the yard, I could see her lips were painted red to match the rest. I loved red lips. Red lips made a fucking mess and they looked great with a black ball gag.

I was getting way too worked up for the situation. There was maybe a millimeter of restraint keeping me from marching across the yard, pushing her down to her knees, and getting a look at how much of that lipstick would rub off on my cock.

Did she come in that car of hers? Jesus. Her in that outfit, climbing out of that hot rod, bending over the hood...fuck, I was making a fucking porno of her in my head.

I finally looked away from her when Emmy ran across the yard again, this time toward Ember, yelling, "You look pretty!"

Kid didn't know the half of it.

Needing to take advantage of my broken focus while I could, I walked away from the clubhouse door and over to the makeshift bar set up on a table. Like always, someone made sure the Jägermeister was there for me. Not surprising, every brother knew it was the only thing I drank. There were two bottles on the table. I didn't bother with cups and shit, I just grabbed one of them and popped it open. A cup of anything wasn't going to be enough with Ember wandering around looking like that.

Ace came around, grabbing a beer from one of the buckets of

ice. He opened it up and took a drink before looking around the yard. When he stopped and his eyes widened, I knew exactly what the fucker was looking at.

"Holy fucking—"

"Don't finish that fucking thought," I warned.

His eyebrows went up at me. I'd known Ace a long time. I was the one who introduced him to the club. We met way back when, in juvie. In some ways, he was even more a brother to me than the rest of the guys. But that didn't change shit if he thought he was going to fuck Ember.

"You claimin' her?" he asked

"No."

He gave me a smug look, telling me I had no ground to stand on.

"Think you got enough women problems." It was a low fucking blow. We both knew it.

"Asshole." Ace left then. I didn't blame him. What I'd said was uncalled for, but it was also true.

Tank sidled up as Ace stormed off. "Shit, what's up his ass?"

"Nothin'," I answered. That was Ace's business. I knew that shit, but no one else did. I wasn't about to go blabbing. I took a long pull on the bottle in my hand.

"Hey there, pretty lady," Tank greeted, and I knew exactly who it would be.

"Hey, Tank," Ember's voice came back at him.

No way I was ready to be that close to her yet. Not with the way she looked and the smell of mangos coming off her. Fuck, she looked good enough to devour and smelled sweet as hell too.

She was testing me, but she'd regret it when she got the results.

"Hey, Jager," she went on to greet me.

I moved my eyes to her, letting her see exactly what I thought of that get up. She read it, the promise of the punishment I'd be doling out for dressing like that, for getting me so damn hard when I couldn't do a thing about it.

The fuck of it was, any other woman, it wouldn't matter. I grabbed one of the club girls and pulled her off in the middle of the party, not one person would fucking care. Courtesy was, with the kids running around now, that shit waited until family time ended, but then it was fair game. Odds were, in a couple hours, Daz would be getting his dick sucked or fingering some chick out in the open.

But Ember wasn't club pussy, she wasn't my old lady, she was a brother's daughter. She wasn't fair game. Roadrunner might know about what was going on with us, but that didn't mean I needed to advertise it to the whole club. Roadrunner wasn't the only one who could serve up shit about that.

Walking away before I broke and took her out of there anyway, I grabbed a seat around the just-lit fire. Daz was there with Stone, Ham, Gauge and Cami, Sketch and Ash, and little Emmy, who had a marshmallow on a stick, waiting not very patiently to reach that sucker over the fire. With the bottle in my fist, I settled in, ready to make the long haul right where I was.

A couple hours later, with the booze still flowing strong, the kids and their parents gone, and the club girls descending, I was thinking settling in had been a bad call. It hadn't taken long for Ember to grab a seat around the fire too. I should have figured that's where she would gravitate seeing as both the women had been there, but even after they left, she had not.

Why I stayed put, I had no idea. I wasn't prone to masochism. Sadism, sure, but I like to inflict, not suffer. Sitting there for hours with Ember a few seats away, looking the way she did, and letting all that sass and personality that had been slowly emerging since she'd been around fly, was the purest torture.

"Alright, but I have a question," Ember, who I was guessing had to be slightly tipsy by that point, though she wasn't showing it, announced. Her eyes were on Daz, who'd been explaining how he'd been banned from giving prospects their road names—something he still hadn't let go of even though it had been years.

"Shoot, beautiful," Daz replied.

"Why do they call you Daz?" she asked.

Tank, Stone, and Ham started laughing. "Yeah, Razzle Dazzle, why do we call you that?" Ham goaded.

"Fuck you, assholes," Daz muttered.

"Razzle Dazzle?" Ember asked.

"That's where we get Daz from," Tank informed her.

"Why on earth would you call him Razzle Dazzle?"

The guys looked from her to Daz.

"You want to tell it yourself or you want us to take it?" Stone asked.

When Daz didn't answer, just gave them the finger, Ham took over. "See, Razzle Dazzle got his name years back. He'd been in lockup a few weeks. Nothing major. What was that for again?" he asked Daz, knowing damn well what the answer was.

"Drunk and disorderly," Daz muttered.

"Oh, that's right," Ham went on dramatically, "you got drunk and pissed on a fuckin' cop."

Ember's jaw fell open. "Are you serious?"

"I didn't know he was a cop," Daz defended. "I was so fucked up, I didn't realize there was a person there."

"Anyway," Ham continued, "he was jonesing for some company after he got out. We threw him a little shindig, got plenty of girls for him to take his pick. Ended up picking two, took 'em away, came back a while later."

Ember, obviously not knowing why that was significant, prompted, "Okay..."

"When he came out again, fucker had goddamn rhinestones on his face."

With wide eyes, Ember looked between Daz and Ham. "Why?"

"That's what we wanted to know," Tank answered. "Started asking him, boy clammed up on us. Swear to Christ, only time I've ever seen it happen."

"Wanna tell her what you finally told us?" Stone asked Daz.

"They were on her fuckin' pussy," Daz spat.

"What?" Ember cried, already laughing.

"She'd bedazzled her fucking pussy," Ham explained, laughing his ass off.

"Oh my God! Why is that even a thing?" Ember laughed.

"A better question is," Stone added, "if you saw that shit, why the fuck would you go down on her? Rhinestones on the face aside, she was clearly fuckin' whacked."

"Whatever, assholes," Daz said. "Pussy's fucking pussy."

Ember snorted, and added, "Even if it's had the Liberace treatment."

The guys roared with laughter, and even I had to grin.

She was too much.

CHAPTER 15
Ember

HE SMILED.

I'd been half-focused all night. From the moment I arrived with Dad, every conversation, every joke, every interaction got only half of me. The other half...that belonged entirely to Jager. Since I saw him across the yard, he'd had my attention. And, if I weren't mistaken, I'd had his.

Then, I'd made him smile.

It was incredible, the smile and the high it gave me. Jager didn't smile. By that, I didn't mean he did not smile often. I meant he just didn't do it, or at least didn't do it with the exception of that rare, total solar eclipse, once-a-year or less occasion. I knew this not only because I had never seen him do it, but also by the way the small grin moved into his expression. It wasn't forced, something fake he was putting there for show. It was just tight in a way that seemed like the muscles in his face weren't one-hundred percent sure how to make it happen.

Even with that, it was the most devastatingly handsome grin I'd ever seen.

I wouldn't let myself hope I was changing the landscape of his world. That somehow I was magically going to transform him into a man who smiled openly and frequently. I would, however, acknowledge the reality in front of me. I had, at the very least, been the cause of one of those rare smiles.

Seeing that, I couldn't contain my own smile. Even after his faded out, his face returning to that familiar, impassive look I had come to expect, mine stayed put.

Some time had passed, the guys who had been around the fire with me dissipating into the party one by one, when a voice came to me from my right.

"This seat taken?"

I looked up and saw Ace standing there, beer in hand, strictly friendly grin on his face. Unlike Daz, most of the guys smiled at me that way, but I felt most at ease with Ace. Maybe it was because he'd been there that first day I'd ventured out of my room. Maybe it was just his nature. I couldn't say.

"Nope," I replied, and he sat in the chair next to me.

He started up a conversation about my car. How long I'd had it, what mods Dad and I had given her—the same line of questions I usually got from car people about my baby. I gave him the whole story, even some of the tale he hadn't specifically asked about, but my head wasn't entirely in it.

No, part of me couldn't let go of that damn smile, and the man who had given it was across the yard now, that high of what I'd caused in him still lasting in the slight upturn to my lips.

"It serious?" Ace asked after talk about my hot rod had run its course and we'd gone quiet.

My eyes had been on Jager, so I swung my head around to him. "What?"

He lifted his beer, motioning with the lip of the bottle in the direction I'd just been looking. I didn't have to glance that way again to know what he was saying.

"No," I replied in all honesty.

One of his eyebrows arched. "Sure about that?"

I focused on the fire still burning bright in front of us. "Certain. Neither of us is going there."

He didn't argue, just made a "hmmm" sound as a response.

I kept my eyes on the flames, trying to get the image of Jager's smile out of my head. *Neither of us is going there.* That wasn't a line of crap I was feeding Ace. That was true. Jager was not a relationship guy, I knew that. And me? I might have been a relationship girl, but not anytime soon—not when my head was still a mess and my life here was barely settled.

No, what we had was absolutely just incredible sex.

Any smiles aside.

Ace chuckled low and my attention went to him, ready to defend myself. He wasn't looking at me or Jager, though. His eyes were settled on the other end of the yard, where Sketch was leading Ash around the corner of the building.

"What's funny?" I asked.

He grinned at me. "Those two think they keep that shit on the down low, but they suck at it."

"What shit?"

He took a pull from his beer before he answered, "That they're disappearing over there to fuck."

"What?" I gasped. That didn't seem like Ash at all.

Ace chuckled again and the sound made me a bit tingly in a way Ace shouldn't have been causing. I couldn't help it. That deep, warm sound would affect any woman with a pulse.

"No one talks about it, but they do a pretty shit job of keeping that secret. It seems the two of them have a thing for PDA at the highest level," he informed me, and my mouth hung open. "Not like they're gonna start a show here for everyone to see, but they won't be far around that corner before they go at it. Guess having us all nearby does it for them."

Wow.

I never would have guessed that.

Okay, maybe I could see it with Sketch. The man was hot, and he seemed to emanate sex appeal. But Ash? No way.

"Have I scandalized you?" Ace laughed.

"A little bit," I returned. "I never would have guessed that from Ash. She's so quiet."

Ace's grin looked far less platonic when he said, "We've all got things that get us off."

I wondered if he knew about Jager's sexual tastes, if he surmised I shared those since I was in Jager's bed. For the sake of not dying from embarrassment right there, I didn't ask. I just gave a noncommittal, "Mmmhmmm," and let it rest.

A while later, my phone—another thing I'd gotten back when Dad grabbed my stuff—buzzed in my pocket. I was hesitant to check it. For all the convenience the thing offered, it also had the very distinct drawback of reconnecting me to the life I'd been stolen from—a life I had then decided not to return to without warning.

Dad had, in the time since I'd arrived, fielded calls from both of my bosses. He'd been listed as my emergency contact at the bar and gym, and they eventually called when I'd missed work several days in a row. He didn't go into detail about what those calls entailed, but he made it clear it was handled. Of course, "handled" meant I was out of work entirely. Regardless of how much he chose to divulge about my sudden departure, it didn't change the fact that I wasn't going back.

This was one of the many things Dad had handled for me I knew I ought to take care of myself, but didn't.

Now, with my things—including my phone—in my possession again, it was time to start changing that.

It could have been anyone on the phone. I didn't have a lot of close, good friends, but I was friendly with plenty of people at both my jobs. My complete disappearance was going to raise eyebrows, and some of them would reach out. Several, I'd seen when Dad had given me my phone, already had. I was going to need to decide what to divulge and to whom, and get to setting minds at ease.

Unfortunately, of all the names I could have seen on the display, of all the calls I could have started the process with, I had to see the one I was least prepared to handle.

My mother.

I took a few steps away from the fire and groups of people standing around before I answered.

"Hello?"

"Hello?" Mom snapped. "Hello? Your father tells me ages ago you were *kidnapped*, he won't let me speak to you because he says *you aren't ready* to talk to your own *mother* after something like that, and then I finally get ahold of you myself and you say *hello?*"

One thing I may have missed mentioning about my mother, she was all about drama. I wasn't even sure it was intentional, or that she was aware of how she came off. What I did know was she consistently blew things out of proportion, particularly the specific facts of how any given situation impacted *her*.

"It is how people generally answer the phone, Mom," I replied, not even sure where to start with the rest.

"Ember Justine, do you have any idea how out of my mind I've been? You were *kidnapped* and I couldn't even speak to you!"

Alright, I would give her that. Her distress sounded genuine and not just about herself. For all her faults, my mom did love me. It wasn't always the most functional love, but it was there, nonetheless. I should have reached out to her. It had been selfish not to think of it.

Though, for the sake of saying it, I didn't actually know she knew anything about it.

"I'm sorry, Mom. Really. I've just been..." How did I put it into words without upsetting her more?

"I had no idea what was going on at first. I was so overwhelmed. And then, I don't know, it was just easier to go along and pretend none of it happened and everything was perfectly normal," I tried.

"I've been worried sick," she replied, her voice making that clear.

"I know, I'm sorry," I said again.

She sighed and I let her have a moment to collect herself.

"Are you alright?" she asked after a bit.

"I'm okay. I'm safe here. Dad's taking care of me."

"When will you be home? I'll come up to Seattle to see you."

Well, here went nothing.

"I'm not going back to Seattle."

"What?"

I took a deep breath. "I'm not going back. Dad went up the other day and got everything out of my apartment, gave the key back to the landlord. I'm paying to break my lease early—if Dad doesn't blow up and insist on doing it himself. I just...I couldn't go back there."

"Oh, honey," she said in a sad voice. We both let that hang for a minute before she asked, "Where are you staying now?"

"With Dad," I answered. "I was at the clubhouse until he got my stuff, then we moved me into my room at his house."

"The clubhouse?" she inquired in a strained voice that made it clear it wasn't a question of where or what that was.

"Yes, the Disciples' clubhouse."

I let my eyes move around the yard while I waited for what I knew was coming. I saw Dad standing with Stone, beers in their hands and smiles on their faces. Daz was flirting with some half-naked woman. I knew he was actually being charming, but I couldn't help but want to laugh at him now that I knew the reason behind his nickname. I saw Jager, his eyes on me across the fire, not looking away as he brought the bottle to his lips.

I saw all of it and none of it. Instead, I took in what was beneath the sight. Brotherhood, happiness, family, protection. It was all right there, and the club as a whole had offered it up to me, each brother in their own way. This was home. I'd known it when I told Dad I wanted to stay and knew it just as acutely right then.

"He's had you there, with those men, after what you've been through?"

I didn't want to fight with her. Well, that wasn't entirely true. I did. I wanted to demand the answers Dad couldn't give about why she kept this from me my whole life. I wanted to scream that she'd threatened Dad's ability to see me as a child until I was hoarse. But knowing she did love me—even if she had a demented way of going about it—I didn't want to do all of that then. I wanted to assure her I was alright and end it there.

"Yes." I tried to make it sound firm, to make it clear to her this was not going to be something we were going to get into. Mom didn't catch that, though—or ignored it.

"What on earth is he thinking, having you there? What kind of place is that for you to be right now?" she demanded.

"Well, as I said, I'm not staying there anymore. I'm staying with Dad at his house. Still, I'll be going to the clubhouse plenty. I like it. Those men saved me. The people who took me brought me here and Dad wasn't around. The brothers at the clubhouse didn't know who I was. They could have sent me away, but they didn't. They care enough about each other that they were willing to drop thousands of dollars to protect me because there was even a possibility that I meant something to one of their own. And they've been here for me since. They welcomed me in. They ran out to get me things—food, clothes, stuff like that. Three of the guys went with Dad to help move all my things. They're a family, and I'm part of that."

She scoffed. "They're brothers to each other, but no one else factors into that life."

"You're wrong. You haven't seen it. The old ladies, the kids, they're all family. They found out who I was and welcomed me completely. They wanted to have me here because I am part of Dad," I insisted.

"I'm really not comfortable with you being there. You have no idea what those men are like," she dug in.

"Well, it's good I'm an adult and whether or not you're comfortable isn't really a factor then, isn't it?" I snapped. "And, honestly, I think it's you who has no idea what *these men* are like. You don't get how fiercely loyal and protective they are. I could have had that my whole life, a whole band of uncles who loved me and looked out for me. Cami and Ash, they had that. You kept that from me."

I knew my voice was rising, enough that a couple people looked over my way. I looked toward Dad and saw Stone nudge him and point to me. He started my way as I turned toward the fire. Jager was still there, his eyes on me, his body unmoving.

Mom went on in my ear, "I was keeping you safe! You have no idea what that club was up to. It was no place for you—for either of us."

For either of us.

Those words stirred something in me, something that made me feel ill.

Dad hadn't mentioned offering her a place with the club. As far back as I could remember, they were nothing more than two people who shared a child. Was there a time, once, when it was more than that?

Dad reached me, not speaking, but showing his concern on his face. I stared at him, trying to understand while hopelessly denying what I feared was the truth.

"You left him," I whispered to Mom. "He wanted us to stay, both of us, and you rejected the club."

Dad's face went blank, but there was no masking the hurt still lingering in his eyes. He hadn't just wanted me around; he'd wanted us to be a family.

Mom's voice didn't soften at all, didn't show any compassion for what she'd done to Dad, when she said, "I only left him because he wouldn't leave that godforsaken club. It was more important to him than you or me."

She really did it. I felt sick to my stomach.

"The club is his family, he wanted it to be our family. You didn't demand he leave some stupid hobby behind. You wanted him to turn his back on his family."

"He did turn his back on his family!" she cried.

"No," I said, my voice still soft. My eyes remained locked on Dad's, wanting him to know I wasn't like her, that I would never fault him for the choice he made. "He never turned his back on me. Not once. You tried to tear him away from family. That's not right. Then, you left. You took me with you and threatened to keep me away. That's even worse."

"Ember—" she tried to break in, but I kept speaking.

"You tried to take me away out of spite, but I always belonged here. Now, I'm here, and I'm staying. Goodbye, Mother."

"Em—" her voice came through the line again, but I hit end.

Then, without a word, I wrapped my arms around my dad.

"Don't matter anymore, Ber-bear," Dad murmured. "Got my girl here now. That's all that counts."

He was right. He was so, so right.

106

IT WAS after three in the morning. I was headed to my bed at the clubhouse, neither Dad or I feeling like making the drive home after the drinking and emotional upheaval. Only, I didn't make it that far.

Jager was waiting for me there, leaning against the door to his room.

It was like he knew.

He eyed me, but waited for me to speak. It was up to me. He'd let me head to bed if it was what I wanted, or he would give me something else entirely.

"I need it," I told him.

He rocked his large body forward, bringing his weight from the door that supported him. With a few steps, he closed in on me. His eyes staring down at me were harsh in the sweetest way.

"What do you need?" he demanded.

"For you to make me forget."

And he did. He took me away from there without delay. He took me to his place, shackled me to one of the beams in his second bedroom, and he unleashed that delicious monster within on me.

Thoughts of my mother, of all she'd kept from me, vanished. They had no place in that room with us. The only thoughts were of Jager, of his hands and his toys and his cock. My world reduced to a couple hundred square feet and the indescribable pleasure I found there.

For hours, until I couldn't keep my eyes open another moment, he made me forget it all.

When he finally released me from my bonds and his demands, my body could take no more and slipped into sleep before he even managed to carry me to his bed.

I SCREAMED AND KICKED OUT, but it made no difference. It was happening again. They were there and they were going to take me. I couldn't stop it.

Conciseness hit me like a shot, my body bolting upright.

It was a nightmare. Nothing but a dream. It was only in my head.

Except, it wasn't. It wasn't some horrible image my mind had conjured up. No matter how many times I told myself I was safe, that it wasn't happening again, I could never soothe away the scar left from the fact that it had happened. Those images were very real.

I couldn't help but wonder, as I sat in that bed with Jager asleep just a few feet away, if this fear would always be my life now.

There was no way to answer that.

All I could do was settle back onto the pillows and attempt to convince myself to fall back asleep, that it would all be fine.

Convincing yourself of a lie isn't easy.

Sleep never came.

CHAPTER 16

Jager

SIX WEEKS LATER

"OH GOD!"

The information I was hunting down and sorting through on my computer was increasingly hard to focus on.

I read the same page again, this one credit records. No new transactions in over two months. Before that, ordinary shit—coffee, groceries, gas. Nothing that...

"I can't. I can't."

I couldn't control myself. I had to look.

We were at the clubhouse, in my room. I was trying to find something I might have missed—anything that might heat up the cold trail leading back to why Ember was taken. This would have been easier if those burgeoning masochistic tendencies weren't fucking with me again, but it would have been much less satisfying.

You see, behind me where I'd finally allowed my eyes to stray again, Ember was trussed up and gasping in a mix of pleasure and the desperate need for me to make it stop.

Her hands were cuffed by her sides, connected to a strap system that went under the mattress. She was on her stomach, her head alternately turned to the side or mashed into the bed to muffle her sounds. Her ankles also bore cuffs connected to the same straps as her wrists. This left her face down, legs spread open, and knees bent upward. She couldn't move an inch, which was the idea. Beneath her pussy, making her lose control for me, was a magic wand massager on high.

For the last thirty minutes, that toy hadn't turned off. I'd only fluctuated the speed. Ember had already come three times and unless I was mistaken, the fourth was right on the horizon.

I let my eyes roam over her, loving the sight of her pussy on display for me, so soaked, there was a visible wet spot on the sheets beneath her.

"Please. Please. I can't take it," Ember moaned.

With great effort, I turned back to my computer screen. Ember, from her angle, was able to just get a look at where I sat. Whether she was in any state to make that effort, I didn't know. If she was, I wanted her to see me occupied, think I was in no hurry to release her. The fear that she'd be stuck there indefinitely would heighten the sensation.

In reality, I was ready to break. She'd been moaning since I'd slid the vibrator beneath her, making sure it was snug against her clit in a way no movement from her would dislodge it. Each orgasm made the sounds louder, more anguished, until she was screaming.

I let her keening moans go on, staring without seeing at the screen in front of me. My head was filled with her sweet, wet cunt and how badly I wanted to storm over there and fuck her until her screams made her hoarse. And I would—soon.

"No. No. I can't. It's..."

The break in her voice had me whipping around. Sure enough, just as I did, I watched her body spasm as it moved through her. She screamed incoherent syllables, her face pressed into the mattress, but it barely dulled the sound. I watched her pussy weep, saw that hole where I wanted to bury my cock that had been hard for too damn long contracting.

While it overcame her, I stripped down. That was the final

one either of us was going to be able to take. She'd come once more, but it would be from me pounding into her.

Her body twitched from the over stimulation as it left her and I finally moved her way to pull the magic wand free. She gave a broken sigh when it was no longer pressed against her. Switching the thing off, I tossed it aside before climbing onto the bed.

"Can't do more," she groaned.

"You'll take my cock, pet."

A little whimper left her, but she didn't protest again.

I palmed my dick, breathing through my nostrils and smelling the intoxicating fragrance of her pussy in the air. I'd meant to take a second to rein myself in, but that scent wasn't helping.

Fuck, there was nothing for it—my control was gone.

Unable to hold back any longer, I pressed into her drenched cunt. She was burning hot and tighter than I'd ever felt. I went in slowly, savoring every inch. We'd dispensed with condoms, but I couldn't get over the feeling of taking her ungloved. Each time I got inside, it overwhelmed me again.

Ember cried out even as I took her slowly. I'd have to be quick. She wasn't going to be able to take me long.

As soon as I was seated deep, her clenched pussy releasing enough to let me in, I let loose. I thrust into her fast, hard. Her pussy craving the stimulation her clit had gotten, it took no time at all before she let out a broken sound and came. I didn't hold back. The second she clamped down on me, my release took over, blacking out everything but the feel of her around my dick.

When I pulled out a few minutes later, I watched with depraved satisfaction as my cum leaked from her, dripping down her swollen lips and onto the bed. It was a sight I let myself relish every time.

Setting Ember free of her bonds, I watched as she curled up right where she was, exhausted from what I'd given her. She made no move to clean me from her until I said. By now, she knew the drill. When I wore her out this much, that meant she'd be clean of me after she slept. Possibly, after I fucked her again when she woke.

Six weeks, we'd been playing our game.

Not every night, but most, would end with Ember in my bed. We both got what we needed—the release, the distraction. She let me tie her up and do my worst. She'd stay put and take what I had to give, held only by my command. She gave it all and never once hesitated.

She gave me the high of absolute control.

I gave her the high of coming so hard she passed out.

Then, for reasons I couldn't, and refused, to try to understand, I let her stay most nights in my bed. It never took her long to find sleep after I was done with her. It always took me much longer to do the same.

This time, I wasn't going to sleep with her. It was mid-afternoon, a first for us. But it had been two days since I'd had her last and we'd both needed it.

Ember was nearly asleep before I had her free. Her eyes only cracking open to look at me when I rubbed her down, making sure her muscles all released.

"I should go," she mumbled.

"Rest, pet," I instructed.

"I shouldn't," she demurred.

She should. She needed rest in a way that had nothing to do with what I'd just given her and everything to do with weeks of fractured sleep.

"Wake you after a bit," I told her.

Obviously too tired to keep at the minimal fight she was giving me, she gave in by slumping farther into the bed with closed eyes.

I went back to my computer, my mind a fuck of a lot clearer, but the task far less interesting. Without her as a distraction, it was back to pouring over information I'd read again and again, hoping the words and numbers might morph from nothing into an answer.

My gut told me I was on the right track. It might turn out that the truth couldn't be found on a computer like I was trying to do, but I was fucking sure this all started with him.

Daniel Ethan Louis.

Ember had confirmed what I'd thought on my initial run on her. The guy was her ex. Nothing I could find on him looked suspicious, but that was just it. Not one thing looked off, at all. I'd never seen a report like it. Everyone had stuff I had to track down. An onset of a weird medical anomaly that went away, weird online shopping charges it took time to hunt down the source of, a family member with a record of fucked up shit. He had none of it. Everything was so spotless, it seemed fabricated.

It was a first rate job. Medical history with scattered trips, always at the right times. A bad flu in January, that kind of shit. Employment history with a steady rise from crappy jobs teens get up to something decent, but not gaining ground too fast. Credit charges for normal things like groceries and coffee that weren't all logged at the same time.

Anyone else would look through it all and dismiss it. Normal guy, normal background, normal everything—but my gut told me it was all a bunch of shit.

I ignored my gut once before, I wasn't fool enough to do it again.

I'd been at it another half hour, trying to find the hole in the carefully constructed lie, when it happened. It would happen at some point in the night. Sometimes quick, sometimes not for hours. But always, every time she slept beside me, Ember's nightmares would come.

Eventually, she would bolt upright without crying out, just

like the first night she shared my bed. Every night. Then, she'd take her time, calm herself, and lay back down.

I never made a move to let her know I was awake.

And when the nightmares I couldn't escape woke me, she did the same.

We went on that way, night after night—both of us pretending to be fine, both of us allowing the other to keep living that lie.

It was fucked, but it was working. Or it was working as well as it could, so we left it alone.

That was why, when I heard the bed move and knew it was her, coming awake in a cloud of fear as usual, I didn't move. I kept my eyes on the screen in front of me even though my mind was not in it.

It was a few minutes before the rustling of the bed sounded again, more distinct this time. Ember had gotten herself together. I turned, feigning I'd only just heard her.

"I should go. I'm making dinner for Dad," she told me. I didn't respond. Ember offered up pieces of her life like that a lot, and not just with me. It was natural to her, not an attempt to get something from me.

She dressed while I watched. There was no embarrassment to it, which I liked. She wasn't shy about my access to her body.

"Come here," I called as she stepped into her shoes. She came right to me. "Got shit going on tonight?" I asked.

"No."

"Then you come to me," I told her, not waiting for a response as I tagged her wrist and pulled her down to me. I took her mouth before I let her leave.

When she was gone, I grabbed my phone and composed a text to a number I'd never used. It didn't matter. She'd have my number programmed along with all the brothers. It was a safety thing.

Me: You busy?
Ash: Running errands with Emmy. Why?
Me: Need to talk.
Ash: I can be at the clubhouse in 20.

And, true to her word, I watched while standing outside as Ash pulled in eighteen minutes later. She got out, coming right my way without going to the backseat. Looking beyond her, I saw Emmy wasn't in it.

She noticed my glance and informed me, "I dropped her with Sketch. He's at work, but doesn't have any clients. She likes being around while Daddy's working."

Sketch's work was Sailor's Grave, the tattoo parlor he'd been at for years. The owner, a man named Carson who was friendly to the club, was handing the place over to Sketch so he could retire. This meant Sketch was there more than normal, and the man had always been there a lot until his woman and kid came back to town.

Without leading into it, I told her, "You gotta talk to her."

"Who?"

"Ember."

Ash's eyes went wide, but she didn't say anything. Odds were, she knew something about what was going on between Ember and me. Club life didn't allow for much privacy. Old ladies might be kept out of business at their man's discretion, but gossip-type shit was always fair game.

"She's not dealing," I went on. "You gotta get her on that path."

I watched Ash shift her posture, weighing out her words before she spoke. "Why me?"

What she really meant was, *why not you?* I'd done that for her, she didn't get why I wasn't giving that to a woman I was involved with, even if she wasn't sure what level of involvement that was.

I gave her an answer, but it wasn't the one she was looking for. "You got through your shit, living free and happy on the other side. You talk to her, show her it's possible, she might start making moves to get there."

Ash didn't let me get away with avoiding it. "You were the one who got me through," she pointed out.

"Helped you because I fired the other bullet and knew it was the one that hit. I can't offer the same to her." It was another bullshit answer.

"We both know that's not the part that mattered," she said, calling me on it.

Fine. She wasn't going to let it go, I'd give it to her straight.

"I gave that once, 'cause I didn't see much other way. I ain't up to giving it again. Ember's got another option in you. That means you need to talk to her, and you need to get on that shit before she stops floundering and starts sinking. Yeah?"

She wanted to argue, but one good thing about Ash was she knew when a man was done, he was done and there was no arguing that.

"Yeah," she agreed.

"Good," I said, starting toward my bike. I needed to get out on the road and clear my head.

I straddled the seat when Ash called after me. I looked her way for her to ask, "Floundering?"

I knew what she meant, so I gave it to her. "Shit happens, you flounder a while. Eventually, you can't sustain it anymore. Once you drown, there's no going back."

I didn't watch that knowledge hit her. I started my bike and took off.

CHAPTER 17
Ember

"WHEN THE FUCK did I turn into your lackey?" Ace asked.

We were at Dad's house, which I reminded myself again was now mine too. Dad was at work—as was Jager, not that that mattered overly much. Dad was also overprotective, so when I didn't go to the shop with him or have plans with one of the girls that had me close to a brother, he had a brother at the house to babysit me.

I would have spoken up and pointed out that this bothered me, but I really wasn't much in the mood to be by myself. So, I let it happen.

For whatever reason, Ace was the most frequent brother to get guard duty. He explained it by saying he'd been out of work from the garage healing after being shot—a story which I'd gotten in full from Ace during one afternoon of him watching me that freaked me out and made me seriously want to hug Ash. Since he'd been gone, they'd gotten used to not having him on hand, so it was easy enough for him to be useful elsewhere. I called bullshit, but I never got a real answer.

With all the time we were spending together, Ace had become my friend. Even more than the girls, he was the person I thought of as being a friend to call on since I'd moved to Hoffman. Because of that, I told myself he had guard duty so often because he felt the same way about me.

"Come on, she needs a bath. It's not like I asked you to wash her for me, but you aren't seriously going to just stand around while I do all the work, are you?" I shot back.

The "she" in question was my car. My baby needed a bath and there was nothing but sun in the forecast for once, so it was the optimal time to do it. I was already in a bikini under my tank and shorts and had the supplies ready to go.

"You're a pain in my ass," Ace shot back, getting to his feet. "Part of this gig is supposed to be that I get out of work."

I threw a sponge at him. "Whatever, asshole."

I led the way outside where I pulled my girl out of the garage and into the driveway. One definite negative of me moving in was the garage situation. Dad had a two-car garage where he typically kept his bike and the bird parked, but my baby wasn't exactly the kind of car you left parked out in the elements. For the moment, he compensated by keeping either his bike or the bird at the clubhouse so there was room. If I was going to stay long-term, we were going to have to sort something better out.

I turned on the hose and let the bucket I'd brought out fill up, the soap I'd poured in sudsing up as it did. While that did its thing, I pulled off my tank and shimmied out of my shorts. I didn't mess around with washing my girl and there was no reason to get my clothes all wet.

"Jesus Christ," Ace muttered, and my head flew his way.

"What?"

"You realize I have a dick, right?"

I put a hand on my hip and gave him a droll look. "No shit."

"You in that bikini, bendin' over to get out of those shorts that were already a show of their own, you think that isn't going to have an effect?" he demanded.

Actually...

"Well, no," I told him.

"You shittin' me?"

I wasn't. He read that in my expression. His turned to one of disbelief, which confused me.

See, Ace had a secret. I knew it, from the first time he'd spent the day with me. I wasn't even sure what made that knowledge so clear to me. There was just something about him that told me it was true. After that, I'd started to take an interest in him. After a couple weeks, I realized it was more than I first thought. Ace definitely had a secret, but it wasn't just from me. It was from everyone. I couldn't tell if anyone else realized he was hiding something, but they definitely didn't know what it was. Naturally, I was now fascinated with the question.

About a week ago, feeling our friendship was cemented enough for me to do so, I'd brought it up.

"You have a secret," I'd said, straight up.

"Everyone's got secrets," he'd answered.

This, of course, was true. Still, it wasn't the same.

"You've got a big secret. Something no one knows about," I'd replied.

"Not no one," had been his cryptic response.

"Not the club," I'd tried, wanting to verify what I thought I'd solved.

"Not the club," he'd agreed.

I'd pushed for a while, trying to get him to tell me, but it had been a no-go. When he was done with my pushing, he'd said, *"Like you, Ember. I haven't made a secret of that. It might be that we keep on being tight and you earn that knowledge. I think you appreciate what that means since you already figured out my brothers don't know that shit. Right now, I'm not ready. Feel me?"*

I'd felt him, so I stopped pressing. But that didn't mean I stopped trying to guess for myself. With time, I'd landed on an answer. There was only one thing that fit, and it definitely gave me cause to be confused about what he'd just said.

"Ember, what the fuck?" he demanded.

"I know, Ace," I told him.

"You know what?"

"Ace," I said, bugging my eyes out for emphasis, "*I know.*"

He was starting to look pissed. "Babe, you need to tell me what you think *you know* because I'm really fuckin' not following right now."

Crap. No one else was around, but it still didn't feel right for me to be the one to say it when it was his secret.

"I know," I started, trying to find the right words, "that you don't...view women that way."

Silence.

Ace stared at me for a long time before he hesitantly asked, "You trying to say you know I'm gay?"

"Yes," I answered, trying to convey through my expression there was no judgement here. We were friends and that couldn't matter less to me.

Then, he burst out laughing.

I had no idea what was going on. Was this some weird expression of relief that his secret was out?

He laughed for so long, he bent double, his arms clutching his sides. I started to worry he was having a psychotic break.

"Are you okay?"

"Ember," he choked out, still hysterical, "I'm not gay. Fuck."

"What?"

He wiped at his eyes as he tried—and failed—to get the chuckles under control. "I'm not gay. That's not my fucking secret."

"But...I..." I stammered.

"You seriously thought that shit?"

"Yes!" I snapped. "It all made sense!"

"Gotta know, how exactly did that make sense?"

"Well, it was the only thing I could think of that you might hesitate to tell the brothers," I explained.

He was still chuckling and it made me want to punch him. Instead, I grabbed another one of the sponges, this one wet from sitting in the bucket, and lobbed it at him. He jumped out of the way, but still got hit with the water flinging from it.

"Goddamn," he said, rubbing at his eyes again, "that was the funniest shit I've ever heard."

"Shut up."

"Just to make it really clear, I'm not gay," he stated. "Don't have a problem if that's who a man is, but that's not me."

"Kinda got that," I replied.

"And if I were, I wouldn't have patched in if I didn't know the brothers were cool with that, which means there'd be no reason not to tell them," he went on.

Well, that made sense.

"Then what can't you tell them?" I asked.

That sobered him, and I felt like crap for bringing it up.

"Look, what I've been hiding isn't about how the brothers would take it. I know not all of them would be thrilled about it, but they wouldn't try to take my patch or anything. Me not sharing that shit is about me not being ready to face the serious, huge fuck up I made."

Then, like what he said was super heavy, he turned and got the sponge I'd thrown from the neighbor's front law. When he faced me again, that somber expression was gone, just wiped away like it hadn't even been there.

Whatever it was he was keeping to himself, it was eating him up inside and had been long enough that he knew how to fake it.

"Alright, let's get this beauty washed," he said, looking at my hot rod.

Knowing as well as anyone pushing wasn't going to help, I let him change the subject. I went back to my bucket, which was already overflowing onto the driveway and grass, turned off the hose, and added a bit more soap to make up for the run off. Then, we got to work.

A while later, while I rinsed the suds from one side and Ace scrubbed the other, I decided to lay it out.

"Whatever it is, it won't matter to me," I said soft, but clear. "Whether it was something you did or who you are, it makes no difference. Whatever happened, you obviously made a mistake and you regret it. That tells me, no matter what it was, you're a good person like I know you to be. So, whenever you're ready, I'll be here."

His eyes told me what those words meant and I felt it run through me. When he was ready, he knew I'd be there for him. But there was more to it than that. I knew, without him saying a word, he was telling me the same. Whenever I was ready, he'd be there to talk.

Knowing I recognized that, he broke the heavy again.

With a grin, he said, "Still can't believe you thought I was gay."

Asshole.

I lifted the hose in my hand, took aim, and opened fire.

CHAPTER 18

Jager

SHIT WAS tense to say the fucking least.

Church could get that way. Not one man with the Disciples' patch on his back took that lightly. That meant the decisions about how we handled club business meant a lot to everyone who sat at that table. When the business at hand involved disrespect or a direct threat, that ratcheted it up further.

"Tell me you fucking found something," Roadrunner requested.

He was at the end of his rope, and not one man in the room could fault him for that. It had been two months since Ember was delivered to our door and we'd managed to sort out a fat lot of nothing.

Well, that wasn't entirely true. We knew exactly who sold her to us. That was all we had. We weren't necessarily looking to go to war with Pasha Kuznetsov or his pseudo-Bratva over what happened. Provided shit went down the way we anticipated— that Ember's name was offered up by someone else and she was brought to us as soon as they learned her Disciples connection— we'd let shit slide.

However, we'd only let it go if we found the fucker who put Ember on radar in the first place.

"Louis is the link. Fucking sure of that shit," I answered. "There just ain't shit that can be dug up that proves anything.

Whoever he is, wherever the fuck he came from, that man is fucking gone. Name's a paper trail, nothing more."

Roadrunner cursed, hitting his fist on the table to punctuate it. Brother was going to blow if we didn't get answers soon.

Stone looked like he was ready to be done dicking around. "Ember's got nothing that can help trace this fucker?"

I expected Roadrunner to answer, giving the group the intel he'd given me. Ember had been with Louis less than three months. Short romance, no fire, fizzled out quick. She'd never been overly interested in him, but had given him a shot. Never got beyond casually dating in her eyes.

It was Ace who spoke. "All she's got is what he told her. She never got close enough to meet family or anything that might open up intel."

What the fuck?

Why was he answering?

Stone moved his eyes to Roadrunner, who nodded his agreement, and Pres shook his head. "Leaves us only one choice."

"Sit-down with Kuznetsov," Tank voiced the answer.

"That ain't gonna go too well," Gauge offered. "Motherfucker has a very loose understanding of what respect means."

"I don't give a fuck," Roadrunner spat. "He wants to fashion himself king of the fuckin' hill, I say let him. We gotta go in there and play it like he's got some power in this region, what the fuck ever. So long as he gives a name, I don't give a shit about the rest."

"Brother, that's a slippery slope," Doc warned.

It was. Giving in to anyone else's sense of power always was. If we gave Kuznetsov the impression he could easily bowl over the Disciples, he might get a mind to do just that. The club took a hit to our status by pulling out of the ventures that got us on radar. There were whispers that we weren't so ready to defend our turf anymore. Word got out that we were kissing Kuznetsov's ass, even a mistaken word, it could mean challenges coming for us. We'd best that if we had to, but it didn't mean it was something we needed.

"We go in there guns blazing and demanding shit, we're just as likely to end up at war with those wanna-be mafia motherfuckers," Roadrunner shot back.

He wasn't wrong.

Stone laid down the law. "We go in with respect. Let him think he's the big man. He oversteps, we deal with that after. Right now, we need that info and he's the only one who has it. I'll set it up, figure out who's in."

"Gonna have to lay down the law with Ember," Ace said to Roadrunner. "Girl's got it in her head that she should try to connect with Louis. She does that, he knows she was taken by now, he could get squirrelly."

Roadrunner rubbed his eyes. "Dammit, Ember."

"Told her not to, but your girl's fucking stubborn," Ace replied.

"When'd she get that bright idea?" Roadrunner asked.

"The other day when we were washing her ride. I'll keep trying to talk her down from that ledge, but it'd probably work better if you give her a firm no on the idea."

Again, what the fuck?

"Maybe you should focus on keeping an eye on shit and less on her."

All eyes came my way, Ace raising an eyebrow in challenge. "You got something to say, brother?"

"You're there, it's because you have a fuckin' job to do, not to shoot the shit with her," I told him, not shifting my position from how I was reclined in my chair even though I was ready to go to blows.

Ace shot to his feet. "Well, someone's gotta get that girl talking before she has a fuckin' meltdown from holding all that shit in. Don't see you making that play while you treat her like

125

free fucking pussy!"

I got up and leaned across the table, ready to fuck him up—brother or not—when Stone stood.

"Sit. Down," he ordered.

Neither of us moved.

His hands slammed on the table, jarring the thing as he roared, "Both of you motherfuckers better sit the fuck down before I bury a bullet in one of you!"

I was tempted to stay where I was, challenge the threat and odds that I'd be the one getting the bullet. I'd brought Ace into the club and I'd fucking take him out of it if necessary.

What the fuck are you doing? I thought to myself. *Throwing down with a brother over what? Some pussy?*

It felt wrong to even think it. What Ember gave me was precious, more than just some chick giving it up to anyone in a cut. But that didn't change facts. Ember wasn't my old lady, and she wasn't going to be. Anything shy of that wasn't what you went against a brother for.

I relaxed my stance and Ace read me. We sat at the same time, a sign of respect after what we'd just had.

"Right. This shit is done. I take care of the meet, we go from there. Anything else we need to see to?" Stone demanded of the room.

No one spoke up, so he banged the gavel and walked out.

One by one, the guys filed out. Ace and I stayed where we were.

When we were alone, I spoke first.

"Sorry, man," I gave it to him straight.

"Don't want to push your buttons, Jager. I've got nothing but respect for you and you know that," he started. "But you need to sort your shit. You want to lay claim to her, I get the distinct feeling she would let you do that. If you aren't into that, then you can't get up in the face of anyone you feel disrespects something you don't even have with her."

He was right, and he knew it. I didn't need to confirm.

Ace stood, straightening his cut in a proprietary way. That cut was as much his as it was mine, even if I let myself get fucked in the head enough to think for a minute it wasn't.

"We're good. Just be careful, man," he said as he walked out.

Be careful.

It was advice I hadn't heard since I was a kid, back when Mom was still around, always worrying about me. The irony was she had no reason to be worried. I was careful. I knew what I had and had no interest in losing it. I was only ever reckless once there was nothing left to fear.

Now, I was getting that advice again.

For the first time in a long time, there was something to fear. Ace had meant be careful of how I treat my brothers over a woman. Be careful not to overstep. That wasn't what I really needed to be careful of.

What I needed to be careful of was Ember herself.

I had something, whether I wanted it or not. Losing it wasn't the real fear. I would lose it eventually, no question. But just how that loss was suffered was in my control. I could let her go, make sure she walked away clean and unharmed, or I could be reckless and risk her going because I destroyed her.

Ace was absolutely fucking right.

I needed to be very careful.

I walked out of the room, flipping the lock before I closed the door behind me. People were hanging around in the main room, brothers and old ladies kicking back. Ember was there, sitting on a couch with Gauge and Cami's kid, Levi, in her lap.

Ace took the seat next to her, taking the boy when he tried to crawl toward him. The man wasn't an asshole, he wasn't sitting there to make a point. Still, the point was made.

My time was up.

There was just a bit more for me to sort before that happened.

My gaze moved around the room, jumping from person to person, everyone chill despite the heavy shit that had gone on behind closed doors. Church stayed locked in there, it didn't come out and infest the vibe of the whole club. Old ladies didn't get hit by it, and club girls didn't either.

Ash was seated on a stool by the bar, her eyes on Sketch, who had Emmy seated on the edge of a pool table, teaching her the game. She was giggling incessantly, enjoying her dad's attention and not learning a damn thing.

I went to Ash and didn't beat around the bush. "You talk to her?"

"Not yet," she answered. She gave me her attention, even though she wanted to watch her family. Christ, she pushed my buttons, but she was a good woman. "But we just made plans for tomorrow night. I'll see if I can work it in then."

"Don't see. She won't give you an opening on purpose or by mistake. You find a time and you make it come up," I told her.

Her head tilted. Ash was quiet, but she knew a lot. This was partly because she was quiet, which let her see a lot instead of her being too focused on her own noise. It hadn't been the same when she first came back to Hoffman. She'd been too focused trying not to see the picture of a perfect life Sketch was doing everything he could to show her. Now, with her life sorted and everything as it should be for her and her daughter, she had her mind turned to other things. Me, in particular.

These days, she saw way too much.

And she saw exactly why I needed that from her, so she gave it to me.

"I'll do what I can."

That was all I could ask.

CHAPTER 19
Ember

DENI WADDLED—THIS being not in any way an exaggeration —to the love seat in her living room with Slick one step behind her. I expected she chose that seat because it was closest to the bathroom she just came from. While she was in there doing her business, Slick stood next to the door like a bodyguard.

"Slick, honey, light of my life, I swear to Christ, if you don't back off soon, I'll be popping this baby out in lock-up after I stab you with a fork," Deni vowed as she half-lowered, half-plopped onto one of the cushions.

"Babe, you think you can get to the kitchen, get a fork, and stab me with it before I could stop you or get out of dodge?" Slick asked, completely unconcerned by the third bodily threat I'd heard that evening alone.

Not acknowledging the truth of his rebuttal, Deni snapped, "You don't have to follow me around or stand outside the door while I pee every ten minutes! Everyone's going to start thinking you've got some creepy fetish soon."

"We had this argument when you were pregnant with Jules, we've had it God only knows how many times since you've had our boy in you, and I'm sure you're going to keep bitching about it any time I knock you up in the future, but the answer is the same. I'll do whatever I feel I have to when you've got one of my babies in you and you'll damn well deal with it."

Well, that was firm. It was also sweet in a way that I kind of melted a bit.

I noticed the guys could cause melty-type feelings—the guys who had old ladies, anyway.

Deni, who certainly had way more practice with her man being sweet than me, didn't melt. "If you don't back off, you aren't going to be knocking me up again."

Slick smirked. "We'll see about that."

With that, he kissed the top of her head, then went to the kitchen.

"Asshole," Deni muttered under her breath. Then, she called, "Grab me the puffy Cheetos!"

"What do you think I'm doin', babe?" he shouted back.

"Hiding the forks," Cami snickered.

We all laughed with her.

"Can I ask," I started after the laughter died down, "how far along you are?"

"My due date's the fourteenth," she replied.

She still had about three weeks. I was surprised. She looked like she could go into labor any second, though I guessed three weeks wouldn't make the baby that premature.

As I was thinking this, Slick walked back in and informed me, "She means we passed the due date six days ago."

"Oh," I muttered. That made more sense. Then, it struck me that she really was ready to pop at any time and my eyes got wide. "Oh," I repeated.

"Yeah, it seems our little boy is feeling comfortable where he is," Deni said, digging into the bowl of Cheetos her man brought her.

I had to admit, I knew nothing about pregnancy. "Is that...problematic?"

Deni shrugged. "Only in that it means his full-size baby booty is sitting on my bladder instead of coming into the world where he can be Daddy's problem too. If he doesn't decide to make an appearance soon, I'm scheduled to induce labor the week after next."

I also had no idea what it meant to induce labor, but I wasn't asking that one.

"You alright, Ember?" Ash asked. "You look kind of pale."

How did I answer that without offending the three mothers sitting with me?

"No offense," I decided was a good place to start, "but the whole having babies thing kind of freaks me out. Not like you being pregnant," I assured Deni, "more the idea of doing it myself."

"Don't worry about it, it still freaks me out too," Ash replied. "I thought I'd feel more confident the second time around but..." Her eyes got huge as she pressed her lips together.

"Wait! You're—" Deni started to demand, but Ash waved her hands around frantically, nudging her head toward Emmy, who was playing on the ground nearby in her pajamas. Levi and Jules, Cami's son and Deni and Slick's daughter, were upstairs sleeping. Based on the couple times I'd seen Emmy's little head droop, she'd be joining them soon.

Slick was grinning. Cami clapped a couple times in excitement. I'd thrown a hand over my mouth in shock.

"Yes," she admitted, shaking her head. "But you can't tell anyone."

"Who are we going to tell?" Cami asked.

"I mean Sketch," she replied.

We all looked at each other. "He doesn't know?" Deni broke the seal to ask.

"Not yet. I just found out a few days ago. I'm trying to think of a fun way to tell him." Her eyes went back to her daughter, her face growing wistful. "He missed all of it last time, and that was my fault. I want to make this one as special for him as I can."

"Honey," Cami said gently, "you know you don't have to keep beating yourself up for that, right?"

"I know," Ash replied. "And I don't. Really. We've moved on, all three of us. But I know he's going to be so excited. I want to do something fun for the reveal."

"Balloons!" Cami cried.

"Balloons?" I asked.

"Yeah," she replied. "Like in videos online. Fill up like a whole room with pink and blue balloons. You could use his room at the clubhouse."

I tried to picture the brothers' faces when an avalanche of pale pink and blue balloons went flooding through the hall.

"I can get the girls in to set it up while you keep him busy somewhere," Slick offered.

As if his voice was the trigger, a small cry came through the baby monitor on the side table. Slick shifted into full dad-mode in half a second, jumping to his feet to answer his daughter's cries. He looked from Emmy to Ash.

"You want me to take her up?"

Ash shook her head and stood too. "Come on, baby," she called to her daughter. "Time for bed."

Emmy—surprisingly, since I knew the girl had sass—hopped right to it.

"Jules has been having trouble sleeping lately," Deni said, looking worried. "We can't figure out what's up with her. The only thing that seems to settle her is her daddy singing to her."

My mind filled with the image of Slick, his imposing, muscular self, rocking the little girl, who had some of her dad's features and all of her mom's cute, and singing to her. He was a married man and I'd never cross that line, even if the woman who had his last name wasn't my friend, but I could appreciate that image to my heart's content.

It didn't take long for Ash to settle Emmy in, and she came

back down, reporting, "Jules is being a little fussy. Slick is going to stay up there for a bit and make sure she's good."

"He's letting her out of his sight?" Cami teased, tilting her head Deni's way.

"He might have made it clear if there were any signs of labor or any issues at all, I was supposed to yell for him immediately." She looked directly to Deni. "He also wanted me to remind you that you aren't allowed out of that seat unless it's to pee."

Deni stuck her tongue out at us when we giggled. "I swear, he'd put me in adult diapers if I let him and take away my right to even do that," she grumbled.

It was long after, when the conversation lapped, that Ash addressed me. "How are you doing, Ember?"

It was an oddly direct question, but I also hadn't really said much about myself all evening. "Good. I think Dad and I have finally found a rhythm for living together. I like it. But I really should sort out a job. I don't have much savings and Dad won't let me use it, so he's been paying for everything."

Ash's eyes looked way too sympathetic and gentle for what I'd said. I felt my muscles tense as she said in a soft, but meaningful, way, "That's good, but I meant how are you doing as in how are you coping..." there was a pause as she figured out how to word it before adding, "with what happened?"

"Ash," Cami rebuked on a whisper.

My throat closed up. I didn't want to talk about it. It was over. Done.

I just wanted to leave it in the past where it belonged.

Ash's gaze stayed on me, apologetic but determined. "He's worried about you."

I forced my voice to work, not needing this to turn into Ash picking the whole thing apart. I didn't need to hear her talk about it.

"Dad is..." I started, but Ash cut in when I paused.

"Not Roadrunner," she said on a shake of her head. "Jager."

What?

"Jager?" I choked out.

Ash gave me a sad nod. "He wanted me to talk to you. Obviously, he didn't want me to tell you that, but you should know. He's worried about you, that you aren't dealing with it and it will continue to haunt you."

"I...he..." I took a breath to collect myself. "It's over. I'm fine. He doesn't know what he's talking about."

Shifting forward so she was right at the edge of her seat, Ash leaned toward me and grabbed one of my hands. "I know this isn't easy. I hate doing it. But Jager absolutely knows what he's talking about. He knows exactly what happens when you let something like that fester. He lives it every day. And I might have been too, if he hadn't helped me."

"What are you talking about?" I asked.

She sighed. "There's not much I can say," she offered apologetically. "It's Jager's story to tell. But, after Barton..." she trailed off, her eyes going far away for a moment. I'd been told the whole story about Ash. About the man who tried to kill her and shot Ace. It was horrible and she needed that moment, so I let her have it.

"After what went down with Barton, I wasn't dealing," she went on when she could. "I was having nightmares and not sleeping. I couldn't get it out of my head. Jager noticed. Honestly, it was probably hard not to notice. He'd been living in the farmhouse then, while Sketch and I still were. One night, when I was a mess, he talked to me. He didn't go into a lot of detail or anything, but he told me his story. I don't feel right sharing that. It's not my place. But what he went through was horrible. He didn't say as much, but now I can see he never dealt with it. Instead, he carries it around, every day, feeling that pain."

He did. I knew he did. I had no idea what he'd been through, but I'd been in bed beside him when it woke him. I could feel the fear radiating off him. But I'd never said a thing because I didn't want him to turn it around on me.

How fucking selfish was I?

"He has nightmares," I told her in a small voice.

She nodded, not already having that knowledge but not surprised by it. "It happened a long time ago, well before he ever joined the club. He's been carrying it around since."

Years. Years and years he'd felt that. The nightmares had probably been connected to that.

Would that be me? Years from now, still unable to find peace enough to sleep through the night?

Reading that I wasn't going to continue our talk, Ash spoke up again. "He wanted me to talk to you, to try to help you work through it. I'm here. Anytime you want to talk, I'm happy to listen. But I don't think I'm who you need," she finished meaningfully.

"We aren't that," I whispered.

"Maybe not," she conceded. "Or maybe just not yet. Maybe you both need this to move on."

Maybe.

Maybe wasn't a given. It wasn't even something to work toward. It was nothing but a fleeting possibility.

"We're all here for you," Cami added, drawing my attention back to her and Deni, who'd been quiet throughout my exchange with Ash. "But the right person can make all the difference. We've all experienced it firsthand. Maybe you need that too."

"Both of you," Deni tacked on.

There it was again. Maybe.

Maybe wasn't what you built on. Maybe wasn't a good enough reason to rip your heart open and let the ugliness taking root spill out.

Was it?

No, it couldn't be.

I didn't argue with them, but I couldn't agree. For my own sake, there was no taking that chance.

But still, somewhere deep, a voice inside me whispered.

Maybe.

CHAPTER 20
Jager

THE MOTHERFUCKER with the Uzi strapped across his chest stared us down while we were disarmed. He wasn't the only one going overkill on the firepower. Every suit-clad asshole guarding the joint was armed to the teeth. I could appreciate security, but Kuznetsov's layout reeked of desperation.

That kind of firepower meant one guy who was a decent shot could guard the single building we were in front of. Instead, I counted eight suit-clad men just on the front side, let alone whoever he had guarding around the sides and back. That said two things to me. One, Kuznetsov had no faith any of his men could hit the broad side of a barn. Two, he wanted to create the appearance that he was big-time shit. More guards implied more threats. Men in high places had a lot of threats. Kuznetsov did not.

Pasha Kuznetsov, if the intel we'd gathered over the years was correct, had been a nobody, a lowly foot soldier to a big man back in Russia. Kuznetsov didn't see himself as a little man in a big world. No, he fancied being the Pakhan, the leader of the Bratva. There was no chance of that shit back home, so he committed the cardinal sin of sneaking out of that life. He set up overseas, claiming power his old superiors would kill him in a second for stating he had right to, and set up his own, little, wanna-be Bratva outside Seattle. He had no backing, no loyalty, no ties of any kind to any other Russian mafia men in the U.S. or anywhere else. He was a little man with a big head and a small battalion. Eight guards with that kind of firepower he absolutely did not need.

We were on his turf, having ridden up for the sit-down Stone had set up. So, for the time being, we had to play by his rules. The first of those rules being delivered by his guards demanding we disarm completely before going in. Not surprising, but irritating all the same.

After pat downs and warnings I didn't pay a lick of attention to, we were finally led inside.

Stone took the lead, as was his place as the pres. Tank was at his back, then Gauge and me at the rear. Roadrunner was not present. Fuck, the man didn't know the meet had been set. Stone had told each of us individually so Roadrunner wouldn't tail our asses up here. The fact was, Roadrunner was too much of a liability. The odds he'd lose it sitting across from the man who'd set having his daughter kidnapped in motion were too high.

My hands clenched into fists at the thought of Ember.

From the corner of my eye, I noticed Gauge's head turn my way. I forced myself to release the tension in my body, relaxing my hands at my sides, but I didn't acknowledge him. He turned his attention back in front of him, but his head shook.

He didn't think I should be there. He'd made that plain to Stone, who'd warned me. I was there because I was the one with the intel on Louis already, and I was the one who'd been tasked with finding more after this sit-down. Stone admitted he had considered keeping me out of this. They thought I was a liability the likes of Roadrunner.

But I wasn't. I was cool. I was fucking ice.

Even if the motherfucker was the reason Ember was having nightmares.

Shit.

I had to get that out of my head before I made a big fucking mistake.

We were led through the building, all the men inside stopping whatever they were doing to stand and watch us walk by. They were all in suits. Kuznetsov was known to be obsessed with appearances.

When we stopped, it was outside a solid metal door. Our guide provided an unnatural knock as a code before the thing was pushed open from the inside.

The room itself was ostentatious at best. Dark wood floors, maroon wallpaper, heavy wood and leather furniture in black, a massive oil painting of St. Petersburg in a horrible gilded frame, and, in the center of it all, behind a huge desk obviously for show since it had not one thing on it, Kuznetsov.

He didn't stand from his high-back leather chair when we entered. He just said, "Gentlemen. Please, sit."

There were two chairs in front of the desk and a leather sofa to the side of the room. Stone and Tank took the chairs, Gauge and I remained standing behind them. We weren't there to get comfortable. We were there to get answers and get gone.

Kuznetsov stared us down, waiting for us to be gracious guests. He lost the first battle right then when he finally looked away.

"You wished to see me?" he asked Stone.

"Cut the shit. You know why we're here," Pres replied.

Kuznetsov's face tightened at the rudeness. "Yes," he went on with his air of superiority. "The girl." There was a hint of a smile to his lips when he said it. He thought it was amusing, what he'd put her through, that we were there on her behalf. I clenched my teeth to keep myself from losing it.

Stone didn't respond to his statement. The asshole was drawing this out, trying to play with us. He knew exactly what we wanted, probably knew we'd be after it even before we set this up. Stone was going to let him play his little power game of forcing us to reiterate.

"Very well," Kuznetsov said, reading the situation and getting down to it. "What exactly is it you wish to know? She was handed over to you, unharmed, and it is my understanding my men were even gracious enough to negotiate a lower price for her return. I see no further cause for issue here."

I pictured myself pulling him from that chair and laying him out on the desk. I could practically feel the crack of his nose breaking beneath my fist. There'd be blood, lots of it—all his.

"Who gave you her as a target?" Stone demanded. "You didn't grab her randomly. I want to know who the fuck put a Disciple woman on your list."

"I would have thought you would be able to get that information on your own," Kuznetsov said with a smirk.

"Oh, we got a fuckin' name," Stone answered, "but you know as well as we do it don't mean shit."

"I'm afraid there is little I can do if you already have the man's name," he lied.

Kuznetsov was trying to get one of us to haul of and lose it. That disrespect would give him grounds to do whatever he wanted. Stone didn't take the bait for a second.

"You know who he is. You might even know where to find him. Right now, we're willing to move past the fact that your men broke into the home of a woman with club protection and fuckin' kidnapped her, intending to sell her. You didn't know. You should have fuckin' figured it out before you took her. The club can overlook this if you give us what we want, or we can decide your ignorance is grounds for you to pay," Stone laid it out.

Kuznetsov's men shifted closer to us, but I didn't move. I saw the one to my left, sized him up, and decided I'd have him down before he could fire the gun in his shoulder holster.

"You believe your little club can take my men?" Kuznetsov taunted.

"Yeah, I fuckin' do," Stone replied. "But it wouldn't be just our club. We got friends. You got enemies. We ride on your little mess here, we wouldn't be alone."

The asshole gave no visible reaction to that, but he knew damn well his shit soldiers wouldn't matter if we got those sorts of reinforcements. He also knew we would if he forced our hand.

"Now, you wanna give us what we came for?" Stone pushed.

Kuznetsov face was stiff when he responded, "Daniel Louis was born Anthony Gregor Yeltz. This was something we did not know when he came to one of our fights and placed a bet he couldn't pay off."

Fuck. I had no clue what I'd find when I ran that name, but it wasn't going to be good. The fights Kuznetsov's crew ran were dog fights. Innocent fucking animals being forced into that shit through starvation. I was losing my hold on cool. I wanted to take this motherfucker down.

"When he established that debt, we looked into him. As I'm sure you know, his history and credit look good at first glance. He offered to work off his debt. He worked in a company where there were men with padded pockets, men who might look for certain vices, but would not do so by finding them on street corners."

More not good. They made him a middle man, getting the girls in their stable and whatever shit they were packaging to go in needles or up noses into the hands of up-their-own-ass business types. That was a market with a lot of potential profit.

"And he didn't come back with the cash," Tank filled in.

Kuznetsov did not hide his sneer at the brother feeling he could speak. Stone wouldn't give a shit, that's not how the club ran. The operation Kuznetsov led was not the same.

"Indeed," the man replied tightly.

"How much are we talkin'?" Stone asked.

Kuznetsov looked to one of his men standing a few feet behind the desk. The suit spoke up. "Three hundred."

Jesus. Walking in the doors, I knew this whole operation was a mess, but who the fuck let someone take them for three-hundred grand?

Gauge muttered a curse beside me and Kuznetsov's eyes cut to him before going back to Stone. His face was hard, not taking having to admit something that embarrassing well.

"As you can guess, we are very intent on finding him."

"As *you* can guess, we're a sight more intent on that shit."

Stone and Kuznetsov stared off.

"The man owes me quite a debt I plan to make him repay." His Russian accent was getting thicker with his emotions.

"That man got my brother's daughter kidnapped. Nearly got her sold into fuck knows what by your people. She hadn't had the presence of mind to give up the club, we might never have found her. I don't give a fuck about your money or the fact that you made a bad decision and got fucked. He fucked with what's ours and that means retribution."

My brother's words were doing nothing to calm the storm in me. I gave no fucks whatsoever about this asshole's money. Yeltz belonged on Disciple's property. He was meant to be chained where I could get my fucking turn tearing him apart. Roadrunner deserved the chance to hear him scream. I wanted to clean his blood off my skin right before I sunk myself into Ember's sweet body.

I'd take down Kuznetsov myself to do it.

"Then we have reached an impasse."

I felt the stiffness coming from my brothers' bodies at his words.

"Meaning?" Stone asked.

Kuznetsov shifted forward, clasping his hands together and resting his chin upon them. "Meaning I have divulged as much as I am interested in giving you. You have a name. If you wish to exact your revenge, you better find Yeltz before my men do."

"You sure that's how you want us walking away from this meet?" Stone asked in warning.

"This meeting is over," Kuznetsov stated as a response.

Stone and Tank stood, following Gauge and I out the door and the whole fucking place, through the same sea of onlookers from Kuznetsov's army. Our weapons back in hand and standing at our bikes, Gauge spoke.

"What now?"

"Now we find him," Tank said, eyes on me.

I didn't need him to lay it out. I'd find Yeltz.

"And the shit that Russian motherfucker just handed us?" Gauge pressed.

"We focus on Yeltz," Stone asserted. "We need to go to war to teach the petulant shit in there you don't fuck with us, we'll do that when the time is right."

I didn't like it. Gauge's hard face said he didn't either. But Pres was right.

For now, all that mattered was finding Yeltz.

CHAPTER 21

Jager

WHEN WE GOT BACK to the clubhouse, Ace was standing outside, leaning against the building, eyes on the road. I had a guess what he was waiting around for, and it pissed me off.

We dismounted and headed toward the door.

"What's up?" Ace asked.

Stone answered first. "Church. Tonight. Seven. Get word around." With that, he went inside. If I had to guess, he was getting Roadrunner there to talk this shit over before sitting down with the whole club.

Tank and Gauge went in, but I stayed behind by Ace. I had to know.

"Out here for a reason?" I asked.

"Ember called," he gave it to me straight, "all excited over something. She said she'd be here in a minute, wanted me out here when she got here."

After he said it, but before I could cool the inferno his words ignited in me enough to respond or fucking walk away like I should, the sound of tires and the distinct growl of her hot rod's engine hit my ears. I turned to see her pulling up and told myself it was definitely time to walk away.

I stayed where I was.

Ace moved past me, walking toward where she was parking a bit away. She all but jumped from the thing, a huge smile lighting her face. She was in another one of those fuckin' outfits. This time, capris and a black shirt with little white dots on it that didn't go up on her shoulders. The little sleeves just wrapped around her upper arms instead. Her hair was down, with a big red flower pinning it back on one side. On her feet were wedge heels with red fabric on the tops that wrapped up around her ankles. She even had on a pair of cat-eye sunglasses.

"You wanna tell me why I'm out here in the heat?" Ace called to her, and her smile got even bigger.

"You have to see him," she replied.

"See who?" Ace asked, now standing right by her.

I stayed where I was. It was close enough to hear, but I wasn't part of their exchange.

"My new baby," Ember said, actually clapping her hands together.

"You get another badass car?"

She laughed at that, then moved around to the passenger door. "Not this time. This baby's actually alive."

Ace groaned. "Don't tell me you decided to get some little prissy dog after all?"

"Well, you're almost right," Ember allowed him. She pulled open the car door, but I couldn't see what she did from my vantage point. At least, not until she walked back around the car, a leash in her hand and a beefy English Bulldog trotting by her side.

A dog. Another piece she was adding to a life she was building here. A life with her Dad close, with a group of women who had welcomed her into the fold, and where she'd found a place with the club with ease. She was getting herself settled into a new life.

I came into her life at the start of that process and gave her something she needed. She was getting to the point where she wouldn't need it anymore. She had people who would let her get that shit in her head out instead of offering a distraction. She had

Ace, who she'd called when she had good news and drove to the clubhouse with her new dog.

I was on the fringes of that. She had good in that moment, so I wasn't needed. She'd keep on having more and more good in her world. I didn't have good to give her, and that was becoming clear to her even if she wasn't acknowledging it yet.

Ace knelt down to pet the pup, while Ember announced, "This is Roscoe."

"Roscoe?" Ace asked.

"Shut up, I like it," she told him. "He's just over a year old, but his old owners couldn't keep him." She also knelt then, rubbing down the dog. From the way he crowded her, it was clear the pup was already getting attached.

Couldn't blame the little guy for that.

"Why a bulldog?" Ace asked.

Ember shrugged. "I went to the shelter thinking something bigger. Maybe a Rottweiler or Pitt," she started, but Ace cut in there.

"You were gonna get a fuckin' Rottweiler?" he asked.

"Yeah. They're cute," she said, like his reaction was weird.

"Girl, I'm not saying a Rottweiler's a bad dog to have. I am saying those motherfuckers are tough and aren't really what I'd call cute."

She shook her head, keeping her eyes down on her dog that had seated himself so most of his weight leaned into her while she pet him. "Whatever. I think they're cute," she muttered. "Anyway, I was there looking around when I saw Roscoe. Well, they had him named Sheldon, but I don't think he's a Sheldon. He seems to be taking to the name change. Aren't you, Roscoe?" she asked, getting her face down close to the dog. She looked back up to Ace. "He was cute, so I went over to his kennel and we bonded. Now, he's mine."

I watched them both shower attention on the dog as he ate it up. After a few minutes, Ember finally fucking looked my way. Her face was blank as she did. She didn't smile or wave me over to meet her new dog. She just looked at me for a few moments, then turned away.

"Well, we should get home. He still has to see where he'll be living," Ember said to Ace.

"You just have him riding in your car?" Ace asked, standing and checking out her ride. "His claws and all that drool aren't going to be good to your upholstery."

Ember got to her feet, her fantastic ass in those jeans grabbing my attention as she did. I wanted her bare so I could turn those sweet cheeks red.

"I've got a blanket down on the seat so he doesn't mess it up," she explained as she led Roscoe to the passenger door. Once he was situated in his seat, she went back to her side where Ace opened her door for her and shut it once she was seated.

"See you later," he said through her open window.

"Later," she replied.

All the while, I stood there like a fucking creep, watching her.

As she pulled away, she looked to me once again with that blank face. She didn't wave, didn't smile.

Then, she was gone.

Ace walked by me, heading back inside. Just before he went through the door, he said, "Pretty sure you're a goddamn genius, but with that woman, you're acting like a fucking idiot."

I didn't argue. He wasn't wrong.

TRACING ANDREW YELTZ was proving to be more of a headache than trying to decipher anything worthwhile from the bullshit identification he made. All there was to find was a background, before he started living as Daniel Louis.

The birth certificate was easy enough to find, no father listed on that. From there, I ran a search on the mother. Five investigations into whether she was fit to have custody of her son. It took some doing and a couple calls, but I managed to get into the records. She was suspected of drug use. A couple teachers noticed Yeltz looking ragged, underfed, and there were bruises from time to time they feared weren't from kids rough housing. From the notes in his file on the interviews with his teachers, they claimed it was unlikely he'd have injuries from playing with other kids since he never did such things. He was a loner from a disturbingly young age.

For whatever reason, most likely a failure of the system, Yeltz stayed with the mom. Records followed him through high school, but no higher education. The bachelor's and master's he had for his fake life were forged in more than just the name on them. About the time he finished high school, the mom died. The official cause of death was labeled an overdose.

From there, there was virtually nothing. Whether this was because Yeltz buried the rest or because he went off grid until he built his fake identity, I couldn't be sure.

What I did know was finding the fucker was going to be a sight harder than anything we'd done before. Kuznetsov might have a line on his whereabouts, but that would be because he'd had the man involved in his operation for who knew how long. Some of his men were bound to know a thing or two about Yeltz. We didn't have that luxury.

My phone rang, clattering on the desk beside my computer. The display read something it never had before: Ember calling.

Seeing her name there, remembering the sight of her with Ace while I stood away, I came to a decision. She had people who could be what she needed. I wasn't that.

It was time.

"Yeah?" I answered.

"Ugh...hey," she said. Knowing well enough by now I wasn't going to take over from there, she went on, "What are you doing?"

"Working," I answered.

"Right," she said, mostly to herself. "So I can't come over then?"

"Got shit to do," and I did. I also needed to stop dicking around with this shit between us.

"That's it?" she asked.

"Yeah."

She met me with silence for a bit.

"That's it?" she repeated.

"Yeah, Ember, that's it."

She got it, all of it then. I knew it when she said to herself, "That's it."

I wrapped my hand around the edge of my desk, clamping on to keep myself steady. My body was itching to get out of my seat and find her. My mind was clamoring to spout shit I didn't need to be saying. I tensed my hand until it ached and managed to keep quiet.

She gave me nothing for a long time, until she offered something that had me even closer to losing it.

"Right. Bye, Jager."

Without waiting, she hung up.

Not letting go of my death grip on the desk, knowing I'd be out the door in a fucking second if I did, my need to unleash the fury meant my phone went flying. It hit the wall across the room, shattering on impact. The sight and sound weren't satisfying, not in the slightest.

They were hardly anything at all against the onslaught in my head. The voice there screamed until it was all I could hear, shouting I was an asshole, that I was the worst sort of fucking person on earth, that I was absolutely right in thinking I didn't deserve her for a second.

That I had just made the biggest fucking mistake of my life.

CHAPTER 22
Ember

ROSCOE WATCHED me from my bed as I repeated the path I'd been walking from one end of the room to the other. I'd been pacing the same pattern for half an hour or more. I wasn't really sure. There wasn't a clock in the room, and if I picked up my phone, I'd do something stupid.

Like call Jager.

Oh, wait, I'd already done that stupid thing.

Hence the pacing.

At first, when I'd hung up on Jager, I'd been upset. I'd been on the bed with Roscoe, feeling a crying jag coming on. That lasted all of a few minutes when I realized I didn't do crying jags. I wasn't the girl who flung herself into the pits of emotional upheaval over some guy. Particularly not when that guy was being an asshole.

Jager was, absolutely, being an asshole.

I was not about to become some weepy, needy thing because of it. Seriously, screw that.

And screw him.

That was when the anger started, which kicked off the pacing.

I had no idea what set Jager off and had him instigating his little "that's it" play, but I knew he could shove it if he thought he was going to just brush me off with less than a dozen words on a freaking phone call.

That wasn't me attributing more to what we had than was there. It also wasn't me thinking ending a fuck buddy relationship required a heart-to-heart where we talked about our feelings. That was me knowing whatever was in his head that had him ending it was something jacked.

The intensity of what we had hadn't gone anywhere, and I knew for a fact he felt the same. Every time we got alone, it was only hotter. So, if it wasn't that we fizzled out, that meant he thought he had to break it off.

That meant he either thought I was starting to get too attached or he had some twisted idea that he was being noble.

"Seriously, fuck him," I said to Roscoe.

Roscoe, obviously, didn't respond. He just watched me from his spot on my bed. He could have been sitting on his own bed on the floor, which I'd paid way more than I thought a dog bed should cost for. He didn't do that. In fact, when he'd realized he could leap up onto my bed, that over-priced dog mattress was scarcely a thought.

"I mean, sure, I've thought about it. Ash with her 'maybe' crap," I muttered, still irritated that word had been bouncing around my head since she'd said it. "But it's not like I thought that was us. He made it very clear it wasn't."

Roscoe kept his droopy face my way as I moved back and forth, probably thinking I was nuts. Though, maybe I was. I was pacing around my bedroom ranting about some guy I'd been fucking to my dog.

That made me stop halfway through one of my laps. There I was, ranting and raving and all worked up. Was that really better than crying? Either way, I was expending all this emotion on some guy. Doing that wasn't going to change anything. It wasn't going to give me answers.

Answers. The word bounced around in my head.

Before I could think it through all the way, I was pulling on my shoes. Roscoe had just been out, so he was fine to chill a while. I wouldn't be gone long.

I drove to the clubhouse, assuming—rightly, I realized, when I pulled up and his bike was parked there—that was where he'd be. It was where he always seemed to be unless he was at the gym or we were both at his loft.

I moved into the building, on a mission. The guys were all around, and had I stopped to think for even a minute, I would have known that would be the case. Dad had left early saying they were having a meeting. That, it was plain to see, was over, but the guys were still mostly hanging out. And, I didn't miss, so were the club girls.

Jager was there. He hadn't gone back to his room. He wasn't feeling it at all. The asshole was just chilling in the clubhouse lounge like nothing was up, his hands wrapped around a glass of his normal drink. Better than any of that was the slut in a crop top and tiny shorts seated on the stool next to him.

Well, it was good for him he found my replacement so fast.

A couple of the guys called out greetings to me as I made my way across the room, but I didn't pay enough attention to see who. That wasn't important.

I approached the bar at a clip and only stopped when I was right in Jager's space.

"Can we talk?" I requested.

"Nothin' to talk about, Ember," he replied, not looking at me. Oh, no.

"There so fucking is something to talk about. You don't get to be a coward and pull that crap on the phone and not even look at me," I snapped.

I could feel the chick beside him watching me, but I paid no mind to that.

Jager downed the rest of his drink, his powerful neck arching back to take back the last of it. I watched it, distracted from my anger for a moment by the desire to run my tongue down that skin.

Dammit, Ember, snap out of it, I rebuked myself.

"Fine," he said after he set the empty glass on the bar. "We'll talk, then you'll go."

I wasn't going to argue. I had no desire to be there once I said what I needed to. Without hanging around to hear him tell his piece for the evening he'd be back, or whatever he would say to her, I took off again toward his room.

As I made my way down the hall and away from the music and noise coming from the lounge, I realized his steps were right behind me. Either he'd moved quick to catch up, or he hadn't given that woman anything. I didn't let myself fret over which it was.

I stopped at Jager's door, waiting for him to unlock it. When I did, I saw his attention on the door across the hall that was still mine, on some level. He looked to me when I didn't approach and realized what I was waiting for. He smartly didn't try bicker that we take this to my room. I wasn't going to have it.

Jager let us in, allowing me to stomp passed him before he followed and shut the door. He then stood there, just inside it, not saying a word. I had to admit, I thought I was used to Jager's silence, but getting it on the phone earlier and right then when any idiot would know what I was there for had me pissed.

"Are you going to say anything?" I snapped.

"What do you want, Ember?" he responded.

Seriously?

"Seriously?" I asked, exasperation and attitude taking equal place in my tone.

"We both knew what this was," he said.

I sucked in a deep breath to keep from knocking some sense

into him and forced myself to put the jumble in my head into actual words.

"Yes, we both knew what this was. I'm not standing here because I got some crazy idea in my head that we were real or anything that was going somewhere," I started. Jager didn't take the pause I put there to interject with anything, so I went on. "What I want to know is what has you pulling 'that's it' out of nowhere?"

His posture, legs planted, arms crossed, and blank expression told me he still felt no burning need to take over the conversation.

Well, I would just keep rolling with it then.

"We both know the sex hasn't run its course. We're both still getting something out of it, and you can't bullshit me into thinking you don't. I've been right there with you and know for a fact it's still just as hot for you. So, what is it then? You think I've somehow attached myself emotionally to you and you need to cut that string? Because, guess what? I haven't. I'm cool. I'm completely clear on what we've got. So that's bull."

"You sure about all that?" Jager asked.

Was he serious?

"Yes," I shot back.

"You're standing here, pissed and half-yelling at me over the fact that I ended things when sex was all it was. If that's all it was, what does it fucking matter?" he countered, and gave me nothing but the words. There was no change to his expression, no flash of anything in his eyes.

But I felt a wave of something rush through me. I ignored it and went back to my tirade. "Because it's good. We both enjoy it. Why end it over nothing?"

Jager moved then, taking two steps closer to me. There were still several feet between us, but even that shift made him feel infinitely more imposing.

"You're telling me you haven't considered it? Haven't even thought maybe there could be more?" he inquired.

My tongue felt leaden. He couldn't know that. There was no way.

"No," I answered.

"Liar," he replied right away.

I retreated a step, but he followed me.

"I'm not."

"You are," he said. "You've thought about it. You'll do it again. You'll convince yourself it's a good idea. That's not a good thing for either of us."

I looked at him, feeling ready to bolt. How could he know? Sure, I'd thought about it, but I hadn't granted it the kind of headspace it would need to manifest in my behavior. I hadn't started acting like some lovesick schoolgirl over him. He couldn't know it was in my head.

Unless...

"You've thought about it," I whispered as it came to me.

Jager froze. It was obvious even without him moving. I could actually see his body tense until he was solid.

"This isn't about me," I kept on whispering. "It's about you."

"It's about you." His voice was tight.

"It isn't. It's about the fact that you...what? Want me but don't want a relationship?" I started to piece together.

"That's not it," he argued.

But it was. It so was. It was all there, all coming together before my eyes.

"It is. You feel it. We could work, and that terrifies you."

Jager didn't respond anymore. His face was still impassive, but it looked like a mask. He was giving it all to keeping what he was feeling from his expression, and that said all I needed to know.

"I've thought about it," I admitted in a quiet voice. "Of course

I have. I haven't been in a place to give it much, but that doesn't mean it hasn't crossed my mind."

The muscles of his arms were so tense, I could see the veins beneath his skin.

"We've both thought about it even if we wouldn't admit it, even if we both just meant to keep it what it was. You know that, and it freaks you out. You wanted to cut and run before either of us owned up to it," I went right on voicing all I'd finally realized, all we'd both been dancing around since the beginning.

"I'm a mess," I admitted something else. It was something I had been avoiding for weeks. "I'm exhausted and you know exactly why, just like I know you haven't slept a full night since we met. I've got a list of things I won't let myself think about that's so long, it's a wonder I can even function some days. You know it. You knew it from the start when you told me to talk to Ash, and you've worried about it. That's why you told her to talk to me."

He slipped then, letting his eyes widen just a touch.

"Yeah," I responded to his involuntary reflex, "I know you did that. She told me because she knew. She didn't say it, but she knew why you'd ask her to do that."

Jager's eyes got dark, and he demanded, "What did she tell you?"

I knew exactly what he was asking.

"*He didn't go into a lot of detail or anything, but he told me his story. I don't feel right sharing that. It's not my place. But what he went through was horrible. He didn't say as much, but now I can see he never dealt with it. Instead, he carries it around, every day, feeling that pain.*"

Ash had said it, and I could see the defenses right before my eyes. He was feeling it, and he was protecting that secret.

"She didn't tell me," I tried to soothe him. "Whatever it is, whatever happened, she didn't tell me what it was. She said you told her some to help her after she shot at that guy, but that was it."

Some of that wild, twisted dark left him, but not all.

"That's why," I surmised. "Whatever it is, that's why you shut me down."

He remained a silent, dangerous presence. He didn't agree, he didn't silence me. Still, there was a threat apparent.

"You think I'd push that, try to force you to talk about it." That much was clear from his reaction. I shook my head. "You really think I would do that, even with what happened to me."

It wasn't a question; it was a realization. He was shutting me out before I could push, something he was sure I would do. Something I wouldn't do, something I couldn't when I walked around every day fearing someone would do the same to me. I knew what it felt like to avoid it, to fear letting it get to you would destroy you.

How could he not see that?

"Instead of realizing I might understand some of what you're feeling, instead of giving us both a chance at that, you'd rather cut and run."

The dark of his eyes changed in a way I didn't understand. Frankly, I was feeling too exhausted by the situation to try.

"If that's what you want, you can have it," I gave in. "We can stick with avoidance, throw away something that helped us both and go it alone."

He didn't want that. I knew it because he lashed out, but the words he said when he did also told me he wasn't willing to fight for some mystical "us" that could be.

"Sure you'll have to be real alone with Ace panting after you like a fuckin' dog," he snarled.

Then, I really was done.

So done, I wasn't even going to fight against that attack.

"Think what you want," I said, my voice sounding as tired as I felt.

I stepped around him, going to the door.

"What are you doing?" he demanded.

I didn't answer that. It was pretty self-evident.

When I had the door open, I gave him only two words.

"Goodbye, Jager."

CHAPTER 23
Ember

HE GAVE ME THREE DAYS.

Not Jager. Jager was content to give me forever. That was done.

No, Ace gave me three days.

They were three days—though I was loathe to admit it—I spent being pathetic and stupid. I spent them almost exclusively on my bed or the couch. I put on a game face when Dad was around so he wouldn't see that I was a mess. I kept myself showered and dressed as normal. I ate even though I had no appetite. For all the world, it seemed like I was just happy to chill at home with my new dog.

Luckily, I had walked away from that shelter with Roscoe. He was the only man I needed. He also wasn't as active as any of the breeds I'd been considering. Instead, Roscoe was happy to laze around with me between his frequent naps.

The only time I'd truly failed at keeping up my facade was that first night. It had taken a long while for me to fall asleep after I'd gotten home from the clubhouse. I had though, in time, unable to fight it off any longer.

I woke from nightmares of being taken, of being awake when they brought me to the club and Jager turning me away, of being dragged from Disciples' grounds screaming, knowing I was facing a fate worse than death.

I woke when Dad burst into my room, a gun in his hand,

ready to kill. And I woke realizing my screams had not just been in my mind.

It took a long time to convince Dad I was alright, and this was in part because I wasn't altogether sure it was true. What I did know was I couldn't have a scene like that happen again. Since that night, I'd set alarms to go off every hour. It wasn't helping my exhaustion, but I hadn't scared Dad again.

That pattern had gotten me to now, seeing through the open front blinds as Ace got off his bike and walked up to the door. The open blinds weren't the best call, I could see now. I couldn't ignore him when he'd already seen me sitting there. Sighing at my short sightedness, I got to my feet.

Ace didn't knock. He just waited for me to get there. When I did, I pulled the door open and greeted him with an artificial cheery, "Hi."

I wanted to wince when it left my mouth. It was too high, too bright, too obviously fake. Ace's raised eyebrow as he stepped in without saying anything told me he heard it too.

I stood by the door, contemplating my next move as he went in and sat on the couch where I'd been. Roscoe was still on the next cushion—not a guard dog in the least. Ace gave him a rubdown.

Not for the first time, I found myself taking a second to appreciate Ace as the fine male specimen he was. He had on a white t-shirt beneath his cut, well broken in jeans, and that hat on his head as always. I would never say it to him—or anyone else who might get the wrong idea—but he was seriously hot. Like all the guys, there was an obvious edge to him. However, his was immediately less forbidding than most. A first encounter with most of the brothers for a woman who wasn't used to being around bikers would send her running. Ace was alluring in the classic bad boy kind of way. He made a woman want to get close even if she knew it was probably risky.

He needed a woman, a good woman. He was the type who could have an old lady and be devoted to her, like Slick, Gauge, and Sketch. He just had to find her.

"Do you want to stand there all day or are you going to talk about it?" he asked, his attention still on Roscoe.

"Talk about what?" I tried for innocent.

He turned his head my way and gave me a look that said *don't bullshit me.*

"I was there, you know. When you stormed in and when you left," he offered as further reason to cut the crap.

Damn.

"There really isn't much to say," I told him. "It's over."

"He instigate that play?" Ace asked.

"Yes." But that wasn't really the whole story, so I added, "But I finished it."

"You finished it, but you're hiding out licking your wounds?" he didn't hide the skepticism.

"I'm not licking my wounds." Okay, that might have been a lie. There may have been a bit of wound licking in my hours of lazing around. "But, yes, I finished it."

"What do you need?" he asked.

What did I need? I needed to move on. I needed to get my life sorted, find a job, keep myself busy. I needed to find a gym.

"I need to hit something," I said when the idea struck me.

"Hit something?"

For the first time in a while, I was jazzed about something. I hadn't been to a gym—with the exception of fight night—since I'd been in Hoffman.

"Can you take me to the gym?" I asked. He looked hesitant, so I pressed, "What?"

"That's not the club's gym, Ember," he told me.

"It's not?" I was genuinely surprised. Between the fights and access to the office, whoever owned it seemed to be on very good terms with the Disciples.

"It's Jager's gym," he explained.

I didn't respond to that. My mind had sort of blanked on me. It hit me that I hadn't even known something that big about Jager.

Actually, if I were honest with myself, I knew almost nothing about him.

"He bought it, set it up, everything on his own," Ace went on. "It wasn't club funds that got it going or anything."

"No one ever said."

He shrugged. "No one ever really says much about Jager. Your girls probably barely know him."

Yeah, for the most part, that was true. Deni, Cami, they probably knew next to nothing about him—like me.

Ash, though, she may not have known it all, but she knew more than most.

Far more than I had, far more than I ever would.

"I can head over there, grab some pads and gloves. You can spar with me," Ace offered.

That was, easily, the best offer I'd had all week.

THE NEXT THURSDAY, I made my first trip back to the clubhouse.

Ace had been by every day to spar and it had felt good to hit something, but even better just to get back to something that had been such a big part of me for so long. After that first day, I'd started getting back into my normal workout routine. I didn't have a gym to practice in, but I had Ace to work with, and I had gotten back to my runs and basic workouts at the house.

I still wasn't sleeping well, but I had more energy than I'd had in weeks.

That afternoon, I ventured back into the viper's den for a good reason that had my spirits high. I'd brought Emmy along, strapped in a carseat in Dad's pickup. Ash was at Sketch's tattoo shop, getting her first tattoo done by her husband.

The tattoo was something she'd planned for a while. It was a tribute to her father, "Indian", his road name, in the same font as the Indian Motorcycle logo. She was getting it on her ribs. It was going to be a beautiful tattoo and it would have all the more meaning for her getting it done by the man she loved.

After that was done, she was bringing him back to the clubhouse, where he would finally learn about her little secret.

But first, we had to set up the big reveal.

I had no idea if Jager would be around. The brothers—all except Sketch—knew what was happening. They had everything set for a party afterward. Anything that served as an excuse to get smashed was fine by them, including the news one of their own was having a baby.

It wasn't fair to expect that he would miss a moment the rest of the brothers seemed pretty excited about just because of our drama. We'd made the mistake of starting something when we knew we'd both be around the club after it ended, now we'd have to live with that. In another circumstance, I might have bit the bullet and stayed home, but the girls were expecting me to be a part of the plan we'd concocted and I wasn't going to flake on them.

Emmy, at least, had been excited all day. Before she'd left to join Sketch at the tattoo parlor, Ash had told her daughter about the surprise. It had been all Emmy had wanted to talk about since.

"*I'm really gonna have a baby sister?*" Emmy had asked from the backseat on our way to the clubhouse.

"*Really really,*" I'd told her, then added, "*though it might be a baby brother.*"

"*Ew,*" she'd said, her little face scrunched up and tongue out.

"*A brother wouldn't be so bad,*" I'd tried to soften the blow.

"*Boys are gross. They don't even like pink.*"

Well, she had me there. I very much doubted Emmy would think boys were gross for long. Though, if she had a brother, he'd probably be the exception to that.

Now, Cami, Deni, and I were hard at work filling balloons with little pumps. Cami had texted us from the party store to say she'd found a balloon drop bag with a rip cord we could attach to the door. It would trigger a release of balloons, which meant we wouldn't have to fill the whole room.

Still, we had about seventy balloons to inflate.

After over an hour of pumping, Cami tossed a balloon up in the air after tying it off, then spiked it across the room. It was the last balloon, a pale pink one, and now all we had left was getting the guys to hang the bag and rig it to the door.

"If I never see a balloon again, it will be too soon," she groused.

"This was your idea," Deni reminded her.

We watched as little Levi motored his toddler booty across the room to the balloon his mom had flung away. At least he and Jules seemed to be enjoying themselves. Emmy had taken off not long after we got here when she realized there was actual work to be done. She'd found Daz who was all too happy to keep her entertained.

Cami's phone beeped and she jumped to her feet when she looked at the screen. "They're coming!" she announced, then stepped into the hall. "Guys!" she called out. "Come hang this! They'll be here soon."

Gauge and Slick came into the room a moment later and I had to contain my chuckle. Something about them hopping to for their women like that amused the crap out of me.

Daz came down the hall a minute later, carrying Emmy on his back. "You guys are so pussy whipped," he muttered.

Gauge and Slick shot him glares as they lifted the huge bag of balloons to the ceiling, and I snorted, trying to contain my laughter.

"Daz! Are you ever going to learn to watch your mouth around kids?" Cami demanded.

"Hey, the little ones are too small, and Emmy knows the score," Daz defended, then asked the little girl on his back, "What's the rule, princess?"

"Don't repeat anything Uncle Daz says," she recited.

That time, I laughed aloud.

Once the bag was all set, we all moved to the lounge, trying to appear totally nonchalant. We heard them pull up, then quiet until they pulled open the door.

Ash's voice came through first, "I don't know why you can't just tell me how to take care of it."

"I'll be there to do it myself," Sketch replied.

The guys were cool, a couple calling out greetings to them, but not all. The girls all turned their way, Deni calling, "Well, let's see."

Ash came over and we swarmed in on her tight. As she lifted her shirt, she whispered, "All set?"

We gave her the all good before taking a look at the perfectly executed tattoo.

"It's awesome," I said.

Ash smiled, her eyes tearing up a bit. "It kind of feels like he gets to be a part of this."

We took turns hugging her, then stepped back and let her head toward Sketch. She went up on her toes to whisper in his ear. I didn't know what she was offering to get him to go back to their room, but I could guess. The wolfish grin that crossed his face assured me my guess was probably right on.

Everyone moved quietly to the end of the hall, trying not to grab Sketch's attention. Cami had her phone out, ready to film the big moment. With baited breath, I watched him reach out and unlock the door. As he pushed it open, the avalanche of balloons fell all over the doorway and spilled into the hall around them.

Ash had her hands covering her mouth. Sketch stood still, looking around at the balloons settling all over. Neither moved or spoke.

Then, breaking the silence, Emmy charged ahead from her spot at the front of our group.

"Mommy's giving me a little sister!" she cried excitedly.

We all laughed as we watched Sketch look to Ash.

"Really?" he asked, his voice gruff.

"Well, she might get a brother," Ash amended.

He swept her up into his arms, wrapping a hand around the back of her neck to pull her lips to his. It was deep, intense, and I started to feel like a voyeur.

"We got a game to finish, little miss," Daz announced to Emmy, pulling her away from the show.

Sketch's head came our way briefly to check on his daughter while Ash seemed dazed. Seeing his girl was taken care of, he carried his woman over the balloon-laden threshold and forced the door closed behind them.

Well, that was one way to celebrate.

I looked to Cami, who was putting her phone away and smiling huge. I felt the same on my own face. Then, as I turned back to the lounge, I saw him. At the back of the crowd, notably less emotive than the rest of the excited group, Jager's eyes were right on me.

I kept the smile on my face even though I strained to do it, not wanting to take anything away from the moment we'd all gotten to be a part of. I didn't even let it slip as he turned without a word and walked away.

CHAPTER 24
Jager

I'D NEVER SEEN her smile like that.

Fuck, I'd scarcely seen her smile at all.

Whether I wanted to admit it or not, it was fucking beautiful. It was full of life. At least, until her eyes came to me. I killed that. Then, it was a fake, tight expression she forced herself to maintain.

That smile had haunted me for days.

I was at the gym. It was Monday, which meant we didn't open until four in the afternoon. I had three more hours with the place to myself.

I hadn't opened my own gym for that. If I wanted a place to work out, I could have set myself up in a house with a good-sized basement. I opened the doors on the place because I knew firsthand the difference having access to a place like that could make. It had made all the fucking difference for me.

But that didn't mean I didn't like having the whole place empty, when I could be alone and work my shit out.

Particularly right then, when the shit I had to work out was that image of Ember's smiling face that hadn't left me.

There was just something about that smile, something about the unrestricted light that flowed from it. I'd seen that before, in a face that looked nothing like Ember's. In a face that looked so much like mine.

The memory came of its own accord. It was such a seemingly insignificant one, but it gutted me all the same.

"BRADEN? BRADEN?"

I didn't get up and go to her. I never did. The few times I tried, she'd get upset and ask why she didn't let me find her. She liked to prove she was gaining some independence as she got older. So, I stayed on my bed and let her come to me.

It took a minute before she came in, her smile lighting up her face. She was always smiling, unless she was throwing a tantrum. Then, she was anything but happy.

When Jamie did something, she did it big.

"What's up, buttercup?" I asked.

She came skipping through the room and hopped up onto my bed. "I'm bored."

I looked into the happy face, so like my own. Yet, the girl beneath it was so unlike her big brother. I was content to be still, to just chill. Jamie hated it.

Though, it might not have been so much differences between us as it was the ten-year age gap.

"I've got homework," I told her.

"Homework is boring," she said, drawing out the O for several beats.

Again, something we didn't agree on. I had no problem with hitting the books. I only hated doing homework for statistics, but that was because Mr. Brookes was a moron and liked to load us with busy work so no one would catch on that he knew nothing about the subject.

"Do you even get homework yet?" I asked.

"Sometimes. And it's so boring." She held out those O's even longer than the first time.

"What's not boring?"

She played with a piece of her hair, adopting an innocent look, like she was only just about to come up with whatever she was going to suggest.

"Ice cream!" she then announced, like the lightbulb had just gone off.

This was Jamie's new game. I'd had my license for five months and she tried to get something out of that fact at least once a week.

I chuckled, not even sure I could say no to her.

My eyes went to my backpack and I inventoried the work I had ahead of me. There was a lot, and even though none of it was going to be a challenge, it was still time consuming, and I had just over an hour before I had to head to the gym for one-on-one training with my boxing coach. Ice cream wasn't in the cards.

"I can't tonight," I told her. "I've got to get as much of this done before I go meet Coach Jones."

She stuck her little lip out. "Boxing," she sneered.

"You like to watch me box," I reminded her.

"I like ice cream more," she argued.

I closed my book, making sure the sheet of paper I'd been doing the problems on was tucked flat between the pages. Then, I focused my whole attention on her.

"How about Saturday, after my tournament, we go to dinner wherever you want and then get ice cream?" I offered

"Or we could go get ice cream tonight, and do that then," she countered.

I laughed again, then gave her a look that told her that wasn't going to happen.

She sighed dramatically. "Oh, alright."

She started to get off my bed, already wanting to search out another form of entertainment, but I stopped her.

"Mee-mee," I called. We'd called her Mee-mee since she was little and couldn't figure out how to say her own name.

When she turned, I held out both of my hands, palms up. She

knew exactly what I wanted, coming back to me with that smile wide. She smacked both her little hands down on mine, we each flipped ours over and slapped hands again. Then we pressed our fisted hands against each other's. It was a handshake she'd invented that we could still do when I had on gloves before a match.

"You and me, date on Saturday. Yeah?"

She smiled big, showing the gap where she'd lost a tooth on the bottom. "Yeah."

I kissed her forehead before she ran off, finishing our handshake.

If I'd known what was coming, I would have just taken her for ice cream, damn the homework. If I'd known, I would have given her every minute of attention, every ridiculous errand she asked for. If I'd have known, I would have soaked up every second of that precious smile I'd never see again.

THE AGONY OF IT, the absolute, unrestricted pain that lashed through me letting those memories in was too much. I couldn't take it.

I threw my fists out harder, pounding into the bag suspended before me with so much force, my wrapped knuckles protested. It didn't stop me. I kept going. Hit after hit, focusing my mind on the combinations, on my form. I didn't think about the aches or the sweat. I didn't think about anything at all. I went into the zone and blocked it all out.

I couldn't say how long I went, only that I stopped when the bag was held steady.

Sketch was there, arms bracing the bag, attention on me.

"Time to stop, brother," he said.

I wanted to protest, but it occurred to me I was panting too heavily to talk. My arms were past the point of exhaustion, feeling like jelly as they hung at my sides. I was soaked in sweat. I'd gone way too fucking hard.

Stepping away from the bag and Sketch, I went over to the full water bottle I had on one of the benches. I drank half of it between attempts to catch my breath. Sketch sat down next to me, but let me relax without saying anything.

Of course, once I got there, he was ready to go.

"You wanna talk about why you're bustin' your own ass to the breaking point?"

No. I really fucking did not. I wanted to get up, go back to the bag, and keep going. I wanted to convince Ember to let me tie her up and torture her until she was physically incapable of orgasming again. I wanted to ride until the road lines blurred and go out in a blaze of glory.

I wanted to do any fucking thing but think about the shit that wouldn't get out of my head, about questioning my decision to let her walk away.

"This about Ember?" Sketch pressed.

Christ, when did the club turn into a fucking episode of Oprah?

"It's nothing," I tried to shut him down, but he wouldn't have it.

"Bullshit. You been dragging your ass around for the last week, which, for a fucker who sleeps as little as you, is saying something. You're a fucking mess, and I ain't the only one who's noticed. You want to talk to your woman about it, be my fucking guest. But I'm thinking that's not gonna happen. I'm thinking if you could, you wouldn't be in here punching the damn sandbag until you're ready to keel over. So, I'll ask again, you want to talk about this shit, asshole?"

That migraine, the one I'd been living with for days, was hitting me full force again. Pinching the bridge of my nose uselessly, I replied to him with the only thing I had. If nothing else, it was the truth. "She's not my woman."

"Really? That's the line of shit you're going to go with? There isn't a man or woman around this club you could convince of that. Fuck, you couldn't get Emmy to believe that and my girl's four."

I let that hang there, not arguing because I really couldn't.

"Jager, man—"

Fuck. There was nothing for it.

"How do you deal?"

"What?" he asked.

"How do you fucking deal with that shit? Knowing what happened to Ash, then that shit with Barton. How do you let it go?"

He kept his eyes forward as he answered. "I don't let any of it go. Not for a fucking minute. It's always there. I'll always know that if I'd held on, if I'd realized how much she was broken after we lost Indian, I'd have prevented that. She wouldn't have left. She'd have been right here where me and the whole motherfucking club could keep her safe. And the shit with Barton...*fuck.*" His head went down and he rubbed a hand across his face. "She was fucking here and I didn't even protect her from that. Ace was fucking shot protecting my woman. If anyone should have taken those bullets, it's me.

"My woman shot that asshole. Whether it was your bullet or hers that hit first, she still fucking fired. I'll have that on my soul for life, brother. I lay awake at night thinking about that shit. Get fucking nightmares about it."

We both sat with that knowledge out there between us, neither of us saying a thing because that said it all. At least, I thought it did, until Sketch said more.

"But I don't lay in that bed alone. I've got Ash next to me, and she sleeps through the night. Since you talked to her after it happened, she doesn't dwell on it. I've got that in my arms, so even if I'm up all night thinking about how I could have lost it, I get by knowing I came out on top. And when I drag my ass out of bed, I get to see my little girl smile at me and call me daddy each morning. I get to hear her laugh and spew all the ridiculous shit that comes out of her mouth. Best part is, I know I get that for a lifetime just like I get her mom. And now I'm going to get another kid to give that to me." He stopped, shaking his head. His face was one of awe over going to be a dad again.

Eventually, he finished, "That's how I get through. I carry that weight without letting it drag me down because, for them, I'd carry the whole goddamn world if I had to."

I said the only thing I had to say. "Glad you've got that, brother."

"Not nearly as fucking glad as I am. And, no joke, you get your head on straight before you fuck it up, I've got no doubts at all Ember's the type of woman who could give you the same. You got shit you're carrying and I get the feeling you'd try to shoulder the weight she's now got, but she'd make it all feel worth it. She'd make it feel like that weight isn't so damn heavy. You just gotta open that door for her."

With that parting shot, he stood and walked out of the gym, leaving me alone with all he'd said.

CHAPTER 25

Ember

AFTER MY FEW days of wallowing, I shook myself out of it. I was back to finding ways to keep busy. I'd spent the day before at Deni and Slick's, trying to keep Deni from losing her mind. Despite the days ticking away, their son had still not made an appearance. It was now two days from "Induction Day" as Deni was calling it, and she was more than mildly impatient to get the show going.

Deni was well past stir-crazy and Slick was even further past giving a shit if his wife was going insane, he wasn't letting up on enforcing the bed rest her doctor had ordered.

Today, as much as I loved Deni and wanted to help her out, there was no way I was going back. One day I could handle, two would be too much. Ash had volunteered to go keep her company, so I went to the garage with Dad.

I alternated between hanging out in the office with Cami while playing with Levi—who the guys had tricked out the office for so Cami could work and watch her son—and moving around the bays to see what the guys were working on. I'd even helped Dad for a bit on a vintage Dodge D-100 he was restoring for a customer.

I was sitting in the driver's seat of that truck, just chilling while Dad was on the phone looking for a part when Ace came strolling my way.

"I'm starved," he announced. "Time to feed me."

"Do I look like your maid?"

He leaned into the truck, his forearms braced on the roof above the open door. "Are you suggesting I get you a little French maid outfit?"

I knocked my arm against his stomach, not hard enough to send him double, but not a flirty touch either. He backed away a step, rubbing his abdomen. "Now, you owe me lunch."

I hopped out of the cab and righted my shorts. "Aren't you capable of feeding yourself?"

He shrugged. "Not particularly."

I shook my head, already giving in. "Fine. We'll go to the clubhouse. I'll make us lunch and bring some back for Dad."

He slung an arm around my shoulders. "That's my girl."

I kind of wanted to punch him again, but I just let it go.

"We're taking my car, though," I announced as we made it to the front of the garage.

"Alright," he agreed brightly.

"And I'm driving," I added.

He cursed and I grinned big.

LATER THAT EVENING, I was laid out in bed searching for jobs online, when someone started banging on the door. It was loud, so loud it startled Roscoe from his snooze, and he started barking with menace.

I hurried down the stairs, wondering who thought that kind

of knock was necessary and worried there might be something wrong with the club. Dad wasn't home, and for a terrifying moment, I feared one of the brothers was there to tell me something happened to him.

That fear, and the desire to ease my startled dog, had me pulling open the door without checking to see who was there.

I should have checked. I really, really should have checked. Dad told me since I was a kid you never open the door not knowing what you'd face.

I should have listened.

Without saying a thing, Jager muscled his way inside. He put a hand on my waist, pressing a bit to get me to back up and give him room. As soon as he passed the door, he threw it shut with a bang behind him.

"What do you want?" I demanded.

I tried to back away, but the hand he'd been using to push me out of his way clamped on to hold me in place.

"You aren't his girl," he growled.

"Excuse me?"

He moved in until the hard, hot length of his body was against mine. Then, in a tone so low it made me tremble—from fear or lust, I didn't know, but I was pretty sure it was a mix of both—he repeated, "You aren't his girl."

Forcing myself to keep my wits about me, I asked, "What the hell are you talking about?"

"Ace," he bit out. "You are not fucking his."

Then, I understood.

I hadn't seen him, but he must have been there in the garage. He'd heard what Ace said. Heck, he might have been the reason Ace was so intent on getting me out of there. He was trying to keep me from an awkward encounter with Jager.

For that, once I survived this, I would make him a hundred lunches.

"Yeah, I was there," Jager confirmed, noting the realization in my eyes.

"Jager," I started, wanting to get this done and him out of my house. He didn't give me the opportunity to finish.

His mouth came down on mine, hard, rough, and deep. He took advantage of the fact that I'd been about to speak, darting his tongue into my mouth right away. I tried to fight it. I yanked back from his hold, but he followed me, turning us so we slammed into the wall. Then, he pressed me there, giving me nowhere to go.

His kiss was rough, but his tongue was gentle, teasing even. He wasn't letting me get away as he tried to coax a reaction from me.

It was difficult to hold back, but I was succeeding. I was staying strong. I expected him to get frustrated. I braced for him to pull back and demand I give him what he was after. His dominance was going to be a test of my resolve, I knew. Still, I felt confident I could fight it.

Except, that wasn't what he did.

Faced with my fight, he didn't turn aggressive. Instead, he gave me something I'd never had from him.

With a gentleness I would not have been certain he was capable of, his hands left my waist and came up to cup my jaw. His touch was light as one of his thumbs swept over my cheek. That show of tenderness was my undoing. I had no idea whether I was making a huge mistake or not, but I couldn't deny him when he was being sweet like that for the first time.

So, I didn't.

I kissed him back.

My kiss had all the frustration, all the anger, all the longing that had been living in me since the last time I'd felt him that close. I wanted to release it all, give all of that feeling to him, and take the sweet he was offering to replace it.

Jager didn't let me. He didn't take control, but he didn't let the kiss turn into the blazing fire I was stoking. He kept it soft and slow. With his hard body closing me in, I felt as secure as I always had with him. What surprised me was his touch made me feel cherished. He held me like I was precious to him.

We should have stopped. If I had half a mind to self-preservation, I would have gotten away from him, doing whatever I had to in order to achieve that.

What I did instead might have been stupid, and I might have come to regret it.

But I did it anyway.

I brought my hands up, slipping them beneath his cut. He didn't hesitate to move his arms, allowing me to pull it off. I didn't let the leather fall to the ground though. I held onto it. Knowing what it meant to all the brothers, it didn't belong on the floor.

I moved my mouth away from his enough to say, "Upstairs."

"Roadrunner?" he asked after Dad.

"He's watching Levi. Won't be back for hours," I explained.

That was good enough for him. I knew it when he bent down, hooked his arms beneath each of my legs, and hoisted me up. I threw my arms around him, his cut still held tight in one hand, and he made his way to the stairs.

I heard Roscoe's tag jingle as he made to follow us, so I called to him, "Stay, good boy."

The jingling stopped. Whoever had surrendered Roscoe to the shelter had at least cared enough to train him when they had him.

I let that train of thought fade away as Jager took the first step. I had no reservations about letting him carry me up, even if we were both going up blind. No matter what had happened, I trusted Jager to never let me get hurt.

Neither of us spoke on the way up. There was plenty to say, maybe even too much to undertake it. I stared into Jager's eyes, seeing more than the wall usually guarding his thoughts. He was open to me, showing me his desire, his affection, the lingering fire of his jealousy. That did more than all the words in the world. At the end of the day, he was letting me see that, and that sight alone told me what I really needed to know.

Jager found the way into my room on his own. I didn't ask how. Dad had been in the same house since I was seven. He was a brother. Him knowing the layout wasn't shocking.

Inside, he laid me out on the bed. I watched the surprise on his face when he realized I still had his cut in my hand before he took it from me and laid it across the chair in the corner.

I started to pull off my shirt, but he stopped me with a soft, "Don't."

He climbed on the bed, forcing me to lay back as he came over me. He hadn't undressed aside from kicking off his shoes and I wasn't sure what to make of that. Jager didn't give me much headspace to do anything with as he started kissing me again. His hands made a slow journey along my side, from my hip to my ribs. My shirt went up with his hand until he cupped my breast. He kept his hand there above my bra, holding me but doing nothing more as we kissed.

Part of me felt silly, like we were a couple of high school kids slowly working our way up to the real thing. Yet, nothing about the skill with which he kissed me was silly. It was deep, powerful despite its gentleness, and it was downright consuming.

I sunk into the feeling, blocking out everything else, not caring if going under meant never resurfacing.

Already worked up and trying to move things along, I ran my hands up his back, not stopping until his shirt caught on his arms. Even then, I tugged at the fabric to make it clear what I wanted. He didn't move.

I groaned in frustration, the sound swallowed by his mouth. Jager pressed his hips down against me and the sharp ache that elicited echoed through my whole body.

I groaned again and he lifted up, breaking the kiss as he stared down at me. "Patience," he chided.

"No," I replied.

Leaning in, he said right against my lips, "Let me give you this."

How could I argue with that?

Jager took his time, kissing me until I thought I might burn up from the heat of my own desire. When he finally lifted my shirt up and off, I moaned at the pure relief of getting it out of the way. He moved his lips from mine, taking his time worshipping the skin he revealed.

His lips felt like they were stirring flames to life beneath my skin. They traced patterns of pure fire along my abdomen. By the time he removed my bra, I couldn't take it anymore.

"Please, Jager," I begged. "I need you. I can't wait."

His eyes were electric, like a storm about to begin the deluge. That dominance innate to him could only just be contained. My pleas made some of that control slip.

His hands were more firm, his movements quicker as he stripped off the rest of my clothes. For the first time, he let me remove his. I reveled in the freedom to touch him, to put my mouth on him. Every other time we had been together, I'd been bound either by actual restraints or his commands to remain still.

As much as I wanted to take the time to enjoy having all of him at my fingertips, I wanted to truly have him far more. It wasn't something I needed to say. I simply laid back on the pillows, moving my arms up to wrap around his shoulders. He understood.

With a slowness that had my eyes rolling back in my head, he pushed inside. Like every time he was inside me, I marveled at the feel of him. He filled me so completely. Unlike any other time, he didn't fuck me hard. He moved in and out with slow, controlled motions.

"Feel me," he commanded on a low groan.

And I did. I so absolutely did. I felt every inch of him enter and retreat. I felt the heat of his body looming over mine, warming me so thoroughly, I forgot what cold felt like. Most importantly, I felt and saw what he was really giving me.

His eyes didn't leave mine. Even as they were consumed with desire, I could see the way he laid himself bare. I had that, all while having his body in a complete, unhindered way I never had before.

And I knew, down to my soul, the gift he gave me as he took me there, building it slowly until that crest broke with a shattering power, was one I would never forget.

CHAPTER 26
Jager

"JAGER?" Ember called.

She didn't need to call out to me. We were still in her bed. I was on my back, Ember on her side pressed half against me, half on top of me. We were close.

Her asking for my attention meant it was time. I'd come back without giving her what she actually needed. She'd let me have her because she trusted that my being there meant I was ready to offer that. And I was.

Ember walking away had been playing on a loop in my mind, shaking the foundation of the life I'd built. Sketch's little come-to-Jesus shit the other day had made the crack in the wall. Hearing Ace call her his—even if I knew he didn't mean it, and the dick probably only said it to get a rise out of me—had sent that fucker crumbling down.

I came to her pissed, but that was a front.

It hadn't sunk in on my way over, but I was there with a fucking purpose that went beyond any game Ace was playing with me.

So, I gave it to her.

"I had a sister."

Her body got tense. I was fighting against my own doing the same, but I managed to keep calm by focusing on her weight and warmth. I could smell her shampoo, her perfume, the scent of her sweet pussy—it all helped.

I tried to help her relax by rubbing my fingers lightly along her spine. The feel of her soft skin centered me further. Her muscles loosened and her back arched a bit into my touch.

"Had?" she asked.

"Had." I swallowed, trying to force down the desire to shut her out. I didn't want to do this. I wanted to take off. But Ember was there, laid bare for me. She'd let me have that even after I'd been a fucking dick.

"She'd make it all feel worth it. She'd make it feel like that weight isn't so damn heavy. You just gotta open that door for her."

Looking at Ember, her face turned up toward me, I felt the truth of Sketch's words settle in. He was fucking right. Even with sympathy in her gaze and the lingering worry over what I would do next, hope shone bright in those ice blue eyes.

She wanted this. She'd give it all to me, I just had to open that fucking door.

The appeal of keeping my shit locked up couldn't touch the appeal of her.

"Jamie," she whispered, even now trying to help me on my way.

I was startled by her having that knowledge. I hadn't told Ash that. I hadn't told a fucking soul that shit.

Seeing my reaction, she explained, "You've said the name in your sleep. Just her name. I thought..."

She took her eyes away from me and I knew why. She thought Jamie was a woman I'd been involved with.

Fuck, my Ember. She thought I was hung up on another woman and, despite claiming she was just in it for sex, she'd stuck around. That knowledge, and the not completely unpleasant burn searing through me with it, gave me the push to keep going.

"Yeah, Jamie. She was my little sister. She was ten years younger than me."

"That's quite a gap," she said. She was trying to make me

comfortable. I wanted to kiss her for it, but there was no way I'd want to return to this conversation that she needed to happen if I got a taste of her.

"I guess. It was just always the way it was for us. I figured it out later that my mom had trouble getting pregnant after me. My parents wanted to have more kids, so they did fertility treatments and all that shit to get Jamie. The way they were so excited about it got me excited. When Jamie came, I wasn't upset about not being the only kid anymore. I wasn't annoyed I was going to have a little girl following me around. I was happy. The first time I saw her at the hospital, I fell in love."

I could still remember, even after all the years that had passed, being ten years old and holding her little bundled body the first time. I'd thought she looked weird, all small and wrinkly, but I also knew she was ours. Me, Mom, and Dad—she belonged to all of us.

"They let me pick her name," I went on. "Gave me a couple options. Kayla, Elizabeth, Alyssa…"

"Or Jamie," she filled in.

"Yeah. I don't know why they let me choose. I never asked, but I think it might have been to help me feel connected to Jamie. I don't know. If that was why, I don't know whether it worked or I just loved her because she was my sister. It doesn't really matter, I guess.

"Mom and Dad were great. She was a stay-at-home mom, mostly. But she'd gone to school for accounting. Dad owned his own construction business. She did the accounts for it, but she was all set up to do that at the house so she was home with us. They loved each other, and us. They were happy. We all were.

"Jamie was a lot like Emmy. She had so much personality. She always said exactly what was on her mind. And she was always smiling."

Fuck, it killed to talk about this.

"You loved her," Ember summed it up.

"I loved her," I agreed. "She always wanted to be around me. Some girls are daddy's girls, but Jamie, she was all about her brother. It never bothered me, her following me around or wanting me to play with her. Maybe I got irritated once in a while, but I never wanted to change that.

"I was sixteen when it happened. Dad was having trouble with one of the guys on his crew. I heard him talking to Mom about it for a couple weeks. Asshole was showing up late or missing days altogether. When he did show, he was hungover. Then, he showed one day, after two days being MIA, and came to the site drunk. Dad was done. The fucker was finally there and it wasn't safe for him to work with any of the equipment. Dad laid him off. He didn't like doing it. He was a good guy, he didn't want to fire anyone, but that shit couldn't go on."

I took a minute to breathe. Getting out the next part was the real battle.

"That asshole didn't take getting canned as a wakeup call to sort his shit. He hit the bottle, and he hit it pissed at Dad for his own fuck ups. He came to the house in the middle of the night and started a fire."

I could feel Ember's body was tense, her breathing shallow. Her hands were gripping onto me tight. All of this registered distantly against the horrific images coming back to me.

"He tried to claim later he just meant to damage the house and scare us, but he doused the fucking thing in gas. He spread that shit all around the exterior, and then he popped open a window to spray it inside before he lit it. The house was engulfed fast. Too fast.

"The smoke detector woke me. I don't know whether we slept through it or it didn't go off right away. Might not have been either. Might just be that was how fast the house went up. I remember there was already so much smoke. I could see the fire downstairs as soon as I left my room. I started to run to Jamie's room, but Dad was already in the hall. He told me to run. To get out. He'd get Mom and Jamie out.

"I didn't want to leave them, but I knew he was wasting time yelling at me, so I did. I ran. Got out right before the second floor collapsed."

Her breath hitched and I pulled her in tighter, even though I worried I was holding her too hard.

"I lost them all. Mom and Dad didn't even make it to the hospital. Jamie did. They had to put her in a coma. They did what they could, but her little body just couldn't take it. The burns were too extensive—"

My voice broke thinking of her small frame in the big hospital bed. All the tubes and wires hooked up to machines that dwarfed her even more. I remembered the beeping of her heartbeat only sustained by technology making it so.

I remembered the last beeps of her heart fading away.

Ember adjusted until she was on top of me, practically wrapped around me. I felt the wet on her cheeks when she buried her face in my neck.

"I'm so sorry."

I clutched her to me. All over me was her warmth, her softness. It broke through the haunting feeling of the scalding heat, the ashes clinging to my skin. Her tears ran down my neck and for the first time since that horrific fucking night, it felt like she was making me clean.

Fuck.

Ember.

I held her a long time, letting her weight keep me from sinking into the memories. She cried her tears for my family, for what I lost. Somehow, it felt like her tears were the release I'd needed for too fucking long.

When her tears ran their course, she broke the silence.

"What happened to him?" she asked. Even with her voice low, I could hear it. She wanted vengeance for the people I loved, who she'd never met.

"He got life. Judge didn't buy his bullshit about not meaning to hurt anyone. Threw the fuckin' book at him," I told her some of it.

"He deserves so much worse," she seethed.

"He's dead."

I didn't tell her I organized it. I didn't tell her I made contacts at that prison, greased palms. I didn't tell her he knew in his last fucking moments I made it happen.

"Good."

I didn't respond to that. It was good. It was the best fucking night of sleep I'd gotten since that day. Getting my revenge took seven years, but knowing that motherfucker bled out in slow agony because I made it so was worth the wait.

And as I held Ember, who had so much emotion over my pain, I knew I would stop at fucking nothing until she knew the same vengeance. No matter what it took, I was going to find that cunt Yeltz, and I was going to make him suffer for what he'd done to her.

There was nothing that could stop me. Not even Kuznetsov. His shitty soldiers got Yeltz first, I'd burn that bullshit operation of his to the ground to get the prick. I didn't give a fuck.

In the morning, I was getting back to hunting him down. It was my top priority.

For the night, there wasn't a fucking thing on earth that could get me to move from where I was. Especially not when Ember spoke again, cementing with two words that I had made the best fucking decision of my life.

"Thank you," was all she said.

She was thanking me for giving her all of that, for burdening her with that horror because she knew what it meant for me to share. She wanted to take it on so she could truly have all of me.

"She'd make it all feel worth it. She'd make it feel like that weight isn't so damn heavy. You just gotta open that door for her."

My brother was so fucking right.

"My Ember."

Her arms tightened harder. Her agreement.

She was mine.

CHAPTER 27
Ember

I WOKE in the middle of the night like I did every night.

This time, though, I couldn't shoot to sitting. Jager was beside me, his arms locked around my torso, keeping me still. He was awake by the time I looked to him, his eyes stormy.

We'd eventually risen from the bed earlier, knowing my dad would be home at some point. There was going to have to be some discussion with Dad about the state of play between Jager and me, and out of respect, that conversation shouldn't wait. However, it didn't need to be while Jager and I were still naked in my bed. It also didn't need to happen when we were both still raw from Jager telling me about losing his family.

Because of that, Jager suggested we go to his apartment for the night.

I'd agreed on the spot. *"Just let me call Dad and make sure he's good with watching Roscoe,"* I'd added.

Jager, who had been pulling on his shirt, gave me a puzzled look I didn't understand until he'd said, *"Why? Just bring him."*

"You're okay with him being at your place?"

"Babe, you keeping that dog?"

I'd had no idea why he would ask that, so I'd answered, *"Of course I am."*

"I'm not making a habit of sleeping here with you. This is Roadrunner's house. I respect my brother enough not to be fuckin'

his daughter in his house all the damn time. You having to bring your dog isn't much of a concession to have you in my bed."

Well, I'd thought, *that was that then.*

Then, he'd gone on. *"Besides, I like dogs. Got no problem having one around."*

Evidence was suggesting Jager could be really sweet when he let me in enough to see it.

We'd loaded up, me riding in my car behind Jager's bike with Roscoe, a bag of clothes and "shit" Jager demanded I pack and supplies for my dog.

All that led to being in Jager's bed, waking from another nightmare.

"You're safe," Jager said in a quiet but firm way.

"I know," I responded.

"Talk to me," he requested.

I felt my pulse pick up and tried to divert him. "You already know what happened."

"Gotta get it out," he replied.

"There's nothing to say. It's just all of it. Waking up with them in my room, being in that cell." I shook my head, trying to fight the images that wanted to keep control of my head.

"Tell me what's really getting to you, Ember," he pushed.

"Jager," I tried.

"Baby," he insisted, "tell me."

"I was kidnapped!" I snapped. "I'm allowed to struggle after that!"

"You are, but you need to talk to me about what's keeping it fresh for you."

"All of it," I told him.

My heart was pounding. My mouth dry.

He needed to stop.

"Tell me," he reiterated.

"She was just a kid!" I let fly. "She was only fifteen and she was in that place! And there was a woman my age who was *sold to them.* By her own family. I had the club to get me out of there. They had no one!"

He tightened his hold on me, pressing me into his chest. "We'll find them. We'll get them out if we can."

I shook my head, knowing he could feel it. "It's too late. Who knows who they were sold to."

"We'll find them," Jager repeated.

I didn't know how I could believe that, but there was a vow in his tone. While I wanted to push, I figured I was going to get served the "club business" line I'd heard since I was a kid. As a Disciple, I knew there were going to be things Jager couldn't and wouldn't tell me. I just didn't want to confront that issue so soon.

"Okay," I gave in.

"I know you aren't ready to believe that," Jager called out the truth, "but I'll prove it."

There was more there than this one promise. He was talking about us. He was talking about proving I'd made the right choice by letting him in.

"Okay." That time, it wasn't resigning.

He gave me a squeeze of approval. "Try to get some more sleep, babe. I'm right here."

I did as he said, letting the comfort of his arms lull me back to sleep.

My nightmares didn't wake me again.

I DIALED for the second time, my anxiety mounting. Ringing filled my ear, paused, started again. Four rings and then the voicemail picked up.

At the beep, I did as instructed and left my message.

"Dammit, Slick! Answer your damn phone! Your wife is in labor!" I half-screeched down the line before hanging up.

I walked back into the living room where Deni was doing that weird hee-hee-hoo breathing they make pregnant women do. She looked at me expectantly and I bit my lip as I shook my head.

"Are you fucking kidding me?" she snapped. "He's barely let me out of his sight for more than a month and now the moment has arrived and he's not answering!"

I didn't really know how to respond since she'd said it all. I knew the guys were in church, but Slick had said he'd have his phone on him anyway. He'd said all the guys agreed having a wife past her due date was reason to break the rules.

Perhaps he was wrong.

Deni released a groan of pain and clutched her belly. Another contraction. I looked at my phone. That was four minutes.

It was time to try something else. Not bothering to leave the room, I dialed Dad. No answer. Then Jager, Stone, Doc. Nothing. Everyone's phone but Slick's were actually off. I gave up on the phone, so frustrated I wanted to chuck it across the room.

Deni was still heeing and hooing. I needed to get myself together. I wasn't the one having a baby. She was the only person here with the right to freak out.

"You're maintaining four minutes apart. Do we need to call the doctor?" I asked.

She nodded in time to her breathing. "Number is on the fridge," she told me.

I headed that way, grabbed the paper from the fridge that read "Baby Numbers" at the top, and started dialing her OB.

Before I could place the call, I heard the front door open. Not even a second later, Deni's voice filled the house.

"Why weren't you answering your phone?" she shrieked.

Well, Slick was home.

"Saw Ember calling and took off," he answered. He obviously surmised the situation and asked, "How far apart are they?"

"Four minutes."

I went back to the living room to see the door still wide open and Slick on his phone. Seemed he didn't need the "Baby Numbers" note to get the number. I wondered for a second whether it was programmed in his phone or he'd just memorized it.

I was guessing both.

"Ember, can you get Jules up from her nap and make sure she's ready to go?" Deni asked.

"Of course," I said, hopping to the task.

As I moved to the stairs, Slick covered the phone and said, "There's a diaper bag all packed up in the closet."

Right. I got about taking over Jules duty so Mom and Dad could focus on the new baby finally making his arrival.

It took under twenty minutes before we were all out the door. The doctor had instructed Slick to bring Deni in, so he set about doing that. I got a very sleepy Jules changed and all set to welcome her little brother into the world. For the first time, it really occurred to me that Deni and Slick were about to have a newborn in the house when their daughter wasn't even potty trained yet.

It sounded like utter madness to me, but they both seemed blissfully happy.

Slick had everything ready for this eventuality. There was a duffle packed for Deni, the diaper bag fully loaded for Jules, he even had an insulated bag in the fridge already filled up to keep Jules fed if things went long. All he needed to do was slip an icepack inside.

I supposed if you were going to have two kids that close, it was good to do it with a man who was on top of things.

When we got to the hospital, I assured them both I was good

with Jules while they were escorted to a room. So, I was sitting in the waiting room alone with a little girl nodding off in my lap when Cami arrived with Levi.

"Here we go again," she said by way of greeting. I hadn't been around for Jules' birth, but knew Disciple births were a club affair.

This was proven to be true half an hour later when Doc came in, followed by Stone, Gauge, Tank, Daz, Sketch, Ham, and Dad. I kept my eyes on the door as they all walked our way, but neither Jager or Ace came in.

There were greetings, questions about any updates, and a brief round of betting over how long it would take for the little guy to make his way out. I put a measly ten bucks on two and a half hours and caught shit from Daz about my pathetic bet. He threw down three hundred on five hours.

Priority number one for the day was Deni and her boy coming out of things healthy. But, seriously, if they could take any amount of time but five hours, I'd love them even more.

Ash arrived with Emmy just after the betting ended. She went right to her husband, who stood to give both his girls a kiss before taking Emmy.

"Any news?" she asked the room.

"Not yet," I answered. "We haven't been here long."

"Good. I didn't want to miss anything, but I needed to get Emmy something to eat and pack up some stuff to keep her busy before we could leave."

Emmy was already seated, digging into a pink backpack and coming out with a coloring book and crayons. From what I could tell, that bag was filled with everything a four-year-old girl could need.

I took it all in. The big, burly group of bikers taking up the waiting room, getting more than a few nervous glances from hospital staff and visitors alike. Not one of our party cared, though. Those people didn't factor. All that mattered was the Disciples welcoming a new baby to the family.

I checked my phone, wondering if Jager had sent a text I hadn't noticed, but there was nothing. Neither him nor Ace had showed yet. I started to worry. What if that anger Jager swept into Dad's house with last night hadn't died? What if, wherever he and Ace were, it was breaking free again?

I went to Dad and immediately demanded, "Where are they?"

He started at my demand, then replied, "Club business, Ber-bear. Can't tell you."

Of course.

I already knew between Dad and Jager—not to mention just being around all the guys—I was going to get really freaking sick of that phrase.

"Dad, seriously. You guys can't just let them fight," I snapped.

Now, he looked confused. "What are you talkin' about?"

Oh, well. Maybe they weren't fighting.

Crap.

"Um...nothing," I tried, like that was going to work.

"Ember," Dad warned.

What was it about a parent saying your name the right way that made you feel like a child?

"It's nothing. Really. I was just worried."

"Why would you assume they'd fight?" he asked straight out.

I couldn't lie. I wanted to, but he'd know. "Ace said something yesterday. I didn't know Jager was there, but he heard it, he also didn't like it."

"Jesus," he sighed, "tell me you aren't starting something with Ace."

"Dad!" I snapped.

"Ember, I'm not fucking around. Tell me you aren't."

"I'm not!"

"Thank Christ," he muttered.

"I'm not just going to jump around between the brothers."

"Baby, you reconsider that, you call me. Yeah?" Daz called.

I turned my head, realizing our conversation getting heated also meant it got louder. So, naturally, the nosey bikers and biker broads were all listening.

Tank wasted no time shoving Daz. "Shut up, dick."

My attention went back to Dad, but I took care to keep my voice down. It wouldn't matter. We already had everyone's attention. And anyway, they'd all know soon either way.

"I haven't had a chance to tell you, but Jager and I are together. As in, *together*. That's why I left last night. We were... working things out."

Dad's response to that?

"Shit."

"Dad," I started, stepping closer to him and placing a hand on his arm, "we talked. He opened up to me. This is real."

Then, in a completely different voice, one filled with genuine surprise, he repeated, "Shit." He went on to ask, "Jager talked about himself?"

I nodded.

"That boy's locked up tighter than a steal trap."

He was. I knew that.

"Not with me. Not anymore."

"That explains it," I thought I heard from behind me.

I turned to see who said it, but no one was looking my way, and no one responded to the statement. I shook it off and focused back on my dad.

"Can you still not tell me where he is?"

Dad gave me an apologetic look. "Sorry, baby girl. I can't."

"Okay," I replied on a huff.

"They're both good," he promised. "They wouldn't be where they are if we all didn't know that."

Right. They were brothers. If the guys weren't worried, I had no need to be.

"Okay, Dad."

"Come on." He wrapped an arm around me and led the way to two open chairs. "Who knows what kind of wait we've got ahead of us. Best settle in."

And that was what we did. Waiting patiently for three hours —making Ham the winner of the bet—until Slick came out to tell us Hunter James had arrived.

CHAPTER 28

Jager

"YOU'RE SURE THIS IS IT?" Ace asked, binoculars pointed on the house.

It seemed pretty self-evident. The place was ostentatious. I knew from pulling the building records it had eight bedrooms, ten baths, and a fucking indoor pool. Seemed like every light in the damn place was on despite the fact that no one was in any of those rooms. This we could see because not one of them had blinds shut.

It was also built with its back to hills that eventually became mountains. Chances were, this choice was for privacy. There was a fair amount of distance between this house and any others. The hills blocked off access from one side.

Unless, of course, you rode something slim enough to navigate the narrow paths on them.

"Certain," I told him.

"How'd you find this place?"

"Kuznetsov's accountant needs better passwords."

The man did too. Disregarding the fact that he was filing taxes for a man with more power and money than sense, no one handling that kind of sensitive information from anyone should have their daughter's name and birthdate as their password for damn near everything. Getting into his accounts was the only way I was able to trace the not-so-short trail through offshore accounts that had Kuznetsov's cash paying for the monstrosity of a house we were looking at.

If the not security savvy accountant wasn't willing to take big bucks to handle the affairs of a dick like Kuznetsov, I might have dropped him the friendly advice to step up his game.

"You think they got a line on Yeltz?" Ace asked.

"Yeltz is off the grid," I explained. "Everything. Regular scheduled charges are coming from his accounts under Louis, but nothing that requires the man in person. Could be he's already setting up elsewhere, or it could be that Kuznetsov's men were too close and he went to ground. If he was settin' up, he'd dismantle everything that was Louis. Wouldn't want that there to trace back to. Louis isn't gone, so I'm guessing Yeltz hasn't gotten far. Not easy to find ground deep and dark enough to hide from the fuckers Kuznetsov has after him. We could go lookin' ourselves, but those men know dark better than we do."

"So, you're thinking we'll have better luck getting Yeltz out once they grab him?" He didn't hide his doubt.

"I think Kuznetsov is cocky, but not that smart. This place has a vulnerability. We just have to find it, and it'll be easier to do that when he and his personal guard aren't here."

"Personal guard," Ace scoffed under his breath.

I couldn't agree more.

"East side, check out the ground," Ace said after a minute, passing over the binoculars.

I focused in on where he'd indicated and noticed exactly what he was pointing out. A gravel path, wide enough for a car. There was an attempt to work it into the landscaping, but it was obvious. That was, it was obvious until it hit a tree line. Then, it purposefully veered in a turn that would take practice driving so the path didn't stand out.

"We need to find out where the access point for that is," Ace said.

I didn't respond, but felt the grin on my lips.

Fucking got him.

IT WAS LATE when I stepped into the apartment. Roscoe came my way the moment the elevator doors opened, barking and growling. That dog was already protecting Ember, even in a place he wasn't overly familiar with.

I bent to give him a rubdown. "Good boy," I murmured low so Ember wouldn't hear if he'd woken her. She wasn't big on him barking at anyone who came in. I thought that was jacked, so I was going to see if Roscoe and I could form our own understanding.

After a minute, I instructed him to go lay down so I could find my woman.

Before I could head to the bedroom, I saw a box on the kitchen counter. Ember must have noticed it downstairs and brought it up.

I knew what it was without opening it and that knowledge had my dick getting hard.

A few minutes later, I entered the bedroom. Ember was spread out in bed, her somewhat groggy eyes on me.

"There you are," she said in a sleep-heavy voice.

She needed sleep and I'd let her get it, but that would be later. Much later.

I moved into the room until I was standing against the foot of the bed.

"Come here, pet," I gave the quiet order.

There was a widening of her eyes that told me she understood. When she moved, she was coordinated, awake. She crawled down the bed and knelt on it in front of me.

"I got you something."

I pulled the lavender leather from my back pocket and lifted it in both hands so the metal, heart-shaped ring was upright. Reaching back, she pulled her hair up and out of the way. Situating the heart so it was centered on her slim neck, I leaned in so my mouth was right at her ear while I secured the buckle.

"I've never collared a woman before," I said, allowing my lips to graze her ear as I did.

She shuddered, and I hoped she understood what I meant.

I'd bound women with a collar on their neck. I'd restrained them with one so they couldn't move their head. That wasn't what this was for.

No, this was a statement, even though she would only wear it when we were alone.

It said she was mine.

My Ember.

My pet.

Stepping back, I saw she had one hand resting delicately on her own neck, her fingertips on the leather and metal.

"How does it feel?"

She looked up at me without tilting her head, just her eyes coming up to meet mine. It made her look innocent. It made me want to sully her.

"Like I'm yours," she responded.

I hooked my finger into the metal heart, having to press into her neck a bit to do so. I'd secure the collar tight enough that she would feel it, but did it with care. I tugged her forward and up, forcing her to rise onto her knees and stretch up toward me.

"Good girl," I praised before taking her mouth.

I kissed her long and deep, feeling her air run out. Even when it had, she didn't try to pull away from my tongue. She just laved it with hers affectionately, trusting me to release her when it was time. She didn't even gasp for air when I let her go. She took a breath and that was it. Meanwhile, she watched me, waiting for what was next.

Without releasing my hold on her collar, I pulled the second, longer piece of lavender leather from my pocket. With a click, I latched the leash onto the metal heart.

"Come," I commanded, and it wouldn't be for the last time that night.

She climbed from the bed and walked behind me as I held the leash. I wasn't pulling her. I didn't need to, and I didn't want to. She followed me across the hall into the second bedroom gladly.

I took her to the side of the room, to a drawer where what I needed was stored. I rifled through it, taking my time to build her suspense. I heard her intake of breath when I produced a bottle of lube. Facing her, I gave a little tug on her leash to get her to look up at me. When I had her eyes, I wrapped both arms around her, sliding one up under the nighty she was wearing and into her panties until I could run my finger between her ass cheeks.

"We've played back here, but I haven't asked. Have you taken more than the plugs I've given you here?" I let my finger slip in to the first knuckle as I asked.

"No," she said on a small gasp.

Fucking perfection.

"I'm going to take this tonight." I wriggled my finger a bit, but didn't press in further with her unprepared.

"Yes, sir."

I placed a kiss at the corner of her mouth, then led her to the door again. From over my shoulder, I saw her looking somewhat despondently at the room we were leaving behind and I fucking grinned. She wanted that kind of play, and she'd get it, even if she was thinking otherwise. The leather adorning her neck was all I needed to give it to her.

Bringing her to the bed, I reeled her leash in to get her lips. Just a quick taste as I pushed the straps of her nighty off her shoulders and let the thing drop to the floor.

"Lay down," I told her before giving her the lead to do so.

She settled in the center of the mattress, her body language revealing she was ready to move as I instructed. Grabbing a pillow from above her, I settled it beneath her head. Above all else, she needed to be comfortable.

In Ember's case, being comfortable enough to give this to me meant something different than most. To give her that, I grabbed her wrists. Her eyes flared as I held them above her chest in one hand. She thought I wasn't going to bind her. She wanted to be.

I brought the leash straight down from her neck, leaving some room before wrapping the leather around her wrists and up a bit onto her forearms. She could move her hands no lower than her breasts.

After a quick minute to discard my clothes, I climbed onto the bed and positioned myself so I was kneeling between her legs. Ember, whose eyes hadn't left me once, was taking in every inch of me, her gaze lingering on the inches she'd be taking.

I dipped my thumbs under the sides of her panties and pulled them off. I could smell her wet pussy with the fabric gone and I had to grip my dick to keep from losing control. With two fingers, I rubbed against her and felt just how wet she was. I didn't waste another fucking second before sinking both inside her slick cunt. She mewled, rotating her hips and pressing against me.

"You're soaked," I praised. "Thinking about my cock in your tight ass makes you hot, doesn't it, pet?"

"Yes," she moaned.

I struck with my free hand, landing a smack so it would sting against her clit.

"Yes, sir!" she corrected on a cry.

Instead of rewarding her, I pulled free of her grasping pussy. She made a noise of protest, but I focused on pouring lube onto my other hand. I thrust two fingers back into her pussy at the same time I pushed one right through her tight ring of muscle and fully into her ass. I moved both hands together, filling her up completely before backing off. As the clench of her ass around my finger lessened, I pushed another in without breaking the steady rhythm I fucked her with.

"Oh God," she chanted on the same beat.

She was fucking cute, losing her mind when we weren't even close to all I'd give her. My cock was throbbing, but I savored it. I knew now how sweet that touch of masochism could be. When I sunk inside her, taking her ass for the first time, I knew it would be the greatest fucking feeling.

On that thought, needing her to be prepared to have me, I pushed a third finger into her lubed hole. She tightened up, trying in a small way to pull away from the invasion.

"Push against me," I coached her.

She did, easily taking what I gave once she relaxed. Our play up to that point hadn't been minimal. I'd been teasing myself by playing with her, prepping her for this moment painfully slow. Now, with her ass slick with lube, her pussy drenched and wanting, and the way she shifted her hips into my hands, I knew she was ready.

I took my fingers from her pussy first, using the wet digits to massage her clit while I finger fucked her ass hard and fast. Her cries grew heady, her hips churning with desperation. She was right at the cusp, but she wasn't going over. She could come when she had me buried deep—not before.

I took both my hands from her, glorying in the agonized sound she made. In a rush, I slid on a condom and slicked lube onto my aching cock before moving into her. Still kneeling, I lifted her hips as I inched forward so her ass was up on my thighs. I went back to teasing her clit while I gripped my shaft and rubbed the head of my cock back and forth between her cheeks.

"Are you ready for me, pet?"

No hesitation at all before she answered, "Yes. Please, sir."

Please, sir.

Fuck. She was *begging* for me to take her ass. I was only too fucking happy to comply.

Lining myself up, I pressed in carefully, minding the angle and being sure not to go too fast. The position wasn't the best. To make it easiest on her, I'd have her straddle me, but I had to have a mind to what got her the hottest, what made her lose any inhibitions and just feel—that meant tying her, taking her. So, I did, but I did it with care.

She was so fucking tight, tighter than anything I'd ever felt. I wanted more than anything to bury myself deep and fuck her until she screamed.

"Alright?" I asked, though it was through clenched teeth. It felt too good. I was going to lose it.

"More," she begged.

With another little thrust, I was in to the hilt. The pleasure was blinding. If I let go of my control, I could come without moving an inch. She was perfection, pure and simple.

Then, she made perfection even more incredible by being greedy. Her hips churned and a moan came from her lips.

That was it, the moment I lost control.

Arching over her, I wrapped my hand around the length of the leash between her neck and hands and yanked on it, bringing her head up. Her eyes came to mine, the blue glazed over with her desire.

"Take me, pet."

She didn't get a chance to respond. With long, smooth thrusts, I fucked her. Each churn of my hips went faster and I was fucking thrilled they were accompanied by her moans getting louder.

Soon, I was taking her fast and deep. It was so fucking good. Her tight ass, her delirious eyes, my collar locked around her neck. She needed to come. I needed to feel her spasms around my cock as I unloaded.

I attacked her clit with quick fingers, working her into a frenzy. I could feel it coming over her and it was going to destroy us both.

"Come," I demanded on a roar, already feeling it at the base of my spine.

Her cry pierced the air, that first clench squeezed my dick, and I was gone.

It felt like I was lost in her forever, wave after wave. When it finally left me, I could barely breathe.

"Oh my god," Ember said on a hoarse whisper.

She was so fucking right.

It took a long time for us to come down, for me to pull free of her cautiously, but Ember was too worn out to care. I dealt with the condom and returned to her curled up, her arms still tied. Releasing her wrists and giving them a rubdown to be sure she was good, I detached the leash and threw it aside.

Ember was already drifting off, unconcerned with removing the collar. Taking in the sight of her in it, I decided it could wait until morning. It didn't bother her and I wanted to fall asleep with the sight of that leather on her neck, claiming her as mine.

Soon, as soon as the fucking thing could arrive, I'd add more leather to her collection to show the world the same.

CHAPTER 29

Jager

THE CALL CAME in the middle of the night. I was awake, going over the intel we'd gathered over the last few days.

The access road that went around back of Kuznetsov's place was more complicated than we could have guessed. The entry to it was nearly five miles away and the route itself was circuitous. Ham had finally found it by being a crazy motherfucker and going on foot, sneaking down the hillside from where we'd been watching, through the trees, and then walking a path through the darkness a few yards away from the road. When he surfaced, I had to pull up the GPS on his phone so we could find him.

Since then, we'd taken shifts watching the house and that access point. If they brought in Yeltz, we had to be ready.

This meant, when my phone vibrated beneath my pillow—a place I'd taken to keeping it so it wouldn't wake Ember—I was on it as soon as I could get the bedroom door shut in my wake.

"Yeah?"

"Daz and Tank got him," Stone reported.

"Where?"

"Taking him out behind the farmhouse. Kuznetsov comes looking, he'll go to the clubhouse. Couple of the guys are grabbing what we'll need."

"Right."

I didn't wait or fuck around. I hung up, got my ass dressed, and got on my bike. I didn't like leaving Ember there alone, but it was something I had to do.

The farmhouse was a big old house on scenic property that had been left to the club by a former president. Brothers lived there at their whim. I'd been there a while before I leased my apartment a few months ago. The property was nice because it was removed, quiet. At least, it was quiet depending on who was living there.

But I wasn't there for quiet.

I rode through the paths on the property, leading to a shed in a far corner from the house. Several of the brothers were standing outside the structure, arms crossed and facing off with Roadrunner.

What the fuck?

I watched Daz move from the line to the shed door and knock. "Hurry it up," he shouted through it.

"What the fuck is this?" I demanded.

The guys looked shifty, eyes moving to one another and avoiding me and Roadrunner. I'd never in my life known a situation where my brothers couldn't look me in the fucking eye like men. Giving up on that shit, I turned to Roadrunner.

"You gonna tell me what this is?"

"Fuckers aren't letting us in," he rumbled.

"What the fuck?"

"Pres's orders," Roadrunner shared, staring daggers at the door to the shed. "Said they need time to get intel from Yeltz before we go at him."

"We don't need any fucking intel on Kuznetsov. Motherfucker's too dumb to hide shit."

Roadrunner didn't voice his agreement, but I knew we were on the same page.

There was nothing to be done until Stone came out and said

otherwise, but that shit did not sit well with me. I moved my eyes to Gauge and Sketch.

"You two fuckin' know. You know exactly what you're doing keeping me out right now," I spat. Each of them had had some motherfucker mess with their woman. Tank wasn't there, or I'd throw it in his face too on Roadrunner's behalf.

"If that motherfucker had info about Barton that could have prevented him nearly taking my woman and Ace taking those bullets, I would have waited to get it," Sketch answered.

"Bullshit," I spat.

His jaw tightened because he knew it was. He could say it now with his woman and daughter safe, all that shit in the past. In the moment, when we brought that asshole back here, nothing would have stopped Sketch from laying into him. Only thing that cut it short was Ash being in trouble.

Things were tense, really fucking tense in a way they shouldn't have been between Disciples until the shed door opened. Stone and Tank came out, not reacting to the sight of us all facing off. They knew exactly what was happening while they were in there.

Neither Roadrunner nor I spoke. Stone, taking that cue, did. "Didn't want to do that to you two. You both gotta know that, but that fucker had info. Shit we can use to take down Kuznetsov before he decides he wants Ember or any of the women here added to his sick as shit auctions." He indicated the shed behind him with his thumb. "We took Yeltz right out from under him. Fuck, we took him off the man's own property. You don't think we need to be prepared for retribution after that, you are dead fucking wrong."

I knew retribution was coming. I even knew exactly what kind of threat that presented to Ember. I also fucking knew we could handle it. Whatever it was, we would handle it. We didn't need Yeltz for that.

"Now, I gotta delay you again," Stone said. I could feel the tension come from Roadrunner as my own body tightened.

Tank decided to step in there. "Ember deserves to know what happened, what that fucker did to her. She deserves her pound of flesh more than either one of you. My Cami got her shot. Ash didn't, but that girl doesn't have the stomach for it. Both of them knew who did them wrong. Ember deserves at least that, but you gotta consider she might need her chance to confront him in order to let this shit go."

Fuck.

I looked to Roadrunner, seeing his face tight with frustration.

He knew, just as I did.

She'd want that. She might even need it.

And we had to give it to her.

"Call her," he said without looking.

As much as I wanted to keep her home in my bed, safe from the emotional turmoil this shit might cause, I knew I had to.

EMBER DROVE up to the farmhouse just over an hour later. She wasn't done up the way I'd learned she usually liked to be. My girl had her style, and she did the work to rock that look daily. I couldn't say that shit wouldn't get frustrating when it took her half a lifetime to get ready and out the door, but I could say I always appreciated the results. But with her in a simple t-shirt and jeans, her hair pulled back into a basic ponytail, I also appreciated that she didn't need to do any of that work.

I appreciated it more right then, because her gorgeous face helped pull my head away from the burning desire to head back out to that shed and do what I wanted. And what I wanted meant there wouldn't be enough of Yeltz left for her to confront.

As she got out of her car and came to where Stone, Roadrunner, Doc, Ace, and I were standing, she looked nervous. I couldn't fault her for that. I'd woken her with a phone call in the middle of the night when I should have been beside her, only to tell her I needed her to get up and come to an address she wasn't familiar with.

"What's going on?" she asked, coming right to me and fitting herself against my side.

Roadrunner told her. I couldn't. It took everything in me to focus on holding her when she got tense learning about Louis/Yeltz. I internalized that, let it feed the fire burning in my gut. I was going to remember it with every nightmare she woke from, the tears she cried into my chest when she realized she was safe. Once she was done here, I was going to let those memories drive every blow, every single thing I would do to Yeltz, and his screams would wash them away.

"We have him," Roadrunner finished. "We wanted to give you the chance if you—"

Ember cut him off, turning in my arms and looking up at me to demand, "Take me to him."

There was fire in her eyes—a fire to match my own.

I did as she asked.

I had just stopped my bike outside the shed when she jumped off, charging right past the brothers still collected outside. Stone, Roadrunner, Doc, and Ace's bikes were all still pulling up behind me as she hit the door. Daz was on it and halted her there.

Not knowing what she might do, I hurried to put down the kickstand and shut my Harley off.

Just as I got to her, she demanded in a firm voice, "Let. Me. In."

Daz looked to me for the go-ahead before opening the door, something Ember saw if her little growl was anything to go by.

Inside the shed, there was a single lightbulb dead center lighting the room. Beneath it, tied to a sturdy wooden chair with knots I'd checked over, was Yeltz. He had a ragged cloth shoved in his mouth to keep the fucker quiet.

Ember froze when she made it in and faced off with him. I stood behind her, giving her space to do or say what she needed to. I had no idea what to expect, which was why she caught me off guard.

Her head turned away from Yeltz, something I thought was an emotional move. I thought she needed a moment to collect herself. That wasn't it at all.

No, Ember was searching, and she found what she was looking for. In one swift move, she reached to the table where the boys had unloaded everything we needed to play with the motherfucker, grabbed a large hunting knife, then swung around and buried it in his thigh.

Brothers cursed while I grabbed onto her. Yeltz screamed behind his gag.

"You motherfucker!" Ember shrieked. "What? You think the fact that I dumped you before you got to fuck me means you can pull some fucked up shit like this? You're fucking disgusting!"

Yeltz's eyes got hard and he tried to spit venom back at her to no avail.

"Shut your fucking mouth!" she ordered. "You tried to destroy my whole life! Now you get to sit there while my family destroys *you!*"

Blood was still streaming from the goddamn knife sticking

out of the guy's leg. A knife my woman had been driven to put there. Her words revealed she knew exactly what we had in store for Yeltz, but that didn't mean she needed to see any more gore than she'd already caused.

I wrapped both my arms around her. "You're done," I told her.

She didn't fight. Whatever had possessed her to that level of violence—while understandable—had run its course. It was time to get her out of there before the whole episode turned traumatic. She let me lead her out of the shed, but that was as far as we got. Her feet stopped and her eyes widened as she stared off in the distance.

"Oh my god," she whispered. "I just...I...I stabbed him."

"Don't think about it."

She blinked a few times and gave me her eyes. "But, I—"

"Baby, don't go there. You're fine even though he almost made you not that way. He deserved that shit, and he deserves worse."

"And you're going to give him worse," she stated in a blank way that had me questioning how she felt about it.

"Ember," I started, but she spoke.

"You have to." Her eyes went to the shed where all the brothers had disappeared inside. "All of you."

"Yeah. We do. You belong to this club, you don't hurt without retribution."

"He deserved that."

"He did."

She nodded.

The door to the shed opened, making me look over. Sketch stepped out, his phone in hand.

"Ash is coming to get you," he said, focusing on Ember.

"I'm okay. She has Emmy," Ember protested.

"Jasmine got to town today," he replied. "She'll be good there if Emmy wakes up before you two get back."

"Okay," Ember agreed.

I gave Sketch a chin lift, a silent thank you for doing that. Knowing my girl was being taken care of meant I could focus where I needed to.

When he was gone again, I gave Ember my attention, making sure she was okay to go when Ash got there. Her head was still turned away, but I used a finger to tilt it my way. Her eyes had been distant, but she focused on me.

"Make him pay," she said.

That was it, just those three words told me what I needed to know.

I kissed her for being so fucking strong, for giving me permission to dismantle that motherfucker who hurt her. She kissed me back, letting me taste her deep. I wanted that sweetness on my tongue while I made Yeltz's blood flow. When it was there in a way I hoped would last, I pulled back.

"I fucking will," I promised.

"Good," was her response.

Good.

CHAPTER 30
Ember

I WALKED through the gym on somewhat unsteady legs. There were guys scattered around, working out or training. Some gave me chin lifts. Some didn't look my way at all, such was their focus. Some let their gazes linger. These were, I was not surprised to see, only men I hadn't met before. They didn't know who I was, and thereby, who I was with. They'd learn. Jager always made sure they learned.

I'd started tagging along with Jager to work since that night with Daniel.

Wait, no. His name wasn't Daniel. It was Anthony Yeltz.

Bastard.

I had no idea what exactly happened to him after I left that shed while the knife I'd put in his leg was still there. I knew, of course, whatever had followed for him had been excruciating. And Jager's words when he'd returned to me that night had been "taken care of".

I tried not to do too much soul searching about it. The fact of the matter was the asshole had me kidnapped. He tried to give me to those people who would have auctioned me off and god knows who would have bought me for things I didn't even want to imagine.

I'd stabbed him—something I tried not to remember the actual sensation of, but I didn't regret. My man, my dad, and the men I'd come to consider family did far worse. Maybe I wasn't a good person, but that reality didn't bother me.

He deserved it all.

And I deserved what I was getting, which, at that moment, was a whole lot of good in the form of watching my man in the ring, working with a younger boxer.

This was one of the many boons of coming to work with Jager. Not only was it a change of scenery, I got to watch Jager work out, I got back into a gym, which I'd missed, and I'd gotten back into the rhythm of working out, often doing it with Jager. So, watching him work out came both while I did it beside him and in moments like right then when I was just a spectator. Both of these were highlights of my days. Jager, I learned, never wore a shirt when he was working out.

Seeing him move, his muscles flexing and glinting with sweat, was almost too much. I couldn't let myself focus on him when we were working out together. When I did, I had to stop what I was doing because it took all my focus not to drool.

This also led to one of my other favorite parts of going to work with him: the one-way mirror in his office window and the lock on the door.

We'd taken advantage of those office amenities more than once and each time was amazing. Though, I preferred when we took advantage of the variety of amenities Jager had at his place.

Since the night he gave it to me, playtime with Jager meant him collaring me. I loved it. Not only the collar and what I knew it meant, but the affectionate way he always put it on me. What followed was the same powerful, hard man I always had and loved, but those few moments only made what we shared better.

I touched where the collar would sit around my throat, remembering how he'd taken his time to kiss every part of the skin it covered the night before when he'd been ready to put it on me, and the similar treatment I'd gotten when he took it off that morning. Whenever Jager took me before bed, he liked me to keep it on while we slept. He always secured it tight enough that it was on, but nowhere near it being uncomfortable, so I was happy to give him that.

Although I always hated to, I'd taken the collar off and laid it on Jager's nightstand where it always stayed unless it was on me. At some level, I wanted to wear it all the time. I wanted to have that sign that I was Jager's and he was mine to be ever present. But a collar wasn't an engagement ring or even a property cut. People wouldn't understand. They'd bastardize it. So it stayed on the nightstand.

Though, Jager didn't need to put it around my neck to get me in the mood, as was evident by the activities we'd done not twenty minutes ago upstairs.

Like I said, I greatly enjoyed his office.

After I used the always-empty ladies' locker room to freshen up, I intended to go back up to it. I'd started taking over some of the administrative stuff for Jager while we were there. I liked it. If the monotony of the desk work got to me, there was a whole gym full of life just outside the door. I'd been thinking about talking to Jager about making my work there more permanent. In preparation for that, I was doing my best to show him how useful I could be.

I was going to head back up and get some more work done, including thinking up some ideas about getting female membership up—a thought I had while I'd been in that locker room by myself. But first, I was going to give myself a little time to enjoy the show Jager was unwittingly putting on for me.

LATER THAT EVENING, after Jager handed over running the gym to Leo—one of the instructors he employed—we were at the clubhouse. Jager needed to do something on the crazy computer set up he had in his room there and we'd decided to hang around for a while with the brothers.

Dad was around and he'd made chili for the guys and me. For the most part, Dad—like I was learning was true for most of the Disciples—was hopeless in a kitchen. The one thing he could make that didn't involve a grill or smoker was his chili. Jager and I had joined him, Stone, Ham, and Daz in kicking back with a bowl while we watched a UFC fight on pay-per-view.

"Did you ever think about going pro?" I asked Jager.

He took his attention from the stat breakdown for the next fighters up to answer, "Thought about it when I was a kid. Boxing, at least. But I'd been focused more on college."

That made sense. Something I'd learned about Jager while getting to spend time with him when he wasn't fucking my brains out was he was kind of a nerd. I say that with all the affection in the world, but it was true. He read a lot, and I'd noted this was all sorts of books. History, science, philosophy, technology, even classic literature had all made an appearance and that was just in the last few days. I hadn't seen him with the same book twice. I wasn't sure whether that was how fast he was going through them or he was reading multiple things at once.

"What were you going to study?"

He shook his head, but didn't blow me off like he might have once. "I've got three degrees."

"What?"

He chuckled. "Computer Science, Electrical Engineering, and Mathematics."

"I thought..."

Well, he knew what I thought.

"Went off the rails after it happened, but I still went to school. That was the only fucking thing that still made sense to me."

"Where'd you go?" I asked.

"Stanford."

"Are you a genius?"

He laughed all out at that and I noticed heads swing our way. "Never been tested, pet."

"I'm going to take that as a yes."

He didn't confirm or deny that, just settled back in to watch the fight, tucking me into his side as he did.

After a bit, I ventured into the kitchen to store the excess food and grab Jager and I fresh drinks. I was closing the fridge when I noticed Daz there.

"You might be a miracle worker, babe," he said.

I tilted my head, giving him a bemused smile. "I'm sorry?"

He leaned against the counter, nodding to the side to indicate the lounge. "Known the brother in there for a long time. If I tried, I could probably count on both hands the number of times I've actually seen the motherfucker smile when it wasn't a sick fuckin' one he was offering to some poor dick he was about to beat the shit out of. Yet, I just saw him laugh. Twice."

That was heavy. It was also beautiful. I loved that I was able to give that to him.

Still, I found what came out of my mouth next couldn't be

helped. "I thought you were the champion of not having more balls and chains around here."

He gave me that cheeky grin he was always sporting. "Maybe the right ball and chain ain't so bad."

He came over, grabbed one of the beers from my hand with a wink, and took off with it.

"Ass," I called after him.

But, as I went to grab another bottle, I couldn't help but think for the second time there was a lot more to Daz than met the eye.

CHAPTER 31
Ember

I WOKE in Jager's bed alone.

Alone was something I was getting accustomed to over the last few weeks.

Since the day Hunter was born, Jager had been busy. In fact, all of the guys seemed to be busy—excluding Slick, who was also busy, but that was at home with his wife, daughter, and new baby boy, so I hadn't seen him to tell how he seemed. The brothers were frequently off doing who-knew-what, who-knew-where, even logging less hours at the garage.

At first, this must have been doing whatever they did to get their hands on Yeltz.

In the aftermath of that, with him gone, I expected the seemingly constant activity for the club would lessen. I knew occasional disappearances and the once-in-a-while late night call out would be par for the course. Still, I'd been around for months and this level of activity wasn't always the way of the Disciples. This difference was not explained to me. It also had not been explained to Cami or Ash. Something was going on with the club that went beyond hunting down Yeltz. And whatever it was was important.

"Doesn't not knowing what's going on bother you?" I'd asked the women one day while we held down the fort at the understaffed garage in Cami's office. Jager was not overly fond of me being alone in the days after they found Yeltz. He explained

this as being concerned that what happened might start to fuck with my head. I thought this was true, I also thought there was more to it he wasn't sharing.

Ash shrugged, but Cami had answered, *"You haven't been around that long. For one thing, we grew up with this. Roadrunner might have kept things from you and even admitted to doing so if you asked, but it's different when you're around and can actually see something is up and no one will tell you what. But for another, there are a lot of times when you will get to know. Being an old lady is a tricky role sometimes. Our men open up to us. Sometimes, they'll tell us club business that maybe not all the brothers would want us being privy to. Then, it's our job to keep that knowledge to ourselves. Other times, we won't get to know. They have their reasons—privacy of their brothers, protecting us, whatever—and I don't always agree with them, but it boils down to the fact that when you love a Disciple, you have to take him as he comes."*

There was a lot there, and not all of it was great. Though I knew she was right.

Regardless of my misgivings, I had chosen Jager. I hadn't done that blind. I'd always known the club at some level through Dad. In the months I had been around, I had gotten to know it far better. I'd made my choice having that knowledge, so I had to accept that.

I also knew she was right about the fact that they would share when they wanted to or felt they could. Jager and Dad could have made a different choice when they'd gotten Yeltz. I knew it. They might even have intended to, seeing as Jager had left that night without me. But when it came down to it, they made the decision to let me know what they'd learned and gave me the opportunity for closure.

That conversation was something I reminded myself of frequently when Jager would state, without explanation, he was "heading out" or "had business to see to" before doing just that.

Accepting that meant I went about getting ready despite having no clue what I'd do with my day. The pattern of feeling that way was getting old. I sent out a few applications for jobs, but hadn't heard anything back yet. None of them interested me much, but I was eating through my savings even without having rent to pay. I also just needed to get out of the house. I was fine on days I'd help out Jager, Dad, or Cami, and even when I'd spend time with Deni, Ace, or Ash. The second I was stuck sitting around the house, I got restless.

My plan had been to go into the gym with Jager since I'd been in the middle of a few things when we'd left the night before. I tried calling him to see if he'd be home soon, but got nothing. I wasn't surprised, but it also meant I was at a loss for what to do. I sent along a text asking him to let me know what his plans were when he could.

That done, I got to sorting out other plans for my day.

I WAS at Ash and Sketch's house, sitting sideways on the couch. Emmy was standing on the cushion behind me. She'd come to me with a brush saying she wanted to brush my hair. Although Ash had given me wide eyes that told me this was definitely a skill she hadn't mastered yet, I said yes. She was so excited, I figured whatever rat's nest she might land me with would be worth it. I'd sort it out eventually.

Jasmine, who I'd met the day after my confrontation with

Yeltz, was still staying with them. She'd been essentially Ash's only friend before she returned to Hoffman, as well as Emmy's regular babysitter. Their obvious love for, and Sketch's gratitude for her taking care of his girls when he couldn't, meant she was part of the family.

She was a petite, African-American woman with the kind of amazing bone structure that meant her face should be plastered across glossy magazine pages. She was also sassy, but sweet, and she was incredible with Emmy because the love our resident princess had for her was definitely mutual.

"And then," Emmy continued the story she was telling us, "Uncle Daz said Twix is better dan Skittles!"

Clearly, to her four-year-old self, this was the height of blasphemy. Jasmine and I gasped accordingly.

"He's so silly," she stated, still yanking away at my hair.

Ash had left the room a few minutes ago, answering a call from Sketch. She walked back in, looking nervous. Jasmine noticed it at the same time I did, and she saw Ash's eyes were on me.

She jumped right to, saying to Emmy, "You want to watch a movie, Ems?"

My hair fluttered down and I felt the couch jostle as Emmy jumped and cried, "Yes!"

"Alright, come help me pick," Jasmine said, leading Emmy to the entertainment center, where all Emmy's DVDs were stored. I got up, following Ash back out of the room.

"What's going on?"

She shook her head. "I don't know. He wouldn't tell me. He just said Ace is coming here for you. But he also said he wants me to be sure the alarm is set when you leave and the three of us aren't supposed to go anywhere until he gets back."

Shit.

That was not good. That was so, so not good, and Ash's voice had a bit of a shake to it that told me Sketch hadn't said those things lightly. It had been a warning, a serious one, and she was taking it that way.

I thought about the text I sent Jager hours and hours ago that had gone unanswered.

Ace was coming for me. Not Jager.

Why not Jager?

"Ash," I started, all of my anxiety bleeding into just her name.

She stepped into me and gave me a hug. She knew where my mind had gone. Hers had already been there on that call.

"Just stay calm," she murmured. "I know it's hard, but we don't know anything. Something's going down, yes. But it might be that they need Jager more. He's got a lot of skills that are important to the club. He might be the one sending Ace, wanting to be sure you're safe."

Right. Jager would do that. If there was something wrong, he'd want to be sure. So would Dad. But wouldn't I be safe with Ash? And if I wasn't, wouldn't Sketch want her elsewhere too?

"Go to my master bath," Ash instructed, her tone even but gentle. "There's another brush in there. You can fix your hair before he gets here."

I thought fixing my hair was unimportant, but I followed her instruction. I had no idea what was going on. Maybe I needed to have it together in more ways than one.

It took some doing to repair my hair from the mess Emmy had left, but I managed. I also managed to keep my mind focused on that task rather than spiraling into fits of panic over whatever was going on. When I was back downstairs, I could hear Emmy singing along to *Under the Sea* brokenly, since she didn't know all the words.

Ace was there. Ash must have seen or heard him pull up and let him in before he could knock. He watched me descend, his face controlled, but tight with the effort of keeping it that way.

"Tell me," I demanded.

"We need to go," Ace evaded.

His lack of answer scared me far more.

"Ace, please, tell me." I didn't attempt to keep the panic from my voice. I was panicking and he needed to know. He needed to know exactly how scared I already was. Whatever he was keeping from me, the lack of knowledge wasn't keeping me calm.

He came close and spoke low, probably so Emmy wouldn't hear. "I know you're freaking, but I need you to keep it together. Right now, you might be the best shot we've got at fixing this."

No.

No, no, no.

That was not good.

"You need to tell me," I begged.

He sighed, not with impatience, but in a way I knew he hated having to be the one to say whatever came next.

"I tell you, you gotta promise me you get on my bike so we can sort this. You might want to break, but you can't. You have to keep it together until we get to the clubhouse and see if you can help. I'll tell you everything when we get there. Yeah?"

I didn't want to agree to those terms. I knew, absolutely, when I heard what he had to say, I wasn't going to want to stay calm, but he said I could help. For Jager, for Dad, for the whole club or whoever was involved in whatever was happening, I would do what I had to.

"I promise."

As if it all happened in slow motion, I watched Ace's control over his face dissolve until the anguish and fury was clear. That shot through me even before he spoke and drove that feeling home.

"They took Jager."

CHAPTER 32

Jager

"WHERE IS YELTZ?" the fucker with the brass knuckles demanded.

I hadn't answered him. Not when he woke me, not when he'd landed the first blow, or the second—I kept my mouth shut.

I didn't make a fucking sound until Kuznetsov dragged his ass down there and stood in the open doorway to the cell they had me in. Only when he was there and I could smile into his smug fucking face while I spoke did I say it.

"He's fucking dead."

That wiped his satisfied expression away in a flash. With a nod of his head, he gave the order and those brass knuckles came flying at me again. I didn't care. It fucking hurt, but it was well worth it.

After the blow, Kuznetsov gave a hand flick that made his men clear out. A fucking hand gesture, like they were deaf dogs or some shit. They locked me in as they left.

Before they were out of earshot, I heard the motherfucker ask, "His bike?"

"We have it," one of his lackeys answered.

"Destroy it."

That was for my benefit. I fucking knew it, but it didn't stop me from fighting the chains they had me dangling from. Any asshole who damaged my fucking bike was getting skinned alive.

I stopped myself from struggling when a door slammed in the

distance. They were gone, and they were obviously just fucking bright enough to make sure the shit they bound me with would actually hold.

I'd been watching Kuznetsov's place. We hadn't stopped after bagging Yeltz even though it was risky. The dick knew we took his prisoner and he no doubt knew we'd done it on his property. He was out for blood. Still, I wanted the man taken down, and I wanted that for my woman.

Fuck, thinking about Ember stung more than anything the prick with the hardware had done.

I knew, without a fucking doubt, the cell I was in was the same as the one she'd been kept in. There had to be more than one down here. She'd been on that dirt floor, staring at bars just like those, having no fucking clue why she was there.

Fuck whoever touched my bike. If I ever got the chance, I was going to skin Kuznetsov alive.

She was probably freaked the fuck out. I didn't want her feeling that shit.

I really didn't want her living through whatever might come my way.

There was not a doubt in my fucking mind that I might not walk out of that building. That didn't scare me. It pissed me off, made me want to rage at the universe for deciding this might be the time when I wouldn't have given a fuck before Ember. It made me want to kick my own ass for not drinking in every fucking moment I'd had since I met her.

Mostly, it made me fucking sick to think of Ember without me. She'd hurt, and that killed. I didn't want that pain for her. I never wanted her to feel that.

I shouldn't have let them get the drop on me. It was fucking stupid.

I'd seen the guards leaving their normal positions and knew what that meant. Something was coming in. I'd gone down near the access route to get a better look. If they were bringing in a girl and I could get pictures, that'd be enough to pop the motherfucker. All we needed was to get him sent away and he'd be dealt with.

There were powers that be—important, Russian powers—that didn't appreciate a little shit like Kuznetsov even thinking he was big shit, let alone acting on that thought. They operated on a code of respect he'd violated. They wanted him gone, but didn't worry over the matter much. But if we could get him locked up, they would sort it out. Kuznetsov was a nobody, but he'd once been a part of something larger. He might have names, and they wouldn't risk that. And they knew, an honorless man like that, he would flip if offered the opportunity.

It had been a trap. I should have been smart and guessed they might try it, but my head was clouded by the shit they'd done to Ember.

I'd have probably been able to take the fuckers that ambushed me too, if it weren't for Kuznetsov's knack of drugging people instead of having a fair fucking fight he knew he couldn't win. The asshole who got me hadn't even been close. He'd shot me from a distance like he was goddamn animal control.

Never in my life had I made such a stupid move.

I just hoped my brothers could figure out a way to fix it.

Not for me.

But for my Ember.

CHAPTER 33
Ember

PASHA KUZNETSOV.

That was the name they gave me.

He was the man behind it all. Yeltz sold me to him. He had planned to sell me to god knows who.

And he was the one who had Jager.

Stone explained this. Dad was at my side, holding my hand. Ace was standing by the door to Stone's office. All three men were emanating serious levels of fury, but were taming it for my sake.

They didn't have to. This fucking Kuznetsov had Jager.

I was more furious than anyone.

"What do you think I can do?" I demanded.

They'd spent a long time on this story. I got it. But nowhere in it had it sounded like there was a reason we were sitting around in an office having this discussion. Jager was out there. There was no telling what they were doing to him. They needed to be working to get him free.

"What we're discussing here isn't strictly legal," Stone forewarned.

I shifted forward on my seat, making sure he could see my expression well.

"I don't care about legal. I care about saving him."

Stone gave me a nod before producing a folder and handing it to me. Opening it, I saw it contained pictures of a house. It was huge and kind of gaudy, like the kind of place some celebrity who was way too into their own fame would get.

"I don't..." I trailed off before I could say I didn't understand what I was looking at.

The last picture had my attention. It was the back of the house. I couldn't tell right away why the picture stood out. It was taken during the day. There were windows, a lot of them, including a bank of glass French doors on the first floor. None of the windows had blinds drawn, though the daylight made it difficult to see inside. There were two men in the photo, their backs to the exterior of the house. Guards.

There should be more. The thought came to me, but I couldn't figure out why.

None of the men spoke, but I was only aware of their silence in a vague way. My eyes were moving over the photo, top to bottom, side to side. There was something about it. I knew it. It was like a puzzle, those ones you do as a kid where one thing has been changed between pictures. Something on the glossy paper in my hand was important.

The door.

There was another door aside from the glass ones. It was painted to match the exterior walls, meant to be nondescript. It was off to the left, easily missed when looking at the photo.

Easily missed unless you'd been through it.

The memory flooded in, having been trapped somewhere in my mind until I saw that door.

I WAS AWAKE, but only just.

I felt sick. Maybe hungover?

I didn't remember drinking, but maybe that was how much I had.

My body was numb. Otherwise, I wasn't awake enough to feel it.

I concentrated on opening my eyes and they cracked open.

It was dark, but there was some kind of light behind me a bit, casting a glow at my back and onto...what?

What was I looking at?

There was a surface, like a wall, just in front of my face.

That shouldn't be there, *I thought.*

My bed was in the middle of the room. There were no walls that close.

My mind was foggy, but I forced myself to focus. That was when it registered. There was sound—a low, even sound. And we were moving.

A car.

I was in a car, and that wall in front of me was leather. I was lying in the backseat.

But why?

I tried to sort through memories. I'd been at the gym, teaching my kids. Janice had been struggling with her form, but it had only been because she felt inferior to the boys. There was nothing wrong except what she had in her own head. But I'd sorted her out.

After that, I'd gone home. I hadn't had a shift at the bar. It was my night off, which meant junk food and catching up on the DVR.

That was all. I'd gone to bed.

And then...

The car turned and the smooth ride ceased. Instead, it seemed we were on jagged ground. More turns, one sharp and jostling. Something about the change had the anxiety I'd been feeling since I woke rising to the point it choked me.

What was going on?

My body was forced against the back of the seat as the driver hit the brakes. We were stopped, and for the first time since I realized I was in a car, I wished we were still moving. It didn't matter that every second the car was moving meant I was probably going farther and farther from home. I just knew stopping meant nothing good for me.

The door by my head opened before I heard anything from the front of the vehicle. I shut my eyes, not wanting them to know I was awake. They yanked me from the car, hoisting me up without care.

I chanced a peak through the jostling. There were windows. A lot of them. All of them brimming with light from the rooms inside. They didn't look like the uniform pattern of an office building. I snapped my eyes shut again before anyone might notice.

"Get her inside," I heard someone say. It was a male voice, gruff, and there was a hint of an accent I hadn't heard long enough to place.

I was shifted until my head was hanging down. I could feel the pressure at my gut that made me realize I was over someone's shoulder. I peeked again, my eyes landing on legs. I was careful not to move, but I looked around as much as I could. There was grass below us and I could make out the corner of a tire. The man who had me was facing the car he pulled me from.

He turned then, and I frantically took in what I could. There were several men around. I was able to look up a bit and saw them all dressed in dark colors, most of them holding large guns.

What the hell was this place?

I also got a glance, just briefly as my captor turned, at a door. It wasn't an ornate entryway. It was more like a service door. There wasn't even much of a distinct jamb around it. I couldn't make out colors in the mix of darkness and yellowed light, but I could tell the door was painted to match the siding around it.

It was meant to blend in.

That door was supposed to go unnoticed. As my captor stopped turning and I lost sight of it, I realized that was where he was headed.

I wanted to fight, to try to get away, but even as I tried, my body wouldn't move. I was trapped in stillness, being taken somewhere I knew without a doubt I did not want to go.

"Did you dose her again?" a voice asked.

"Net."

"Hang on."

My captor stopped and I held my eyes closed. I didn't know what happened, but not long after he started moving again, despite my terror, I faded out.

"THEY TOOK ME IN THERE," I whispered my realization, my eyes still glued to the image of that door.

"Fuck," Dad spat harshly.

"Ember," Stone called.

Robotically, I lifted my head to him.

"You're sure?" he asked. He was gentle, but there was murder in his eyes.

I put the stack of pictures on his desk, the one that had sparked the memory still on top. With a hand I saw was shaking, but too numb to feel, I pointed to that fucking door.

"I didn't remember it before. I woke up in the car. I couldn't move, but I was able to open my eyes. When they took me from the car, I saw that door," I explained. "That's where they took me."

Stone's eyes moved up and behind me, landing on Ace. "Make the call," he ordered.

Ace didn't respond, but I heard the door open and shut.

"What's going on?" I got out. "How do you have pictures of that place?"

"That property is Kuznetsov's," Stone explained. "We've been watching it. We managed to find a hidden access road that goes to the back of the house."

The turns and uneven ground, I put together.

"That's where Jager was when he went MIA," Stone went on.

Wait. They knew where he was?

"You know where he is?" I demanded.

"Ember," Dad tried to calm me.

"Why haven't you gone in and gotten him out?"

My head flew between the two of them, wanting an answer.

"We can't," Dad said.

"Why the fuck not?"

"We'd never make it in," Stone answered. "Kuznetsov usually has the place guarded, but he's got every fucking one of his men on that house now that he took Jager. We don't have the men or firepower to get in there."

My heart sank, the anger bleeding out. Of course. If they could storm in and get him out, they would have.

"I'm sorry," I choked out. My emotions were all over the place. In my mind, all I could see was Jager in a cell like the one they'd kept me in. I imagined men in dark clothes beating him, wounding him.

Killing him.

The sob broke out before I could get myself together.

I couldn't lose him.

Dad reached over, pulling me against his solid chest. I fought to hold it together even though I wanted to shatter right there.

"We can't help him, Ber-bear," he said low to me, driving that knife deeper. But, then, he continued, "But you can."

I lifted my watery gaze to him. "What?"

"There's a team of feds investigating him," Stone answered. "They've been on him for months, trying to catch a break. If they were able to follow the same paper trail as Jager and connect that house to Kuznetsov, then your testimony that they took you, held you there, and what you can tell them about the other women in that cell, is enough for them to get a warrant to go in."

"You can't tell them we showed you those pictures," Dad put in. "That shit's not technically legal. You gotta describe what you know. Then, they might show you pictures of their own to verify. But you can't mention this."

What they weren't saying, but I understood, was I was breaking the law by omitting that from my statement. I might even have to lie if asked about how I'd remembered.

The image of Jager in that cell filled my head again, tearing through my heart.

I could do it. I could keep that secret. I could lie under oath if I had to.

Anything for Jager.

Anything to save him.

CHAPTER 34

Ace

EMBER WAS HOLDING IT TOGETHER. At times, it seemed like by a wing and a fucking prayer, but she was strong. Stronger than anyone could be expected to be in the circumstances.

It only took two phone calls to get word to the right people. Not ten minutes later, Special Agent Roth, who was all over a witness who could get him access to Kuznetsov's place, called. I set it up.

Now, we were waiting at Roadrunner's house for the man to get there, moving Ember there to understate the club's involvement in the situation.

Ember was pacing. Roscoe had been following her at first, but the dog had tired of it and collapsed at the midway point of her path to watch as she went back and forth across the room.

"Where is he?" she demanded.

"He's coming," I answered. It wasn't the first time she'd asked.

She was impatient. I knew that feeling. It was simmering beneath my surface, amping up as I watched the distress play out in her. She wasn't wrong to be upset. Every fucking second Roth took to get there was one Kuznetsov could use to off Jager. We were all feeling it.

It took everything in me to keep my ass planted and mind focused on the bigger goal rather than taking off and charging into that house guns blazing. That shit wouldn't work. We went in like that, not one of us would walk out—Jager included.

This play—the legal play—was the only one we had.

And Ham and Daz had eyes on the place, reporting the prize was going to be even fucking sweeter if we pulled it off. Kuznetsov wasn't expecting our move. He was preparing for an ambush, and he was drawing in every soldier he had to prepare for it.

When Roth had what he needed to raid the place, he was going to bag every man on his list without having to hunt those fuckers down.

"He's taking too long," Ember pushed, the nerves and frustration at constant war.

Unable to take it, I got to my feet and strode right into her path.

"Babe, you're holding it together like a fucking champ," I told her. "I know you want to lose it, I do too. But right now, you gotta keep it locked down. For Jager. This dude gets here to take your statement, it can't be about Jager for him. It's got to be about you. You were kidnapped. You remembered this detail. You made the decision to step forward and report what happened. It ain't about the club. It ain't about your man. Right?"

She nodded, but I could see her biting the inside of her cheek.

"The second he's out that door again, you wanna fall apart, I'll be right here. But until then, you have to keep fighting through this. Jager'll be fighting. You fucking know that. No matter what, he's fighting to get his ass back here to you. You have to give him the same by staying cool."

"Right," she whispered back.

Right.

I led her to the couch and got her to sit, though she did it with her knee bouncing and hands fidgeting the whole time.

Roadrunner was by the door, eyes keeping watch outside. He had the task since it was his house and he knew the neighborhood. He'd spot a car that wasn't supposed to be there before anyone else clocked it. We all waited in silence as agonizing minute after minute ticked by.

I watched Roadrunner tense before the headlights could be seen on the drive. They were there. The nervous energy coming from Ember felt like the air itself was vibrating. I grabbed her hand and held on.

Roadrunner let Roth, two other agents, and an attorney from the DA's office in. Roth made the introductions and established right away he'd be the one handling the situation. Then, he took a chair Roadrunner brought into the room for him and sat across from Ember. I went to move away, but she clutched onto me.

After the spiel about falsifying statements, he got right to it. "Ember, tell me what happened."

And she did. She told the story straight from the beginning. The kidnapping, the cell, telling Kuznetsov's men about the club, and waking up at the clubhouse. She stuck to her own experiences, not filling in the blanks that we had paid Kuznetsov's men for her release. In fact, she carefully stayed away from the asshole's name entirely.

When she reached the end of the story without mentioning the house, Roth prompted, "Is there anything else you remember?"

"Yes," Ember answered. "I only recently remembered waking once while they were transporting me. I woke in the car and saw part of the outside of the building they took me into. It was around the back of a large house. There was a door there they took me through. It was painted like the rest of the house, blended in."

Roth already knew this and was prepared because I'd given him that. So, he turned to the attorney who handed him a folder.

"Do you mind looking at a few pictures to see if you recognize any of them?" he asked.

She shook her head and he began showing her images one by one.

Most of them were just random houses. Maybe they were involved in other investigations, but they were only meant to assure she could identify the right place. Ember took her time, even though she didn't need it. She studied each one, rejecting them after full consideration. The fourth image was Kuznetsov's. Ember still took her time, giving not one thing away before she spoke.

"That's it." She leaned in to point at the door. "That was where they took me in."

"You're sure?" Roth pushed.

She looked him right in the eye. "I'm certain."

Roth focused on the attorney and nodded. The man immediately stepped outside, already on his phone.

They had what they needed for a warrant.

EMBER WAS BREAKING.

She'd gone back to pacing after Roth and his men cleared out. He'd told us they'd had a judge on standby to issue the search warrant after I called and his team was ready to move on Kuznetsov's place the moment they could.

Still, it had been over an hour, and no word.

The brothers had all left their posts around Kuznetsov's place as the feds moved in, converging at Roadrunner's and waiting for word. Gauge and Sketch had gotten their women and brought them over, but the posse did nothing to calm Ember.

None of us could help. We were all feeling it too.

At some point in her pacing, the tears had started. She wasn't sobbing. She wasn't screaming. She wasn't giving sound to her pain even if she had every right to. Her tears were silent, rolling down her face like she wasn't even aware of them as she made her path back and forth. The whole time, she had her right hand resting against her neck.

Some of the brothers had tried to talk to her, but they hadn't even gotten a word in response. Cami rushed right to her when she showed and tried to comfort her. It had stopped Ember from pacing for a moment, but did little else. Ash had just left her to it, as I had been.

We could try to distract her, try to assure her everything would be fine, but the fact was that girl was not coming out of her head until her man was standing in front of her.

As for what would happen if that never came to pass, I wasn't even going there in the hypothetical.

My phone ringing broke the tense silence. Every set of eyes came to me, except Ember's. One footstep halted for half a second, but she resumed her pacing. That was when I truly understood. If she stopped, she'd fall apart. Focusing on the next step was the only thing keeping her in one piece.

I answered on the second ring, not wasting even a fucking second to check who it was.

"Yeah?"

"Pasha Kuznetsov has been arrested," Roth announced in my ear. "Four captives were found in the house. I believe one of them might mean something to you."

He knew Jager was a Disciple. He'd been keeping tabs on

Kuznetsov, which meant he noticed us circling. There was no telling what else he knew. At very least, he had to guess we'd been planning our own retribution and that was why Ember hadn't made a statement sooner. He'd obviously figured out why we'd given up on that.

"Status?"

"On the way to the hospital," Roth replied. "Needs to get checked out, but he'll be fine."

"Right." I went to hang up, but he stopped me.

"She'll have to testify at his trial," he stated.

"We both know he won't make it."

And we did. Pasha Kuznetsov was a dead man once he was locked up. It didn't matter what kind of protection they tried to offer. There were people who could be bought everywhere.

"Tell me you aren't threatening him to a federal agent."

"Not a moron," I assured him. "Just stating facts. It won't come from the Disciples, but it'll happen."

He sighed before he clicked off, and he did it because he knew I was right.

I pocketed my phone, everyone still watching me. They needed answers, but I had to be sure Ember was with me. Once again, I inserted myself in her path.

She looked up at me with red-rimmed eyes begging me not to give her news she didn't want to hear.

"He's okay," I stated.

Her knees gave out right there.

I didn't fuck around, just knelt down and picked her up with arms at her back and beneath her knees.

"They're taking him to the hospital now," I announced to the room. "Someone sort out which one is closest, text me the information. We're leaving now."

Roadrunner was already on the move, keys in hand for his

244

truck. He opened the door as I carried Ember out. I got her in the passenger seat with his help as he handed off the keys.

"I'm right behind you," he said, already going for his bike.

I got us on the road. We were just out of Hoffman when Ember spoke up.

"I need you to talk," she requested in a strained voice.

I knew what she meant. She didn't have her pacing to keep her together now and neither of us knew what sort of shape Jager was going to be in when we got there.

I gave her the only thing I had.

"How about I tell you a secret?"

IT TOOK two hours to make the nearly three-hour drive.

It felt like a fucking lifetime.

Ember walked into the emergency room at my side, half her weight leaned into me. One of the agents who had been at the house, Matthews, was there to meet us.

We didn't fuck around with saying a thing to the desk staff. We went right to him.

"I'll take you back," he stated before we had to ask.

With a couple flashes of his badge, he did just that.

It wasn't far before we hit the bay of curtain-divided beds. At the end of the line, angled so he was facing us and saw as we entered, was a big, tattooed motherfucker I was real fucking happy to see.

Jager was sitting up on the bed while a doctor and nurses looked him over, but he didn't give a shit. He stood, ripping what looked to be an IV from his arm and pushed through them. He marched his way right toward us as Ember's weight increased against me and her tears became audible sobs.

The brother was bruised, bleeding, and he sure as fuck wasn't seeing out of one eye, but that didn't matter to either of them. He charged right for his woman and grabbed her from my hold. She collapsed against him, crying into his bare chest.

"I love you," she sobbed there.

"Fuck, I love you too, pet," he answered.

CHAPTER 35
Jager

EMBER DIDN'T LEAVE my side. This was in part because she didn't want to, but it was mostly because I wouldn't fucking let her. I made the doctor and nurses do their shit with Ember in my lap, shifting her from one side to another as needed.

The third time I tried to switch where she was seated, she offered, "I can stand just over there out of the way. I won't leave."

I didn't answer that shit.

I'd lived for hours thinking there was a good chance I was going to die in that dirty cell. I wouldn't get to have her that close again. I'd never get to have the words she gave me when I first got her back in my arms.

"I love you."

Even hearing it come through her fucking tears was beautiful.

So, no. The damn hospital staff could work around her. I didn't give a shit. And I went right on not giving a shit until I signed the papers a few hours later stating I was checking myself out of the hospital against medical advice.

"Sir, your body needs rest and time to heal. You were fortunate there was not any severe damage to your internal organs, but there is still a great deal of bruising as well as four cracked ribs," the doctor kept at his shit even as I handed the signed form back to him.

"Not the first time I've had broken ribs, doc," I replied. "And I know there ain't shit you can do to fix them, so I'm not staying."

He backed off, but Ember wasn't ready to.

"Are you sure? Maybe we should stay just tonight," she suggested.

"Babe," I said low, just to her, "I don't like hospitals."

Her eyes widened and I knew she got me. I'd sat by Jamie's side, watching my little sister die in a place like that. No fucking way I was going to get any rest there.

"Okay," she capitulated.

We got out of there, emerging into the waiting room packed with the Disciples. Daz came at me first.

"Fuckin' A, it's good to see your surly ass."

He started the damn love fest I let my brothers have until I noticed Ember was completely dead on her feet and shut that shit down.

"Time to go," I demanded, pulling her into me until she had no choice but to give me the weight she was barely keeping upright.

Ace took off on cue, bringing Roadrunner's pickup around to the front doors. I got Ember up on the bench seat with me and we drove off with a caravan of bikes at our rear.

We weren't even halfway back before Ember knocked out, her body going lax against me. Adrenaline crash. Her weight there fucking ached, but I wasn't about to move her.

"You wanna fill me in?" I requested from Ace.

He did, telling me all about them showing Ember pictures of Kuznetsov's place, bringing the feds in, her reliving all that shit to get me out.

"She gonna get blowback from that?" I asked.

"Nah. Roth's a good character. He's not an idiot, he knows there was more we weren't sharing. He also gets she didn't come forward sooner because we intended to take care of shit ourselves, but we have assurances from him already that it won't be an issue. Victims don't always report right away. His records will chalk it up to that," he explained. "Attorneys battling Kuznetsov's side might try to make a different case, but that's only if shit goes to trial."

"Which it won't," I muttered.

"Not after the call Stone made that'll assure the right folks are aware of what's become of that little thorn in their side."

"They get anyone else out of that place?" I asked.

"Four women," he answered. "Three, I'm told, match the descriptions Ember gave of the women she'd been housed with, one they must have grabbed after that."

They'd all made it. I hadn't lied when I told Ember Kuznetsov hadn't had the opportunity to sell, but I'd been worried even still that all three women might not make it out of there. Knowing they were safe, that Ember would be able to know she was the reason they were free when she'd harbored guilt for abandoning them before, almost made that shit of being taken and not knowing whether I'd be able to come home to her worth it.

"Got one other piece of news," Ace offered.

"Yeah?"

"They found your bike," he told me, a grin in his voice. "There are a couple of scratches to see to, but it's all in one piece."

Thank fucking Christ.

IT WAS light out when I was finally in bed with my woman beside me, her dog sprawled on the floor next to the bed. Ember was drifting off again, but I had something to say before she could.

"I was fucking terrified," I said, and felt her surprise. "Not about what they might do to me. That didn't matter. I was terrified I'd never get the chance to be right back here."

She nuzzled against my chest, being cautious of my bruised body.

"Even death didn't scare me, just the thought of leaving you behind."

"Jager," she whispered.

"We both had to survive that shit, but you got us both out. You're the reason we're both where we are right now," I told her.

"Home," she said.

"Yeah, pet. Home."

CHAPTER 36

Ember

WARMTH MOVING down my back woke me. Jager and I were in bed at his apartment. As I came to, I felt the softness of his lips trailing kisses along my spine. The tickle of it made me arch and I felt him smile against my skin.

"Good morning, pet."

Oh, it definitely was. How could it not be waking up like that?

How could it not be when I was waking up with Jager safe beside me?

Even though more than a week had passed, I still woke with that being the first thought in my head. I wondered if it would always be.

Of course, as he was prone to do, Jager moved my mind elsewhere in no time.

"Dammit, I want to fuck you," he growled as he settled back up behind me.

I rolled forward onto my stomach and lifted my hips a touch. A sharp crack sounded as he landed a smack on my ass, the sting sending a ripple of pleasure through me. I gave a small gasp, pressing my ass up higher in hopes of getting another.

"Fuck," he groaned.

"Please," I replied.

I felt him move away, and then I was being pulled around.

He settled me over him so I was straddling his hips as he reclined on the bed. He'd put me on top, something we'd never done.

"What?"

He gave me a devilish grin. "Supposed to be resting, pet. Fucked you hard last night. I do it again this morning, that's not resting. We have places to be, but not until after you bring it home riding my dick."

I rocked my hips against him, rubbing my clit along his already hard cock. It was almost embarrassing how fast I was wet and ready for him, but I felt nothing like shame. Jager loved how I wanted him. That was all I needed.

Taking him in my hand, I slid down on his cock. I loved the way he filled me. At first, I was so caught up in the feeling, I didn't even move. I just sat astride him, feeling his cock stretching me.

"Ember, you don't start moving, I'll take a crop to your ass until you can't sit down for days," Jager threatened.

Oh lord, why did that sound so good?

I rolled my hips, getting used to him. Then, I started an easy rhythm, moving up and down his length. I planted my hands along his ribs to hold on as I bounced on his cock, taking him deeper.

"Faster, pet," he commanded, but this was my show. I was going to enjoy it.

I gave my head a little shake and kept my rhythm. Up and down, slow enough that I could feel the drag with every nerve ending. Each time I took him all the way in, I rocked forward a bit to rub my clit against him.

It was amazing.

I wanted to stay right there riding his cock all day.

"Fuck, Ember. Take me faster," he repeated.

I ignored him. Jager didn't like that. He started to shift under me to sit up, but I planted both hands onto his chest hard and pushed him down. Closing my eyes, I went back to focusing on the feel of him.

That was a mistake.

Jager surged up, his cock never leaving me, then flipped us over so I was on my back. He grabbed onto both of my wrists, pinning them to the mattress above my head.

"I told you to go faster," he chided, circling his hips and making me moan. "Now, you're going to take what I give you."

What he gave was deep, hard thrusts. He unleashed everything on me, each inward motion pushing my body up the bed. He was relentless. He was overwhelming.

I fucking loved it.

In a matter of minutes, I was crying out my climax as he drove himself there with me.

Still panting out harsh breaths, his dick still twitching inside me, Jager leaned down to my ear. "Even when I sit you up there, you don't top me, pet."

No, I didn't.

With the way he took me, I'd never need to.

"Up, babe," Jager said after a while. "We're on a schedule."

There was no part of me that felt like leaving the warmth of that bed. After what he'd just given me, I was ready to doze back off. I grumbled some random noises at him, hoping that would suffice. It didn't.

One minute, I was lying down, and the next, I was in the air and he was carrying me out of the bedroom.

"Jager!" I screeched. "You're not supposed to do any strenuous activity!"

He chuckled and I almost forgot I was pissed. I wondered if I'd ever get used to that sound. If someday, way down the road, I'd grow accustomed to the fact that I gave that to him.

I doubted it.

"Ember, carrying you is hardly 'strenuous activity'."

"I think your doctor would disagree," I argued.

"That guy was a moron."

Ugh. There he went with that rant again. "All he said was it would be easier to take care of you, thereby get you better faster, if you didn't have me all over you."

Jager deposited me on the bathroom counter as I said the last word and went to turn the shower on, getting the water warm.

"Exactly," he replied when he came back to me. "Anyone who would think having you across the room would be better for any man than having you in his lap is a fucking moron."

This wasn't an argument I was going to win. It also wasn't one I really felt all that inclined to win. If he wanted to think that about me, I was just going to take the compliment.

"Whatever."

After our shower, which Jager kept disappointingly PG—well, not PG, seeing as we were both naked and there might have been a little bit of grabby hands on my part—he told me to get ready. In this, included the instruction that I "had some time" but not enough to do one of my "fucking crazy sexy get-ups". Accordingly, I blew out my hair and put it up in a ponytail. I tacked on a few minutes to add some lift to my pinned back bangs and tie a headband on.

When I was dressed in jeans, my kick ass biker boots, and t-shirt, I found Jager in the living room with Roscoe. It was clear I had used up every minute he was going to give me.

He got to his feet as soon as I entered, moving right to me.

"Gotta do this quick. We need to get on the road."

Only then did I notice he had something in his hand because he lifted it up. The black leather tumbled out until it hung from his hold. It was a vest. A leather vest in my size. The air got thin. He turned it around so I could see the back, displaying the patch for me.

"Property of Jager".

Not knowing what to say, I decided to act. I turned around, lifting my arms behind me. He took the hint and settled the property cut onto my shoulders. I spun back to him, not trying to contain my smile.

"Doesn't go with your look," he mused.

"Of course it does," I disagreed. "I'm yours. That's part of my look."

He grinned and shook his head at me before hooking me around the neck with one hand and pulling me in for a kiss.

"We need to move," he said after. "We're behind schedule and if I look at you in that thing much longer, I'm going to strip you down and fuck you in just that and your collar."

"Do we have to go?" I liked his plan way better than whatever we would leave the apartment to do.

"Later," he promised.

I could live with later.

WE TOOK JAGER'S BIKE. As much as I loved my hotrod, his bike was my favorite way to get around. My baby was just that to me, but taking her didn't come with plastering myself against Jager, so she lost the battle on that fact alone.

We'd been riding for a while. I was pretty sure we'd passed into Washington, but I wasn't paying much attention to where we were. I was content to watch the scenery fly by.

I was confused and a bit worried when we got off the

highway and started driving through suburbs. I had no clue where we were headed, but it didn't seem much like Jager to be going anywhere like this.

He stopped on a quiet street. It was a typical neighborhood, maybe slightly below middle class. The houses were small and a little weathered, but not rundown. The lawns were all trimmed, but they weren't manicured with perfect gardens.

"What are we doing here?" I asked.

He didn't answer as such. He just pointed to a house across the street and up a ways. "That house," he said.

"Yeah, what about it?"

"Just wait," he instructed.

I waited. Minutes passed and my confusion grew. Then, a car pulled up, parking in the driveway. From it, a man in his very early twenties—twenty-two at the absolute oldest—alighted from the driver's side. It was on the tip of my tongue to ask again why we were there when the passenger door opened.

A girl stepped out, and I recognized her instantly.

The last time I'd seen her, her light brown hair had needed washing, her skin had been dirty, and she'd been hiding behind her own hands in fear.

"Oh my god," I whispered.

She looked better. Maybe not as healthy as a normal fifteen-year-old should—she'd need time—but her transformation just from being out of that wretched place was astounding.

She moved around the car. Her approach was hesitant. I guessed that would be a part of her for a while. Maybe forever.

The guy who'd been driving went to her, despite the fact that the front door was the other way. He grabbed onto her hand. He didn't tug her on, just walked beside her with his hand in hers for support.

"The others?"

"Both of them are safe," he assured me.

I swallowed to stop the choking tightness in my throat.

"Who is he?" I asked.

"Her brother," Jager answered.

Her brother. She had a brother who obviously cared.

"Her parents?" I asked.

He shook his head. "Already gone before they took her. Car accident took them both. Her brother was her guardian. When she disappeared, the cops didn't take it seriously at first. Thought she was just a troubled teen who ran off."

"When did they take her?"

"About a week before you."

They'd had her so long. I hated that she had to experience that, that she'd have to live with that for the rest of her life.

"Her brother never stopped trying to find her," Jager went on. "Ran himself ragged doing everything he could to find her, blew the insurance money they got from their parents' accident paying investigators to look for her."

I was glad she had that. She would need it.

"In the next few days, they'll find those funds have been...restored."

I squeezed my eyes tight and took a deep breath. I let the knowledge that she was safe, she was loved, and that Jager had already made sure the two of them would be okay settle over me.

For the first time since I woke up to the sound of a picture frame knocking against the wall, I felt at peace.

"Thank you," I told him, hoping I could convey with just those two words the weight of everything he had done for me.

"Love you, pet," he replied.

I let that settle in too, feeling the peace become much more.

"Let's go home."

Without a word, as my man was wont to do, he revved the engine and we rode back to Hoffman, the Disciples, and home.

BONUS SCENE
SKETCH

I WAS KICKED BACK in my chair, my station already cleaned after my last client left, taking a minute to rub out the tension in my hand. Only one more appointment left for the day, then I'd get home to my girls. I loved my job, couldn't imagine doing anything else, but that didn't mean I didn't relish the moment I got out of the fuckin' shop each day.

Looking to my left, my eyes landed on the painting I did of Emmy months ago on the first day I brought her to Sailor's Grave. I'd let her go to town with paints, and my princess hadn't held back. The smear of pink on her cheek lay testament to that.

"Your next appointment is here," Jess said from behind me. When I turned to her, she was already strutting away. I told her more than once she didn't have to wear those tall ass shoes, but they definitely played well with the men who came in. Half our repeat customers were there to try to get in her pants as much as they were for the quality of work we put out.

I followed her up to the front a minute later, hoping this would be a short, simple appointment. The last fucking thing I was expecting was the sight that greeted me at the reception desk.

There was only one person in the front of the shop with Jess. One gorgeous fucking woman leaning over the desk with a smile on her face as she chatted with my tricky fucking head of house.

"Ash?"

My woman beamed up at me. "Surprise."

Well, it was definitely that.

I went to her, wrapping her up and taking her sweet lips. "What're you doing here?"

She shrugged, but it didn't entirely hide her nerves or the emotion just beneath the surface. "I thought it was about time you gave me that tattoo we drew up."

That was it then. That emotion was about the tattoo.

We'd been talking about it for months. Ash wanted a tattoo in memory of her father, but she'd struggled with what to get and where to put it. Then, I drew up an idea and the tears had been immediate. I fucking hated that shit. Ash had come a long way in moving past Indian's death, but it would never stop hurting her. Every time she had to remember her dad was gone, it was going to tear her up.

I cupped her cheek, loving the way she responded by nuzzling into my touch.

"You sure you're ready?" I asked.

Tattooing was a painful process without the added emotion Ash would have. With the weight of what that ink meant, it was going to be a trying experience for her.

"I'm sure," she said with that determination she always seemed to pull from within.

Every fucking time she did, it made me want to pull her into my arms, take her somewhere private—or private enough, anyway—and fuck her until she saw stars. For the moment, I settled on stealing another kiss.

"Where do you want to put it?"

Like the beginning of a very real fantasy I'd had more than once, she started lifting her shirt right there in the shop.

In the fantasy, I let that shit play out. I let her strip right there, not giving a fuck who else was around, then I...

Fuck, I did not need to finish that thought.

"Babe, what the hell are you doing?" I asked, making her hands halt their attack on my good sense.

She cocked her head. "Moving my shirt. I decided on the ribs. I know you said it'll hurt, but it's going to hurt anywhere, right?"

I got all that, but half my brain—and all of my dick—was focused on the skin she'd revealed. I wanted to lick her. I could trail my tongue right from her belly button and down to her sweet pussy.

Focusing, I brought my eyes up to meet her baby blues. "Firefly, I love our daughter more than life itself, but if she fuckin' crawls into our bed again tonight, I'm going to lose my mind."

Surprise hit Ash's face first, then something that looked a whole lot like pity.

Four days. Four fucking days had passed since I'd last sunk myself into my woman. And that last one had been a shower quickie. It got the job done, but it wasn't enough. Emmy was having trouble sleeping and I hated that my baby was suffering, but I was not particularly partial to my dick suffering either.

Ash took a step toward me, but I forced myself to move back. If she touched me, I was going to drag her out of the room and fuck her until this ache went away.

"I'm hanging on by a thread here," I told her.

She laughed in response. Laughed. We'd see how much she was laughing when I finally got her naked again and fucked her until she passed out.

"Alright," she said as she stepped back with her hands up in a placating gesture, "hands to myself."

Like that would matter.

"Just sit your cute ass down so we can get this torture started."

And it was torture. The sweetest fucking pain.

Never in my life had I tattooed with a raging hard on until I had Ash laid out for me, her shirt tucked up around her tits. It was the ultimate test to stay focused on the piece I was giving her, but I wasn't about to put anything less than my best on her perfect skin.

That Ash seemed to find the whole process cathartic helped keep my mind centered. As soon as I had the stencil sized properly and lined up on her side, she started with the stories. I knew nearly all the ones she told, had been there for most of them, but I never tried to derail her. Though she never made it a secret how much she missed her father, she still hesitated to relive all the happy memories she had of him. I knew it was because it hurt her to face what she'd lost, but I also knew it was important that she be able to think of him without drowning in the pain.

I was adding the last highlights when she sighed.

"What, babe?" I prompted when she didn't immediately follow the sound with an explanation.

"All those stories," she started, "I've never shared those with Emmy. I've told her some things, but she really doesn't know much about him."

"She's still young, Firefly," I insisted. "We've got time to share him with her."

"She's been asking ever since we came back to Hoffman. I should have been sharing him with her."

Christ, but no one could ever be as hard on Ash as she was on herself.

"Roadrunner stored all the shit from the house when you left. All the pictures, videos—it's all safe at his place," I said, not sure anyone had informed her of that in the months she'd been home. "I'm sure plenty of the brothers have shit too, and we've all got stories. We'll get all that shit together, make sure everyone knows we want Indian to be a part of Emmy's life. They'll make sure she knows her grandfather."

ASH and I had to ride to the clubhouse separately so we wouldn't have to leave her car or my bike behind. I didn't want to spoil whatever she had planned, but I knew Ash was up to something. When I'd said I would just meet her at home after she grabbed Emmy, she'd all but shouted at me that I had to come. She tried to play it off after that, but my girl was a shit liar.

I spent the ride over trying to figure out what she was up to. I'd thought it was weird that she decided to have Jess put her down for an appointment without telling me, but now I was thinking it was all part of whatever she had planned.

Ash pulled up right after me, climbing out of her car and leveling me with an exasperated look I knew well. She walked past me to the front door as she said, "I don't know why you can't just tell me how to take care of it."

She was referring to her tattoo, which I hadn't given her any instructions on how to care for.

"I'll be there to do it myself," I replied. And, if I didn't give her that information, I would have to be. The topmost parts of the design were barely an inch beneath her breast. I was perfectly happy to make the sacrifice to ensure her ink stayed healthy.

As soon as we got in the door, the women were swarming Ash, demanding to see the tat. I stared down my brothers as Ash pulled her shirt up to show it off. Those fuckers didn't need to see it. They didn't need to be looking at anything under Ash's shirt.

Checking out that tattoo turned into hugging for whatever reason women always did that crap, and then Ash came back to me. She was giving me a little smirk, trying to be sexy, and it made me want to fucking laugh. Of course, it also had my dick stirring.

She got right up against my chest and onto her toes to whisper, "The girls are fine watching Emmy a little longer."

Any thoughts of her being up to something swept clean out of my head. My princess was occupied and happy where she was and I could finally get some relief. I didn't say a thing. I just hauled Ash down the hall, grinning like a fucking fool.

My key was out before I hit the door and I got that sucker unlocked with one flick of the wrist. When I pushed the door open, I froze.

Balloons. Everywhere. They were fucking pouring down and out onto us. Some sort of rig had them up on the ceiling.

In the chaos, it took a second for their colors to register. Was that...pink?

It was. The balloons were fucking pink and light blue. I immediately thought it was some bullshit prank by the guys, but my mind stayed on those colors.

Pink and light blue.

No, not light.

Baby blue.

"Mommy's giving me a little sister!"

Emmy's voice shrieking out that news jarred me from my stupor.

I turned to Ash. She had a hand up over her mouth, but I could tell she was smiling even as tears filled her eyes.

"Really?" I choked out.

Please, please let this be real, I thought. *Please, tell me I'm going to be a father again.*

"Well, she might get a brother."

I grabbed her then, needing to fucking feel her, needing to assure myself this all wasn't just a dream. With an arm around her waist and a hand at her neck, I pulled her sweet lips to mine. Ash melted into me, letting me release all I was feeling into her.

Distantly, I heard, "We've got a game to finish, little miss."

I pulled back from my woman's lips long enough to see Daz leading Emmy away.

Knowing our girl was fine, it was time to show Ash just how fucking excited I was. I picked her up, giving her the half second she needed to wrap her legs around me, then forced myself through the mess of balloons and managed to get the door shut behind us.

I laid Ash out on the bed, not stepping out of the hold she had on me with her legs. I pulled her shirt up and off. Settling both my hands on her sides, I stared down at the smooth plane of her stomach. I'd had my eyes on it at Sailor's Grave, but it was like the very sight had completely changed.

Our baby was in there. Our second little miracle.

I'd be able to watch Ash's body change this time. I'd be able to take care of her while she took care of our son or daughter. I'd be able to see our baby come into the world.

"How far along are you?" I rasped.

"Seven weeks."

I sunk down to my knees, my forehead resting against her stomach.

Seven weeks.

"Did you see him yet?"

"Him?" she sassed back.

"Him. Fuck, I need a him. Emmy already looks just like you, but isn't fucking shy by a long shot. She gets older, I'm going to be screwed. I need a boy, not another daughter to worry about."

"You'll be fine," Ash assured me. "But I haven't seen her yet. I have an appointment Monday and we'll be able to."

Monday. Just a few days and I'd get the first look at our baby.

I looked up to my woman's eyes. "I love you."

She gave me a watery smile. "I love you too."

I placed a kiss on her belly, letting myself revel in the life she had in there for just another second. Then, I got back to my feet, my hands going to the button of her jeans.

It was time to celebrate.

"Gabe," she moaned, already as desperate for me as I was for her.

I wanted to tell her how much I needed her. I wanted to fucking worship her for all she was and for the little life she carried inside her. I wanted to give her slow and gentle.

I would do all those things, but first, she was going to take her man the way he came.

I was a biker—her biker. I was a man who loved and lusted after his woman. And I hadn't had her properly in too fucking long.

Wrestling the jeans that seemed to be painted on her damn legs away, I went back down to my knees. I could smell her, that sweet aroma of her desire that always made my mouth water. My dick protested the decision even as I made it, but I had to taste her first. I yanked her underwear off and barely threw them aside before my mouth was on her.

Ash cried out, her body bowing off the bed, but I didn't let up for even a second. I feasted on her sweetness, reveled in her reactions. I could eat her for hours.

"Please," she begged, "I want you."

My dick pulsed in response, pressing up against my jeans until it hurt. Luckily, the pain was just enough to keep me from blowing my load.

I moved my eyes up her body, across the smooth skin of her stomach I could already imagine expanding with our second child, over the ink I'd put into her skin, over her beautiful fucking breasts that needed to be free of that damn bra, and up to her bright, blue eyes.

My Ash. She was perfection.

I was on my feet in a heartbeat, removing my clothes. Without having to tell her, Ash sat up and released her bra. My breath stuttered watching her tits sway as they were freed. Those were going to grow, too. Christ, I didn't know how I was going to be able to handle it. I could barely keep my hands off her as it was.

Picking her up as I climbed on, I moved Ash into the center of the bed and settled over her. Just the feel of her warmth, her softness against my skin, was almost too much. I shifted onto my knees, looking down at her as my hands roamed over her body.

"Please," she repeated, her hips churning and drawing my eyes to her glistening, wet pussy just inches from my cock.

With my hands spanning her hips, I pulled her in until that distance was gone and sunk into her with one thrust.

"Fuck," I groaned, lost in the hot, tight grip she had on me.

"Gabe," she sighed, like having my cock made everything right.

I couldn't hold back. My thrusts were quick, deep, almost savage. I fucked her with all I had. She moaned in complete abandon, angling her hips to take me deeper still. There was not a thing in the world that mattered more in that moment than the way I was sinking myself as far as I could into my woman.

"Oh God," Ash whispered, "I'm..."

I fucked her harder still, stealing the words from her. I wanted—no, I fucking needed her to come for me. I needed to feel her pussy milk my cock. And I needed it right then. I couldn't contain it much longer.

Her cry barely registered above the ecstasy of her pussy clamping down around me, rippling with the pleasure she felt. It only took that first spasm to set me off. I was coming with her— absolutely blinded by it.

I collapsed as it left me, barely managing to keep my weight on my forearms instead of my pregnant woman.

Pregnant.

Fuck. That word was going to be like fucking Viagra for me, it seemed. I could already feel the need building again just thinking about my Ash being pregnant.

Leaning all my weight onto one arm, I brought a hand to her stomach.

"We're having a baby," I muttered, still in awe of it all.

"We're having a baby," she confirmed.

"Fuck, Firefly."

She gave a soft laugh that I felt right down to my balls. My dick lurched and I rolled my hips to press him in further.

Ash gasped. "Again?"

I brought my lips against hers. "We're just getting started," I replied, dragging my cock back to thrust in again. Her mouth opened in surprise, and I took that too.

We had a lot more celebrating to do.

HOURS LATER, when my balls were finally empty and I'd made Ash come until she begged me to stop, we cleaned up and went to find our Emmy. We'd needed our time alone, but now we both wanted to be at home as a family.

"How did Emmy take the news?" I asked Ash as we walked into the hall.

"She's excited, but if you get your boy, she won't be."

Of course not. My princess wanted a real life doll.

I chuckled, and kept doing it when we made it to the lounge where my daughter was clearly in the midst of an episode with Daz.

"What you saying, Uncle Daz?" she demanded, hands on her little hips.

That she'd perfected that move at such a young age was another reason the idea of Ash carrying another girl scared me. The levels of sass in our house were high enough as it was.

"Say what you want, little miss, you can't get me to take it back," Daz shot back.

Lord only knew what that asshole had Emmy up in arms about.

"Nothin's better den Skittles!"

Seriously. Candy?

They were arguing about fucking candy.

"Twix is the best," Daz returned.

"That's just ridic-lus," Emmy shook her head.

I looked down to Ash's belly. "Come on, little one. I need you to be a boy."

Ash just laughed as she said, "Good luck."

Then she left me to call down our daughter before proclamations of war started.

I watched her wade into the fray and knew one thing for sure:

I didn't need luck. I had all the fucking luck in the world.

ABOUT THE AUTHOR

Drew Elyse spends her days trying to convince the world that she is, in fact, a Disney Princess, and her nights writing tear-jerking and sexy romance novels.

When she isn't writing, she can usually be found over-analyzing every line of a book, binge watching a series on Netflix, doing strange vocal warm ups before singing a variety of music styles, or screaming at the TV during a Chicago Blackhawks game.

A graduate of Loyola University Chicago with a BA in English, she still lives in Chicago, IL where she was born and raised with her boyfriend and her fur babies Lola and Duncan.

Website: DrewElyse.com

Facebook: facebook.com/DrewElyseAuthor

Facebook Group: bit.ly/DisciplesClubhouse

Twitter: twitter.com/DrewElyseAuthor

Mailing List: bit.ly/DrewElyseNews

BOOKS BY DREW ELYSE

The Disciples' Daughters Series

Clutch
Shift
Engage
Ignite
Combust
Cruise

The Dissonance Series

Dissonance
Harmony

Made in the USA
Lexington, KY
13 July 2018